UNREMEMBERED

Jessica Brody is a bestselling US author of nine novels – two for adults, the rest for teenagers. She works as a full-time author and producer and lives in both Colorado and Los Angeles.

www.jessicabrody.com

Books by Jessica Brody

Unremembered
Unforgotten

J E S S I C A B R O D Y

UNREMEMBERED

MACMILLAN

First published in the US 2013 by Farrar Straus Giroux Books for Young Readers
First published in the UK 2013 by Macmillan Children's Books

This edition published 2014 by Macmillan Children's Books
a division of Macmillan Publishers Limited
20 New Wharf Road, London N1 9RR
Basingstoke and Oxford
Associated companies throughout the world
www.panmacmillan.com

ISBN 978-1-4472-6552-8

1 3 5 7 9 8 6 4 2

To Bill Contardi,
a real-life action hero
(also known as my agent)

The heart that has truly lov'd never forgets.

– Thomas Moore

CONTENTS

AWOKEN

The water is cold and ruthless, lapping against my cheek. Slapping me awake. Filling my mouth with the taste of salty solitude.

I cough violently and open my eyes, taking in the world around me. Seeing it for the first time. It's not a world I recognize. I gaze upon miles and miles of dark blue ocean. Peppered with large floating objects. Metal. Like the one I'm lying on.

And then there are the bodies.

I count twenty in my vicinity. Two within reach. Although I don't dare try.

Their lifeless faces are frozen in terror. Their eyes are empty. Staring into nothing.

I press a palm to my throbbing temple. My head feels like it's made out of stone. Everything is drab and heavy and seen through a filthy lens. I close my eyes tight.

The voices come an hour later. After night has fallen. I hear them cutting through the darkness. It takes them forever to reach me. A light breaks through the dense fog and blinds me.

No one speaks as they pull me from the water. No one has to. It's clear from the looks on their faces they did not expect to find me.

They did not expect to find anyone.

Alive, that is.

I'm wrapped in a thick blue blanket and laid on a hard wooden surface. That's when the questions start. Questions that make my brain hurt.

'What is your name?'

I wish I knew.

'Do you know where you are?'

I glance upward and find nothing but a sea of unhelpful stars.

'Do you remember boarding the plane?'

My brain twists in agony, causing my forehead to throb again.

Plane. Plane. What is a plane?

And then comes the question that awakens something deep within me. That ignites a tiny, faraway spark somewhere in the back corners of my mind.

'Do you know what *year* it is?'

I blink, feeling a small glimmer of hope surge from the pit of my stomach.

'1609,' I whisper with unfounded conviction. And then I pass out.

PART 1

THE FALL

1
ANEW

Today is the only day I remember. Waking up in that ocean is all I have. The rest is empty space. Although I don't know how far back that space goes – how many years it spans. That's the thing about voids: they can be as short as the blink of an eye, or they can be infinite. Consuming your entire existence in a flash of meaningless white. Leaving you with nothing.

No memories.

No names.

No faces.

Every second that ticks by is new. Every feeling that pulses through me is foreign. Every thought in my brain is like nothing I've ever thought before. And all I can hope for is one moment that mirrors an absent one. One fleeting glimpse of familiarity.

Something that makes me . . . *me*.

Otherwise, I could be anyone.

Forgetting who you are is so much more complicated than simply forgetting your name. It's also forgetting your dreams.

Your aspirations. What makes you happy. What you pray you'll never have to live without. It's meeting yourself for the first time, and not being sure of your first impression.

After the rescue boat docked, I was brought here. To this room. Men and women in white coats flutter in and out. They stick sharp things in my arm. They study charts and scratch their heads. They poke and prod and watch me for a reaction. They want something to be wrong with me. But I assure them that I'm fine. That I feel no pain.

The fog around me has finally lifted. Objects are crisp and detailed. My head no longer feels as though it weighs a hundred pounds. In fact, I feel strong. Capable. Anxious to get out of this bed. Out of this room with its unfamiliar chemical smells. But they won't let me. They insist I need more time.

From the confusion I see etched into their faces, I'm pretty sure it's *they* who need the time.

They won't allow me to eat any real food. Instead they deliver nutrients through a tube in my arm. It's inserted directly into my vein. Inches above a thick white plastic bracelet with the words *Jane Doe* printed on it in crisp black letters.

I ask them why I need to be here when I'm clearly not injured. I have no visible wounds. No broken bones. I wave my arms and turn my wrists and ankles in wide circles to prove my claim. But they don't respond. And this infuriates me.

After a few hours, they determine that I'm sixteen years old. I'm not sure how I'm supposed to react to this information. I don't *feel* sixteen. But then again, how do I know what sixteen feels like? How do I know what *any* age feels like?

And how can I be sure that they're right? For all I know, they could have just made up that number. But they assure me that they have qualified tests. Specialists. Experts. And they all say the same thing.

That I'm sixteen.

The tests can't tell me my name though. They can't tell me where I'm from. Where I live. Who my family is. Or even my favourite colour.

And no matter how many 'experts' they shuttle in and out of this room, no one can seem to explain why I'm the only survivor of the kind of plane crash no one survives.

They talk about something called a passenger manifest. I've deduced that it's a kind of master list. A register of everyone who boarded the plane.

I've also deduced that I'm not on it.

And that doesn't seem to be going over very well with anyone.

A man in a grey suit, who identifies himself as Mr Rayunas from Social Services, says he's trying to locate my next of kin. He carries around a strange-looking metal device that he calls a cellphone. He holds it up to his ear and talks. He also likes to stare at it and stab at tiny buttons on its surface. I don't know what my 'next of kin' is, but by the look on his face, he's having trouble locating it.

He whispers things to the others. Things I'm assuming he doesn't want me to hear. But I hear them anyway. Foreign, unfamiliar words like 'foster care' and 'the press' and 'minor'. Every so often they all pause and glance over at me. They shake their heads. Then they continue whispering.

There's a woman named Kiyana who comes in every hour. She has dark skin and speaks with an accent that makes it sound like she's singing. She wears pink. She smiles and fluffs my pillow. Presses two fingers against my wrist. Writes stuff down on a clipboard. I've come to look forward to her visits. She's kinder than the others. She takes the time to talk to me. Ask me questions. Real ones. Even though she knows I don't have any of the answers.

'You're jus' so beautiful,' she says to me, tapping her finger tenderly against my cheek. 'Like one of those pictures they airbrush for the fashion magazines, you know?'

I don't know. But I offer her a weak smile regardless. For some reason, it feels like an appropriate response.

'Not a blemish,' she goes on. 'Not one flaw. When you get your memory back, you're gonna have to tell me your secret, love.' Then she winks at me.

I like that she says *when* and not if.

Even though I don't remember learning those words, I understand the difference.

'And those eyes,' she croons, moving in closer. 'I've never seen sucha colour. Lavender, almos'.' She pauses, thinking, and leans closer still. 'No. *Violet*.' She smiles like she's stumbled upon a long-lost secret. 'I bet that's your name. Violet. Ring any bells?'

I shake my head. Of course it doesn't.

'Well,' she says, straightening the sheets around my bed, 'I'm gonna call you that anyway. Jus' until you remember the real one. Much nicer soundin' than Jane Doe.'

She takes a step back, tilts her head to the side. 'Sucha pretty girl. Do you even remember whatcha look like, love?'

I shake my head again.

She smiles softly. Her eyes crinkle at the corners. 'Hang on then. I'll show you.'

She leaves the room. Returns a moment later with an oval-shaped mirror. Light bounces off it as she walks to my bedside. She holds it up.

A face appears in the light pink frame.

One with long and sleek honey-brown hair. Smooth golden skin. A small, straight nose. Heart-shaped mouth. High cheekbones. Large, almond-shaped purple eyes.

They blink.

'Yes, that's you,' she says. And then, 'You musta been a model. Such perfection.'

But I don't see what she sees. I only see a stranger. A person I don't recognize. A face I don't know. And behind those eyes are sixteen years of experiences I fear I'll never be able to remember. A life held prisoner behind a locked door. And the only key has been lost at sea.

I watch purple tears form in the reflecting glass.

2
COVERAGE

'Mystery continues to cloud the tragic crash of Freedom Airlines flight 121, which went down over the Pacific Ocean yesterday evening after taking off from Los Angeles International Airport on a non-stop journey to Tokyo, Japan. Experts are working around the clock to determine the identity of the flight's only known survivor, a sixteen-year-old girl who was found floating among the wreckage, relatively unharmed. Doctors at UCLA Medical Center, where she's being treated, confirm that the young woman has suffered severe amnesia and does not remember anything prior to the crash. There was no identification found on the girl and the Los Angeles Police have been unable to match her fingerprints or DNA to any government databases. According to a statement announced by the FAA earlier this morning, she is not believed to have been travelling with family and no missing-persons reports matching her description have been filed.

'The hospital released this first photo of the girl just today, in the hopes that someone with information will step forward. Authorities are optimistic that . . .'

I stare at my face on the screen of the thin black box that hangs above my bed. Kiyana says it's called a television. The fact that I didn't know this disturbs me. Especially when she tells me that there's one in almost every household in the country.

The doctors say I *should* remember things like that. Although my personal memories seem to be 'temporarily' lost, I *should* be familiar with everyday objects and brands and the names of celebrities. But I'm not.

I know words and cities and numbers. I like numbers. They feel real to me when everything around me is not. They are concrete. I can cling to them. I can't remember my own face but I know that the digits between one and ten are the same now as they were before I lost everything. I know I must have learned them at some point in my eclipsed life. And that's as close to a sense of familiarity as I've gotten.

I count to keep myself occupied. To keep my mind filled with something other than abandoned space. In counting I'm able to create facts. Items I can add to the paltry list of things that I know.

I know that someone named Dr Schatzel visits my room every fifty-two minutes and carries a cup of coffee with him on every third visit. I know that the nurses' station is twenty to twenty-four footsteps away from my room, depending on the height of the person on duty. I know that the female newscaster standing on the kerb at Los Angeles International Airport blinks fifteen times per minute. Except when she's responding to a question from the male newscaster back in the studio. Then her blinks increase by 133 per cent.

I know that Tokyo, Japan, is a long way for a sixteen-year-old girl to be travelling by herself.

Kiyana enters my room and frowns at the screen. 'Violet,

baby,' she says, pressing a button on the bottom that causes my face to dissolve to black, 'watchin' that twenty-four-hour news coverage is not gonna do you any good. It'll only upset you more. Besides, it's gettin' late. And you've been up for hours now. Why doncha try to get some sleep?'

Defiantly I press the button on the small device next to my bed and the image of my face reappears.

Kiyana lets out a buoyant singsongy laugh. 'Whoever you are, Miss Violet, I have a feelin' you were the feisty type.'

I watch the television in silence as live footage from the crash site is played. A large rounded piece – with tiny oval-shaped windows running across it – fills the screen. The Freedom Airlines logo painted on to the side slowly passes by. I lean forward and study it, scrutinizing the curved red-and-blue font. I try to convince myself that it means something. That somewhere in my blank slate of a brain, those letters hold some kind of significance. But I fail to come up with anything.

Like the slivers of my fragmented memory, the debris is just another shattered piece that once belonged to something whole. Something that had meaning. Purpose. Function.

Now it's just a splinter of a larger picture that I can't fit together.

I collapse back against my pillow with a sigh.

'What if no one comes?' I ask quietly, still cringing at the unfamiliar sound of my own voice. It's like someone else in the room is speaking and I'm just mouthing the words.

Kiyana turns and look at me, her eyes narrowed in confusion. 'Whatcha talkin' about, love?'

'What if . . .' The words feel crooked as they tumble out. 'What if no one comes to get me? What if I don't *have* anyone?'

Kiyana lets out a laugh through her nose. 'Now that's jus' foolishness. And I don't wanna hear it.'

I open my mouth to protest but Kiyana closes it with the tips of her fingers. 'Now, listen here, Violet,' she says in a serious tone. 'You're the mos' beautiful girl I've ever seen in all my life. And I've seen a lotta girls. You are special. And no one that special ever goes forgotten. It's been less than a day. Someone's gonna come for you. It's jus' a matter of time.'

With a satisfied nod of her head and a squeeze of her fingers, she releases my lips and goes back to her routine.

'But what if I don't remember them when they do?'

Kiyana seems less concerned with this question than the last one. She smooths the sheets around my feet. 'You will.'

I don't know how she can be so confident when I couldn't even remember what a television was. 'How?' I insist. 'You heard the doctors. All my personal memories are completely gone. My mind is one big empty void.'

She makes a strange clucking sound with her tongue as she pats the bed. 'That doesn't make any difference. Everybody knows the memories that really matter don't live in the mind.'

I find her attempt at encouragement extremely unhelpful. It must show on my face because Kiyana pushes a button to recline my bed and says, 'Don't be gettin' yourself all worked up, now. Why doncha rest up? It's been a long day.'

'I'm not tired.'

I watch her stick a long needle into the tube that's connected to my arm. 'Here, love,' she says tenderly. 'This'll help.'

I feel the drugs enter my bloodstream. Like heavy chunks of ice navigating a river.

Through the mist that's slowly cloaking my vision, I watch Kiyana exit the room. My eyelids are heavy. They droop. I fight the rising fatigue. I hate that they can control me so easily. It makes me feel helpless. Weak. Like I'm back in the middle of the ocean, floating aimlessly.

The room becomes fuzzy.

I see someone in the doorway. A silhouette. It moves towards me. Fast. Urgently. Then a voice. Deep and beautiful. But the sound is slightly distorted by whatever substance is pumping through my blood.

'Can you hear me? Please open your eyes.'

Something warm touches my hand. Heat instantly floods my body. Like a fire spreading. A good kind of fire. A burn that seeks to heal me.

I fight to stay awake, wrestling against the haze. It's a losing battle.

'Please wake up.' The voice is far away now. Fading fast.

I can barely see the face of a young man. A boy. Hovering inches above me. He blurs in and out of focus. I make out dark hair. Damp against his forehead. Warm maple eyes. A crooked smile.

And without thinking, without intention, I feel myself smiling back.

I open my mouth to speak but the words come out garbled. Half formed. Half conscious. 'Do I know you?'

He squeezes my hand. 'Yes. It's me. Do you remember?'

The answer comes before I can even attempt to respond. It echoes in some back corner of my mind. A faraway flicker of a flame that is no longer lit. A voice that is not my own.

Yes.

Always yes.

'This wasn't supposed to happen.' He speaks softly, almost to himself. 'You're not supposed to be here.'

I struggle to make sense of what is happening. To cling on to the unexpected surge of hope that has surfaced. But it's gone just as quickly as it came. Extinguished in the dark void of my depleted memory.

A low groan escapes my lips.

I feel him moving around me. Fast, fluid motions. The tube

that was in my nose is removed. The IV is gently pulled from my vein. There's a faint tug on the cord attached to the suction cup under my gown and then a shrill beeping sound fills the room.

I hear frantic footsteps down the hall, coming from the nurses' station. Someone will be here in less than fifteen steps.

'Don't worry,' he continues in a whisper, lacing his warm fingers through mine and squeezing. 'I'm going to get you out of here.'

I suddenly shiver. A chill has rolled over me. Slowly replacing every spark of heat that was lingering just under my skin.

And that's when I realize that the touch of his hand has vanished. With all my strength, I reach out, searching for it. Grasping at cold, empty air. I fight to open my eyes one last time before the darkness comes.

He is gone.

3
ACCESSORIES

I wake up the next morning feeling drowsy. The drugs linger in my system. My arms and legs are heavy. My throat is dry. My vision is blurred. It takes a few moments for it to clear.

Kiyana enters. She smiles upon seeing me. 'Well, look who's awake.'

I push the button on the small box next to me. The back of the bed rises until I'm sitting upright.

Kiyana retreats to the hallway and returns a few seconds later with a tray. 'I brought you some breakfast. Do you wanna try eatin' some real food?'

I look at the items on her tray. I can't identify a single one. 'No.'

She laughs. 'Can't say I blame you. That's hospital food for you.'

She takes the tray back out to the hallway and returns, writing things down on her clipboard. 'Vitals are good,' she says with a wink. 'Like always.' Her fingertip does a *tap tap tap* on the screen of the heart monitor next to my bed. 'A good strong heart you've got there.'

The machines.

The cord.

There was a boy in my room.

I reach up and touch my face. The tube in my nose is intact. I glance down at my arm. The IV has been reinserted. I peer around the room. It's empty except for Kiyana.

But he was here. I heard him. I *saw* him.

Who was he? Did I know him? He said I did.

I feel the warmth in my stomach again. Hope on the rise.

'Kiyana?' I say, my voice inexplicably wobbly.

'Yes, love?' She flicks her pen against the bag filled with clear liquid that's attached to my IV.

I swallow dry air. 'Has anyone . . . ?' My lip starts to quiver. I bite it quickly before trying again. 'Did anyone come in here last night? Like a visitor?'

Her face scrunches up as she flips a page on her clipboard. Then she slowly shakes her head. 'No, love. Jus' the night nurse. When you knocked out your IV in your sleep.'

'What?' My throat constricts but I push past it. 'I did that?'

She nods. 'I don't think you took well to the drugs.'

I feel my face fall. 'Oh.'

But the image of the boy is so clear in my memory now. I can see his eyes. And the way his dark hair fell into them as he leaned over me.

'But listen,' Kiyana says pointedly, her gaze darting discreetly towards the open door, then back to me. A cunning grin erupts on her face as she bends down and whispers, 'I did hear some good news this mornin'.'

I peer up at her.

'They started interviewin' some people who claim to be your family.'

'Really?' I sit up straighter.

'Yeah,' she confirms with a *pat pat pat* on my blanketed leg. 'Hundreds of people have been callin' after that newscast yesterday. The police have been interviewin' them all night.' She steals another glance at the hallway. 'But I'm not supposed to tell you that, so don't be getting me in any trouble.'

'Hundreds?' I ask, suddenly confused. 'But how could there be hundreds?'

Her voice is back to a whisper. 'So far, they've all've been impostors. Media-hungry fakes.'

'You mean people have been *lying* about knowing me?'

The boy's face instantly dissolves. Just like the warm touch of his hand on my skin.

She shakes her head in obvious disapproval. 'Well, I'll tell you. I blame that news coverage. You've become a celebrity overnight. People can be so desperate for attention.'

'Why?'

'Now that's a question that needs a whole heap of an explanation, love. One that I don't know if I can give you. But I'm sure that one of those calls will prove to be the real thing.'

I feel my shoulders sink and my body slouch. Like my spine has given out on me.

Impostors.

Liars.

Fakes.

Was that really what the boy was? Someone trying to meet the famous survivor of flight 121? The thought fills me with a surge of emotion. The idea that he was able to make me feel a sliver of hope – *false* hope – leaves me feeling foolish. And furious.

But then again, maybe he was never here at all. The drugs could have caused me to hallucinate. Invent things.

Invent people.

I fall back against my pillow, deflated. I reach for the remote control and turn on the television. My photograph is still on the screen, although it's been resized and placed in the top right corner. A new female reporter is standing in front of the same Los Angeles International Airport sign.

'Once again,' she is saying, 'anyone with information about this girl's identity is encouraged to call the number on the screen.' A long string of digits appears below the woman's chest. The same ones as yesterday.

And I'm struck with a thought.

'Kiyana?'

She's writing something on her clipboard and pauses to look up at me. 'What's that, love?'

'How do they know the callers are impostors?'

She glances back down at her clipboard and continues scribbling notes, answering my question distractedly. 'Because none of them know about the locket.'

My gaze whips towards her. 'What locket?'

She still doesn't look up, oblivious to the alarm in my voice. 'The one you had on when they found you.' Her voice slows as she comes to the end of her sentence and notices the ghastly expression on my face. Something she clearly wasn't expecting to see.

Her hand goes to her mouth, as though to recapture the words that she has inadvertently set free.

But it's too late. They're already imprinted on my barren brain.

I feel my teeth clench and my eyes narrow as I turn my glaring expression on her and seethe, 'No one told me anything about a locket.'

4
MARKED

'The only reason we didn't tell you about it,' Dr Schatzel says as he dances his hands around in some kind of apologetic gesture, 'is that we didn't want to overwhelm you.'

This overwhelms me. I hear the faint, rhythmic beeping of my heart monitor start to speed up. 'You had *no* right to keep it from me. It's *mine*.'

The doctor puts a hand on my arm in an act I assume is meant to calm me. 'Relax,' he coaxes. 'The police are having it analysed in the hope that they can possibly identify where it was made or purchased. They thought maybe it could help us locate your family. Don't forget that we're all on the same side here. We're after the same goal. And that's finding out who you are.'

I can feel the rage building up inside me. 'I don't believe you!' I cry out. 'If we were all on the same side, you wouldn't be stealing my stuff and not telling me about it. You wouldn't be making me lie in this bed for two days when there's absolutely nothing wrong with me.' I shove the covers off my legs and sit upright.

'Violet,' he urges, 'you really need to calm down. It's not good for you to be getting so worked up. We were going to bring you the locket once you had stabilized more. You've been through a very traumatic experience and your system is—'

'My *system*,' I interrupt, fuming, 'is fine! I'm already perfectly stable! In fact, I've *been* stable since the moment I arrived here.' I launch to my feet. 'See!' I yell, motioning to my fully functioning body, covered by a wispy piece of pale blue fabric. 'Perfectly healthy. *You* and your parade of nurses and specialists are the only things that have been making me *un*stable. And yet you insist on keeping me here anyway. When are you going to start believing me? THERE IS NOTHING WRONG WITH ME!'

I yank the suction cup from my chest. The machine next to my bed screams in protest. Kiyana looks anxiously to Dr Schatzel, who eyes the emergency call button on the wall.

I point at the IV needle in my arm. 'This?' I tug the cord free and let it fall to the ground. 'Completely unnecessary.' Then I pull the air tube from around my face. 'And this is ridiculous. I can breathe perfectly well on my own. Better, now that I don't have a tube up my nose.

'And what is the purpose of this?' I flick my finger against the strip of white plastic wrapped around my wrist.

'Hospital ID bracelets are standard procedure for all patients,' Dr Schatzel responds.

'Well, then,' I say, ripping furiously at the flimsy button clasp. 'I won't be needing it any more, will I? Since I'm clearly not . . .'

My voice trails off as the plastic snaps and the bracelet falls from my wrist, revealing the small patch of skin underneath. It's pink and slightly tender from my struggle but that's not the part that concerns me. That's not the reason I gasp in horror and collapse back on to the bed the moment my eyes catch sight of it.

'What is this?' I ask, my voice no longer thunderous. It's

now weak. On the verge of breaking.

Kiyana leans forward and examines the inside of my wrist. I expect her to react as harshly as I did, but her expression remains neutral. 'It looks like a tattoo,' she says casually.

'A *what?*'

'Relax,' Dr Schatzel assures me. 'It *is* a tattoo. No reason to get hysterical.'

I gaze downward once again and run a fingertip across the inside of my wrist. Across the strange black line that stretches horizontally parallel to the crease of my palm. It's about an inch and a half long and razor thin. And it seems to be etched right into my skin.

'What's a tattoo?' I ask, glancing hopefully between them.

'It's a permanent marking of sorts,' the doctor is quick to explain, sliding back into his professional and informative demeanour. 'Some people choose to decorate their bodies with them. Oftentimes people choose favourite animals, or Chinese characters with a special significance, or names of people who are important to them. Other times, people choose designs that are –' his chin juts ambiguously in the direction of my wrist – 'more obscure.'

I look at the mysterious marking. 'So that's all this is then,' I reply, infusing my voice with certainty. 'A decoration. Something I *chose* at some point in my life.'

Dr Schatzel offers me a half-smile. 'Most likely.'

But I can tell he doesn't believe that. I can tell, from the way he averts his gaze and nervously shifts his posture, that he's already considered this option . . . and ruled it out.

Because if he's even half as reasonable as he looks, he's probably come to the same conclusion that I'm coming to right now. As I examine this strange black mark that's stamped into my skin like a label. Like a *brand*.

It certainly doesn't look very decorative.

5
EMPTY

It takes a little over an hour, but my locket is finally brought to me in the late morning. Dr Schatzel sets it down on the tray next to my bed and rotates the swinging arm so that the tabletop is directly under me.

'Unfortunately the police weren't able to figure out where it was purchased so I'm afraid it's another dead end,' he explains, taking a step back as though to give me time alone with my one and only known possession on this earth.

I carefully reach out and lift the necklace by the chain. I extend my finger, allowing the glossy black heart-shaped charm to swing like a pendulum in front of my face.

I study it carefully. On one side of the amulet's surface is a curious symbol carved out of a matte silver metal. It's a series of interwoven loops, swirling around each other, with no beginning and no end.

I turn the locket upside down but the design doesn't change.

'What kind of symbol is this?' I ask the doctor.

'It's actually an ancient Sanskrit symbol. Called the eternal knot.'

'Does it represent something?' I ask, disliking the contemptuous quality of my voice.

He forces a smile. 'The Buddhists believe it symbolizes the interweaving of the spiritual path, movement, and the flowing of time.'

I frown, feeling disappointed. I was hoping his answer would be more helpful than that.

'But to put it simply,' he offers, almost sounding sympathetic, 'it represents eternity.'

Kiyana squints at the locket. 'It almost looks like two hearts,' she asserts with a confident nod of her head. 'One on top of the other.' She smiles. 'Pretty.'

I stare at the symbol, trying to see what Kiyana sees. It *does* kind of look like two hearts. One upside down and the other right side up. Intersecting at the cores. 'It is beautiful,' I agree.

'Yes,' Dr Schatzel concurs, although the sharpness in his voice is back. 'At first the police believed it might be an antique. But I'm told it wasn't registered in any databases so that can't be confirmed.'

Like me, I think, instantly feeling a special affinity to the necklace.

I reach for the tiny clasp on the left side and manage to pop open the locket with the edge of my fingernail. My hopes fall once more when I see that the hollow space carved inside is empty.

'Was there something in here?' I ask, shooting an accusatory look at Dr Schatzel.

He shakes his head. 'It was empty when they brought you in. I assume if there was anything inside it must have fallen out during the crash.'

Another piece of me. Lost.

I close the locket and give it a flick, sending the empty heart into a spin. The silver-link chain twists and wraps around itself, winding all the way up, threatening to strangle my finger.

It's not until it slows and eventually starts to unwind that I notice something on the other side.

An engraving.

I catch the charm midtwirl and bring it closer to my face so I can read the small calligraphic characters etched into the back.

S+Z=1609.

Kiyana and Dr Schatzel watch me carefully, awaiting some kind of reaction.

'What does this mean?' I ask.

The doctor appears disappointed. 'We were hoping you could tell us that.'

I can feel the frustration start to build up inside me again. 'Why does everyone keep saying that to me!?' I yell. 'Does no one around here have *any* answers to anything?'

He shakes his head regretfully. 'I'm sorry. It's not a mathematical or scientific formula that we're familiar with.'

'S+Z=1609.' I enunciate carefully, reading the text letter for letter, number for number, hoping it will trigger *something* in my memory. Something in this black void I have in place of a brain.

And after five long, quiet seconds, it does.

'1-6-0-9,' I repeat slowly. Familiar images start to snake into my mind. Rapid flashes of faces.

I can feel excitement building in the pit of my stomach.

Am I having a memory? Is this what it feels like?

Yes! I remember. I remember water. I remember bits of floating debris. Bodies. A bright white light. Voices.

'What is your name? Do you know where you are? Do you know what year it is?'

And then suddenly, like a *whoosh* of air exiting the room, the excitement is gone. Thrust out of me by a single disheartening realization.

I'm recollecting what happened *after* the crash.

After I awoke among the wreckage of a plane that I don't remember boarding.

'That number, 1-6-0-9 – does it mean anything to you, love?' Kiyana asks, interpreting the strange progression of emotion that must be registering across my face.

'Yes,' I answer with an unsettling sigh. 'I think it's a year.'

6
TOUCHED

It's been five days since the crash and they've finally agreed to release me. Inevitably coming to the same conclusion that I've already come to: I'm fine. That despite inexplicably surviving a ten-thousand-foot plunge from the sky, there's nothing wrong with me. They've assured me that my memory will eventually start to return and when it does I'm expected to call the hospital or the chief of police immediately.

I smile and agree even though I'm exceedingly less confident.

I would be happy simply remembering my real name.

Violet seems to have stuck though. Now pretty much everyone is calling me that. I don't mind. I suppose it's as good a name as any.

A woman from Social Services arrives and brings me some clothes to wear out of the hospital. A pair of blue pants that she calls jeans, a plain white T-shirt, a bra that Kiyana has to teach me how to clasp behind my back, underwear with red-and-orange stripes on them, socks, and white lace-up shoes with pink lightning bolts on the sides. None of the items seems to fit right except for the socks. Something the woman apologizes profusely for, muttering, 'Sorry, I had to guess on all the sizes.'

I don't mind, however. I'm just glad to be out of that flimsy paper dress.

Mr Rayunas, the man who was unsuccessful in finding anyone related to me (although he promises they have not given up), tells me that I'm to be transferred to the care of a state-appointed 'foster-family.'

I have no idea what that means. But the significance becomes obvious when a man and woman enter my room later that afternoon and introduce themselves as Heather and Scott Carlson. They show me pictures of a house that exists one hundred and seventy-five miles north of here, a front yard with a rope swing hanging from a tree, and a young boy with big blue eyes and messy blond curls whom they introduce as their thirteen-year-old son, Cody.

These are the pieces that will make up my temporary family. My temporary life. This is where I'm expected to feel at home, until a real one can be located.

I take in their kind-hearted smiles and warm, engaging body language and decide there are worse places I could be asked to go. Plus, no one appears to be giving me a choice in the matter and I'm just anxious to get out of this hospital room.

'We've chosen the Carlsons because of their remote location,' Mr Rayunas explains. 'They live in a small town called Wells Creek. It's on the central coast of California. No one outside of this room will be given the specifics of your whereabouts. As you've probably guessed from watching the news, this has turned into something of a media circus. And we want to give you the best possible opportunity to take things easy. Heather and Scott will make sure you're able to keep a low profile. In the meantime, we'll be doing everything we can to find your family.'

He signs a document attached to a clipboard and hands it back to Dr Schatzel, who looks disgruntled. I have a feeling that if it was up to him I wouldn't be going anywhere until this mystery was solved.

I'm glad it's apparently not up to him.

'Do you have anything you'd like us to help you pack up?' the woman identified as Heather Carlson asks me, stepping towards my bed and offering another smile.

I shake my head and indicate the heart-shaped black locket I've been clutching in my hands. 'This is all I have.'

Heather presses her lips together and retreats to her husband's side, looking sorry she asked.

Kiyana enters my room, carrying a bag made of brown paper. 'These are the clothes they found you in.'

I peer inside and see a bundle of dark grey fabric, neatly folded into a tight square. I make a mental note to sort through it later.

'Although,' she continues, 'I'd get some new ones if I was you.' She nods towards the bag in my arms. 'They're not the most flatterin' things I ever saw.'

'We'll take you shopping for new clothes,' Heather promises eagerly.

I try to smile. 'Thank you.'

'We're gonna miss you around here.' Kiyana steps close and wraps her arms tightly around me. She squeezes hard. I stiffen. It's the first time she's touched me with so many body parts at once. The first time *anybody* has. Normally she brushes her hand lightly against mine. Or grazes the side of my face with her fingertip. But now she's everywhere. Her arms suffocate me. Her hair irritates my cheek. Her scent overpowers me. I can't move. I feel the sudden urge to break free. To shove her to the ground.

Then a pleasant sensation begins to travel up my legs. It

tingles, relaxing me nearly instantly. My eyelids begin to feel heavy. As though I can't keep them open. Or don't want to. They sag. Along with my torso. And right as they're about to close, Kiyana releases me and steps away.

'What was that?' I ask, somewhat dizzy from the encounter.

She laughs and touches my hair. 'It's alrigh', darlin',' she whispers so no one else can hear. 'It's just a hug.'

It isn't until we step out the front doors of the hospital that I fully understand the meaning of the term *media circus*.

I blink against the strange flashes of light. They blind me again and again. It takes my eyes a moment to adjust. It takes my mind a second longer to translate what I'm looking at.

People.

Hundreds and hundreds of people.

More than I'm sure I've ever seen at one time before.

I feel a tightness in my chest. I start to count them. Trusting the sum to calm me. If I can determine how many there are, then I might be able to think. Breathe. Function. But I'm so anxious I lose count after 142. And Mr Rayunas is tugging on my arm, coaxing me to walk *through* them. Which only ratchets up the tension behind my ribs.

I hear voices everywhere. There are so many I can't tell if they're real or in my head. They're demanding things of me. Things I don't have to give.

'Do you remember anything?'

'Were you running away from home when you boarded that plane?'

'Do you have any clues about your true identity?'

I clutch the locket in my hand tighter, concealing it entirely behind my flesh.

'She has no comment,' Mr Rayunas repeats over and over again as we struggle past. If he's hoping this will dispel them, I think someone should tell him that it's not working.

He eventually catches on and adds another obviously useless response. 'Please, everyone,' he implores, 'she's been through a lot. Allow her to recover in peace.'

For a moment I actually think that this appeal might work. But that moment is short-lived. Because the assault continues.

'Can you tell us what's going on in your head right now?'

'Do you have any comment about how the airline is handling this investigation?'

'Are you sure they're not lying to you?'

I stop. Lift my eyes from the ground for the first time. Despite the persistent tugging on my arm, willing me to keep moving, keep walking until we've reached the vehicle at the end of the walkway, I don't move. Someone has shoved a long black stick in my face.

'What did you say?' I ask.

'Are you sure they're not lying to you?' a woman with big blonde hair repeats, looking proud that it was *her* question that finally caught my attention.

The crowd has fallen silent. They're waiting for my response.

Why would they lie to me? I wonder.

But I can't answer that question either.

The sea of faces around me starts to spin. Faster and faster. Appearing to me in a blur. I feel myself falling. Losing balance. Losing my sense of direction. The sky is no longer up. The pavement is no longer down. I know nothing.

There's a faint pull on my arm. The world stops spinning. Individual faces come back into focus. I steady my feet.

'You OK?' Mr Rayunas asks.

I catch my breath. 'Yes. I just got a little dizzy.'

'C'mon,' he says. 'Let's get you into the car.'

I follow willingly, keeping my eyes glued to the ground. It moves rapidly under my feet. I feel my legs tingle. They send signals to my brain, telling me to run. But I keep them in pace with my escort.

We reach a long black vehicle at the end of the walkway and I'm told to watch my head as I get in. I fall into the seat. The door is slammed, startling me.

Heather and Scott are already inside. Feeling protected by the glass window that now stands guard in front of me, I find the courage to look out at the wall of people we just walked through. They're still calling my name, demanding my attention. Although now their voices have melded into one loud muffled hum. I can no longer make out individual questions. I watch Mr Rayunas attempt to make his way back to the hospital. My eyes scan the crowd, scrutinizing faces. Features. Eyes. Do any of them resemble mine? Kiyana says she's never seen eyes like mine. The colour of violets. Surely I received that trait from one of my parents. So maybe that's how I'll know them. When they come for me.

If they come for me.

I allow my clenched fingers to part ever so slightly as I glance down at the locket in my hand.

Who gave it to me?

Who was important to me?

If I was wearing it when I boarded the plane, then it probably mattered. *They* probably mattered.

We begin to move. People disappear out the window. Old faces are replaced with new ones. And yet they share one commonality: they're all watching me.

We turn a corner and that's when I see his face.

The boy who came into my room. The same thick sable

hair. The same intense maple eyes. And, as my gaze meets his, the same soft, crooked smile.

Am I hallucinating again?

Or is he real?

A strange burning sensation begins between my eyes. Growing warmer by the second. Like a blazing spotlight pointed right above the bridge of my nose. I wince and touch my hand to my skin. It feels normal. Cold even.

But the longer I stare at him, the hotter my forehead grows. It's like a fire. A fever. But it's not violent. It's . . .

Calming.

Almost peaceful.

As though suddenly sixteen years of a forgotten life no longer matter. Nothing does.

I eye the door handle. Rest my fingers gingerly on the shiny silver latch. But then I hear Kiyana's voice in my head – *media hungry . . . impostors . . . desperate for attention* – and the fever breaks its hold over me.

He's nothing, I tell myself.

His smile means nothing.

My hand falls back on to my lap. With effort, I manage to tear my eyes away from him. And as soon as I do, my forehead returns to normal.

I clutch the locket and squeeze, the metal clasp digging into my skin.

We keep moving. The people keep changing before my eyes. As we pick up speed, there are fewer and fewer, until they all disappear completely.

7
HOME

The Carlsons tell me they live in an old ranch house that was built in the early 1900s. According to them, the small town of Wells Creek used to be run by farmers, but in the last fifty years it's been taken over by city refugees longing for space and quiet.

I'm told it will take three hours to get there. The Carlsons ride in the back seat with me while someone named Lance operates the vehicle. Heather calls it a car.

I like the way it moves. Smooth with occasional bumps that Scott says are due to insufficiencies in the California state budget. I nod as though this makes sense to me, even though it doesn't.

The inside is very pleasing. Black leather that feels soft and silky against my fingertips. Buttons that make things move like the ones next to my hospital bed. I ask Heather and Scott if this car belongs to them and they seem to find amusement in my question.

'Don't we wish!' Scott replies. 'The airline sent it. I suppose it's the least they can do.'

'Why is that?' I ask.

He rubs his hands on the knees of his pants. 'Well, some people are saying it was negligence on their part. The fact that your name wasn't on the manifest. Although to be honest, it was probably just a computer glitch. Happens all the time.'

'Scott works in computers,' Heather clarifies, touching her husband's leg.

'What's a computer?'

Scott smiles. 'Oh right. Basically it's a device or a machine that processes data and performs operations. But you can pretty much programme them to do anything you want these days.'

'Really?'

'For the most part,' he says with pride. 'Computers are quickly surpassing human intelligence.'

I find this statement odd. 'How do you programme a computer to be smarter than you?'

'You programme it to think for itself and then eventually it evolves and becomes smarter than you. Computers can absorb information faster and with much higher efficiency than a human being.'

'If they're smarter than you,' I begin pensively, 'aren't you afraid they'll eventually destroy you?'

They both laugh. 'You should get a job in Hollywood,' Scott says. 'But no. It doesn't quite work like that. Only in the movies. You see, computers may be smarter than humans but they don't react like humans. They don't feel emotions like greed and envy and anger. Those are the kinds of emotions that might lead someone to want to destroy.'

I nod and turn to look out the window, just managing to see Heather and Scott exchange a glance out of the corner of my eye.

*

We arrive at the house and I immediately understand what they mean about the quiet. Their quaint home is nestled into the side of a hill and surrounded by hundreds of towering trees that almost completely hide it from view. I notice the rope swing from the photograph they showed me, hanging from a branch of one of the larger trees. Scott tells me he built it for his son, Cody, when he was younger, although he hardly ever uses it any more.

Heather points towards a leaf-covered trail that disappears over the edge of a small knoll. She tells me it leads to the creek. 'That's where Wells Creek gets its name,' she informs me. 'It runs through most of the town. Cody and his friends used to like to race home-made sailing boats in it.'

My bedroom is on the second floor of the house. It's decorated in white and soft blues. There's a bed in the centre, a small table in the corner, a dresser and a chair that rocks when you sit in it. There's also a door to a bathroom that you can walk through to another bedroom.

'Cody is at summer camp,' Heather tells me, gesturing towards the half-ajar door at the other end of the bathroom. 'Science camp.'

I lean forward to peer inside and catch sight of a desk covered in several pieces of unidentified circuitry.

'He likes to take things apart,' she adds, following my gaze. 'I just wish he liked putting them back together as well.'

I smile, sensing it's a joke from the way her eyes crinkle when she says it. I like jokes. Kiyana used to make them in the hospital. But they seem very complicated to me. Like something you need a special skill for. I wonder if I ever made jokes.

'Maybe *you* went to summer camp,' Heather muses.

'Maybe,' I allow, as I unite the definitions of the two words, creating a visualization of what they might mean. *Summer camp.* Taking shelter in tents for the summer?

'He gets home tomorrow,' she goes on. 'I'll make sure he uses our bathroom so you have privacy. You can keep this door locked if it makes you feel better.' She closes the door to Cody's bedroom and flips the small knob under the handle, demonstrating how the lock works.

I shrug in response, wondering if I was a private person.

I run my thumb back and forth over the thin black tattoo on my wrist, as though the answer is just beneath the surface of my skin.

'Are you hungry?' she asks. 'I can make lunch.'

'Yes,' I say, placing my locket on the dresser and following her down the stairs into the kitchen.

Twenty minutes later, I sit at the table with Scott. Heather sets a plate in front of me. 'If I knew your favourite food, I would have made it.'

I glance warily at the unfamiliar object that I'm expected to consume.

'If I knew my favourite food, I would have told you,' I reply, causing Heather and Scott to chuckle. Their laughter takes me by surprise.

Heather slides into a chair and places a napkin in her lap. Scott does the same so I follow suit, assuming it's the appropriate thing to do. 'This is Cody's favourite so I took a shot. It's a grilled cheese sandwich. Pretty basic.'

I study my plate, noticing how the gelatinous orange cheese drips over the edge of the bread and seems to cling to the sides. I pick up one half and hold it tentatively between my fingers. This is my first real food since the plane crash.

Heather and Scott watch me closely as I take a bite.

The flavour explodes in my mouth, overwhelming me and filling me with a sense of elation that I can't quite understand. The texture is both crunchy and creamy, and every time I chew it releases more and more delicious aroma on to my tongue.

I know I don't remember anything, but I'm certain this is the most wondrous thing I've ever eaten. I don't know how it can't be. Is it possible for anything else to taste so delectable?

I let out a small, involuntary moan and Heather and Scott both laugh.

The flavour eventually starts to evaporate and the piece in my mouth turns soggy. I swallow it down and immediately lunge forward for another bite. This one is just as enjoyable as the first and I let out sigh of contentment.

'I guess that means you like it,' Heather confirms.

I don't speak, in fear that opening my mouth might allow some of the delicious flavour to escape. I simply nod and smile. Heather and Scott chuckle again.

'I'm so glad,' Heather says.

I swallow my second bite. 'It's the most wondrous thing I've ever tasted,' I say zealously.

Heather beams and picks up half of her own sandwich. I can't help but marvel at how happy she looks. And I find myself feeling happy too. Maybe that's what food is supposed to do.

That night when I retire to my room I empty the brown paper bag that Kiyana gave me at the hospital, spilling its contents on to the bed.

I stare numbly at the unfamiliar pieces of dark grey fabric.

The clothes I was found in.

I so wish they had meaning. I wish I could remember picking them out. Putting them on. Did I keep them in a dresser like the one in this room?

Without thinking, I slip my white T-shirt over my head, step out of my jeans and strip down to my red-and-orange-striped underwear. I guide my arms through the short sleeves of the grey collared shirt, remarking at how soft and worn it feels.

Does that mean it was my favourite?

There are white buttons all down the front. I work quickly, fastening each one. Then I step into the matching grey cloth pants, pulling them up around my hips and securing them with the fabric string that ties at the waist.

I peer at myself in the full-length mirror that hangs on the door to the bathroom. The ensemble is comfortable, but certainly not flashy. In fact, looking at my reflection, I can see it's very drab. Almost gloomy.

Was I a gloomy person?

Or maybe this is what people wear on long flights to Asia.

Obviously it's what I wear.

But for some reason now it feels all wrong. The clothes fit *physically* but the longer I wear them, the more uneasy I become. Suddenly I have a desperate urge to shed them as quickly as possible. I throw the shirt over my head, yank the pants down and kick them from my ankles, feeling better almost immediately.

I stand in my underwear breathing heavily for a moment before putting on a pair of pink cotton pyjamas that Heather loaned me to sleep in.

It isn't until I'm bending down to scoop up the discarded grey garments from the floor that I notice the small white flap attached to the inside lining of the pants.

I pick them up and examine the flap closely.

It's a pocket.

And after rubbing the fabric between my fingertips, I conclude that there is definitely something in there.

I squeeze my fingers inside and draw out a crumpled and tattered piece of yellowed paper. The stale texture tells me that it was in the water with me.

I bring the paper over to the dresser and work to unfold it, smoothing it against the wooden surface.

I lean forward and squint at the shaky, faded letters, handwritten in thick black ink. The salt water certainly took its toll but I still manage to make out the only two words visible on the page.

Trust him.

A lump forms in my throat but I quickly swallow it back. I read the note over and over again, feeling more discouraged with every pass.

Trust him?

Trust *who?*

Who wrote this?

I squeeze my eyes closed, trying to shut out the frustration that is welling up inside me but it's pointless. Emotion takes over. Scratching underneath my skin. Burning me from the inside out.

Why does everything have to be so cryptic? Why can't anything just make sense?

I crumple up the note and bury it in my fist. Then I grab the locket from the top of the dresser and sit down in the chair that rocks. I sway until the exasperation has subsided.

I open the heart-shaped charm and stare into the emptiness, thinking about what might have been inside. What might have been lost at sea along with the memories of my favourite foods, car rides and summer camp.

Something Heather said as I was helping her wash dishes after lunch today is echoing in my mind.

'We're not here to replace your real family,' she explained to me. 'I want you to know that.'

I told her I already knew.

'We're just here to help out until they can be found. And I'm 100 per cent positive that they *will* be found. But we're here for you as long as you need us.'

I thanked her and placed the plate in my hand into the dishwasher like she'd shown me a few minutes earlier. I liked how each dish had a place that was made especially for it. A perfectly sized slot.

As I hold my locket in my hand and read the inscription again, S + Z = 1609, I find myself wondering if such a place exists for me. Maybe it did. But maybe it, too, was forever lost.

Everyone around me is so confident that one day I will remember. That my family will be found, my memories will be restored and my life will be returned to me.

But unfortunately I don't share this conviction. I don't believe what they so strongly believe. Because for some reason, my memories don't feel temporarily misplaced. They feel *gone*.

And if that's the case, then my only chance of having a life that I can call my own is to create one myself.

I place the crumpled piece of yellowed paper inside the locket and snap it closed. Then I stand up and walk back to the dresser. I pull open the top drawer and slide the necklace inside, vowing to forget it along with everything else from my past.

Vowing to move forward to find my new perfect place.

8
CRAVED

I am back in the crowd. Trying to leave the hospital but I can't get through. The swarm of people is too thick. They ask me questions. Pull at my clothes. Grab my arms and legs and hair. They yank me in different directions.

My escort has been swallowed up ahead of me. I am alone.

I try to fight them off. But they are too strong. Because there are so many of them.

I plead, begging them to let me go. But they don't answer. I try to capture somebody's attention, but one by one they fade before my eyes. Until they have all blended into one giant, dark stranger. With cold, ruthless blue eyes and a wide, sinister smile. His features are cast in shadow but I know he's watching me.

Always watching.

He doesn't speak. He never speaks. He only observes.

There's a hunger in his presence. A greed. He wants me. He anticipates me. And every day his desire for me grows stronger.

I squirm under his gaze, eager to get away. But there is nowhere to go. I am trapped. His prisoner.

His voice emerges from the darkness like a snake slithering into the light. 'When will she be ready?' he asks.

I scream and wake up.

This is my first dream.

9

SCANNED

Today Heather has to go to something called a supermarket to buy food for Cody's return. Scott is at work and she doesn't want to leave me home alone so she takes me with her, promising that no one will recognize me.

I still feel better when she offers to lend me a navy-blue hat with a white logo on the front. 'Scott's favourite baseball team,' she explains as she pulls the rim down to my eyebrows, cloaking most of my face in shadow. Then she slides something she calls sunglasses over my eyes and the world becomes a few shades darker.

'Now I can imagine how all those celebrities must feel,' she says with a laugh as I get out of the car.

Heather has loaned me a few more articles of clothing to wear until we have a chance to buy some for me. The pants are too big and have to be held up by a belt and the green collared shirt is long but it covers the belt.

We enter the store and I immediately stop and take in the overwhelming site.

Market: a location to buy and sell merchandise.

Super: very large.

Heather places her hand gently on my elbow. 'It's all right. Just stay close to me.'

I do as she says, watching with immense curiosity as she places item after item in the cart. She adds commentary along the way about Cody's love of certain foods and his allergy to others. She makes guesses about what I might like, referencing things she's heard or seen on TV about what teenage girls prefer to eat.

Despite its daunting size, I quickly decide that I like the supermarket. There are words to read and things to count everywhere. I appreciate that someone has taken the time to label everything. Every aisle. Every package. Every ingredient. It's extremely helpful for someone like me. I devour the words hungrily. Some of the simpler labels make sense. Like eggs and milk and orange juice. I have a hard time extracting meaning from others. Like Apple Jacks and root beer and Thousand Island dressing.

'I would buy you some make-up,' Heather says as we stroll down an aisle identified as Beauty Products, 'but I swear you don't need any. Your features are so flawless.'

Then she chuckles softly to herself. 'Funny, that's what my mother used to say to me when I was a teenager. I always hated it.' She plucks a few packages from a rack and tosses them into the cart.

'Do you eat meat?' she asks as we approach a large glass case filled with an assortment of fleshy red slabs.

I peer through the glass, reading the variety of offerings. 'It doesn't look familiar,' I admit, feeling a bit queasy all of a sudden.

'Well, it doesn't look like that when you eat it,' Heather explains. 'You cook it first and it turns brown.'

I nod. 'Oh. Right.'

'Well, you can try it and see,' she offers. 'If you don't like it, you don't have to eat it. A lot of people around here don't eat meat. It's called being a vegetarian. Perhaps you were one.'

I shrug. 'Perhaps.'

Once our cart has been filled to the top, Heather pushes it towards the front of the store and parks it behind another person. I observe the woman in front of us as she empties the contents of her own cart on to a moving conveyor belt. A young female cashier takes each item and swipes it along a metal surface, eliciting a *beep*. I notice a small screen that displays a name and number after each swipe.

Beep. Grape jelly: $2.99.

Beep. Raw sugar: $4.79.

Beep. Oatmeal: $5.15.

'Is that all?' the girl asks several minutes later, after the cart is empty.

The woman nods. 'That'll be it for today. What's the total?'

The cashier presses a few buttons on a machine in front of her and I hear a soft voice whisper, '$187.22.'

It isn't until this very number appears on the screen and the girl repeats it that I realize the voice I heard was my own. The realization takes me by surprise although I'm not sure why. I suppose it's because I wasn't aware I'd been counting.

Heather gives me a look of admiration. 'Impressive.'

She pushes the cart forward and starts to unload it. 'Scott can add large sums in his head too,' she says. 'Math was never my strong suit. Looks like we discovered your favourite subject in school.' She turns and gives me a wink.

The cashier starts to scan our items.

Beep. Canned tomatoes: $1.29.

Beep. Doritos: $2.79.

Beep. Pop-Tarts: $3.85.

Another conveyor picks up the items on the other side of the metal scanning slate and a young man in a red apron places each one into a bag. It looks like the bag Kiyana used to pack up my dull grey clothes.

Beep. Green chillies: $0.99.

The cashier places the can of green chillies on the second conveyor but it gets caught between the edge of the metal and the beginning of the belt. I watch in fascination as the small can spins in helpless circles, trying to free itself.

'Um, would you mind getting that for me?'

I look up to see the young man in the red apron gesturing towards the revolving can.

'Yes, sorry,' I say. But when I reach out to grab it, I'm stopped by a startling high-pitched sound.

BEEEEEEEEEEEEP!!!!

The noise takes me, Heather, the young man and the cashier by surprise. I drop the can of green chillies and quickly withdraw my hand.

The register continues to shrill while the cashier bewilderedly punches buttons on her keyboard to no avail. The screen displays the words *Error. Unreadable.*

'That's strange,' she says. 'It must have malfunctioned. I have no idea what happened. Let me just call my manager.'

As she picks up a nearby phone, I surreptitiously glance down at my left arm. The one that was extended directly over the scanner when the noise started.

I turn my hand over and study the inside of my wrist. The skin around the tattoo is pulsating. I run my thumb across the thin black marking. It feels hot. Strangely hot. I recoil swiftly, a small gasp escaping my lips.

'What's the matter?' Heather asks, looking at me with her eyebrows pinched together.

I shake my wrist. The subtle stinging sensation has already started to fade. 'Nothing.'

The register finally falls silent and the cashier hangs up the phone. 'Sorry about that.' She picks up the next item and scans it.

Beep. Frozen pizza: $4.82.

It travels down the conveyor and into the awaiting brown bag.

Everything appears to be back to normal.

'Your total is $102.49,' the cashier says brightly.

The man in the red apron places the bags into our now-empty cart as Heather swipes a small plastic card through a machine mounted on the counter and punches a series of numbers into the keypad. This seems to finalize the transaction. She thanks the cashier and beckons me forward, pushing the cart in front of her.

We walk to the parking lot in silence. The fresh air feels good. Heather presses a button on her key chain and the trunk of the car opens. She begins to transfer the bags of food from the cart.

'Oh!' she exclaims suddenly, throwing her hands in the air. 'I forgot the sour cream for the onion dip. Do you want to finish loading the groceries and I'll just run in and get it?'

I shrug. 'OK.'

'I'll be two minutes,' she promises, and then scurries away, heading back into the store.

I lift a bag from the cart and place it carefully inside the car, just as I observed Heather do a few seconds ago. I position it against the far wall to maximize space. When I turn to reach for the next one, I notice someone standing behind me.

I jump and inhale a sharp breath.

I recognize him immediately. It's the boy. The one who was in the crowd yesterday. And in my hospital room.

The one I still think I could easily have hallucinated.

But now he's here. Close. I could reach out and touch him if I wanted to. And for some incomprehensible reason, I *do*. I feel my fingers tremble with the anticipation of it. But I force my hands to stay where they are.

'Sorry,' he says. 'I didn't mean to scare you.'

He's staring at me with a funny loose smile. His eyes are sparkling. He takes a step towards me and I suddenly feel queasy.

I step back, reminding myself that he lied. He's one of *them*. The media-hungry fakes. A fraud.

'Who are you?' I demand.

I watch the smile vanish from his face. Replaced by a dismal frown. His thick brown eyebrows knit together, forming a deep crease in his forehead. 'It's true, then, isn't it?'

I don't know what he's talking about so I stay quiet.

He runs his fingers through his thick hair. 'I can't believe this is happening.' His voice cracks. He looks to the ground. When he speaks again it's barely a whisper. 'You really did lose everything.'

'I'm sorry,' I say, trying to make my voice rigid as I pull the brim of my hat further down and adjust my sunglasses, 'but I don't know you.'

It's the truth, I tell myself.

'You do though,' he insists. 'You just have to try harder.' Even through the dark glasses, his eyes lock on to mine, making me feel funny. Dizzy almost. 'Do you remember me?' he asks. Slow. Purposeful. Pronouncing each syllable as though it's a key that unlocks a secret door.

And then I hear another voice. Distant. Faint. Smothered.

Yes.

Always yes.

I shake my head, breaking his gaze. 'No,' I mutter, turning to grab another bag. I place it in the car, rotating the others so that they all face the same direction.

I hear a sigh behind me. And then, a few moments later, a faint laugh. 'You've always been stubborn. Hard-wired to distrust, I suppose.'

I do my best to ignore him.

'But if I have to start all over again, I will.'

Cart. Bag. Trunk.

He speaks again. There's desperation in his voice now. It pierces something inside me. Something I can't pinpoint. 'Please, Sera. *Try.*'

I spin back around slowly. 'What did you call me?'

'Sera,' he whispers. 'That's your name. It's short for Seraphina.'

I wait for a reaction. Certain that if he was telling the truth, my real name would cause me to feel *something*.

But it doesn't.

'Do you remember *any* of it?' he asks. 'What we discovered? Why we fled? How you ended up here?'

'I survived a plane crash,' I say flatly.

He releases a low guttural laugh. 'Oh, come on. You were never on that plane and you know it.'

I swallow, feeling a swelling in my chest. We're both silent for a long moment. His eyes challenge me to negate him. To look away.

I can't do either of those things so I just say, 'I want you to leave.'

It's the truth, I tell myself again. But this time it sounds far less convincing.

I don't know him. I don't remember him. I can't trust him.

I clear my throat. 'I know you're an impostor trying to get on the news.'

'If that was true,' he says, 'then I would have gone

straight to the press. Not come to you.'

I turn my back to him, reach deeper into the cart. I'm running out of bags.

'And,' he continues, 'I wouldn't know about the locket.'

I freeze. Blinking again and again. The surrounding cars grow blurry.

He's close behind me. I think I feel his breath on my neck but I convince myself it's just a passing breeze. A beautiful, sweet summer breeze.

'But I *do* know about it,' he presses on. 'Because I'm the one who gave it to you.'

I turn and open my mouth to reply even though I don't have the slightest idea what to say. The warmth between my eyes returns. It quickly grows hot.

What is that?

Cringing, I tear my sunglasses from my face. I push up my hat and place my finger to my forehead.

He notices and a strange, knowing smile surfaces on his lips. His eyes begin to sparkle again. 'So you *do* remember,' he says. 'At least some part of you does.'

He reaches towards my face. I panic and pull away. My breath quickens and despite my efforts I can't seem to get it under control.

I see the supermarket doors open. Heather exits, carrying a small plastic tub in one hand – the sour cream she mentioned, I presume – and a receipt in the other.

This time I really do want him to leave and I know that she will make sure he does.

He follows my gaze across the parking lot and I watch his expression shift. His palpable calmness suddenly turns to alarm. Which only confirms what I've been trying to tell myself all along.

He's a fraud.

'OK,' he says hurriedly. 'I was hoping to have more time, but apparently I don't, so please listen.'

He focuses back on me, his gaze gripping mine so intensely it stops my breath. 'Sera, you're in danger. You're not who you think you are. There are people looking for you, and trust me when I say, you do *not* want them to find you.'

I shake my head dazedly. What is happening? Why is he saying these things? Why do I feel so woozy?

I don't know him. I don't remember him. I can't trust him.

I repeat it over and over again. Like a mantra.

'Which is why,' he says emphatically, 'it's very important you don't attract any attention to yourself. And especially not any press. Or photographers. Keep wearing the hat. Do whatever you need to do to conceal yourself.'

What is taking Heather so long? She should be here by now.

I look up to see that she's stopped halfway across the parking lot to talk to a woman carrying a baby. Judging by their body language, I assume they know each other. Heather reaches out to tickle the small child, who laughs giddily in response.

'I know you won't believe anything I say,' the boy continues, pulling my attention back to him. 'At least not until you figure it out on your own. And I know you're going to try to talk yourself out of whatever you're feeling right now. That's simply the way you are. But I also know the memory is in there somewhere. *I'm* in there somewhere.'

I drop my gaze to the ground, but he bends his head to catch it.

'You just have to find it,' he urges.

His voice is grave. Pleading. It makes my hands shake.

Heather has finished her conversation and is making her way towards us. She studies our interaction carefully, seemingly noticing the boy for the first time. She doubles her pace.

He glances in her direction, then back at me. 'Sera, you need to *try* to remember.'

I can't take it any more. The tingling skin. The heat. The eyes. It's too much. I turn away from him and grab the last bag from the cart. I place it in the trunk, trying to block out the sound of his voice. But it continues to infiltrate all my mental barriers.

'Don't trust anyone,' he urges. 'Try to remember what really happened. Try to remember *me*.'

I focus on a box of frozen pizza that's peeping out from the top of one of the bags.

290 words.

1,432 letters.

The counting seems to be working. I can no longer hear him. My forehead is starting to cool.

108 instances of the letter *A*.

87 instances of the letter—

'Who was that?' I hear Heather's voice behind me and I swivel around.

'Who?'

'That boy who was just here talking to you.'

I think about telling her the truth. Repeating everything he said to me. But his voice still rings in my ears.

'Don't trust anyone.'

I peer up at Heather's kind, gentle face. I may not remember much about anything, but I have a hard time believing she could possibly be dangerous.

Still, for some reason I find myself saying, 'He recognized me from the news. I told him to leave me alone and he left.'

Maybe it's because that's what I want so desperately to believe myself.

She seems satisfied with my response and reaches up to

close the trunk. I subtly scan the parking lot, searching for some trace of the boy, but I don't see him anywhere. If Heather hadn't asked about him, I might finally have been able to convince myself that he never even existed.

But he did.

And more than that, he knows about the locket.

Heather opens the car door for me and I nearly fall in, grateful to have something sturdy underneath me.

'Well, Violet,' Heather says with a chuckle as she gets in on the driver's side and fastens her seat belt, 'you survived the supermarket. You can pretty much conquer anything now.'

I smile politely and turn to gaze out the window. *Violet*, I repeat silently, the temporary name suddenly feeling as ill-fitting as my borrowed clothes.

10

WRITTEN

Heather and Scott's son is home when we return from the supermarket. He's smaller than I thought he would be. His photograph made him appear bigger somehow. But standing up, he's only as high as my shoulder. His arms are skinny. His face is young. Childlike. Although I don't technically know what thirteen is supposed to look like, Cody does not strike me as someone who is only three years younger than me. But perhaps a person does a lot of growing between the ages of thirteen and sixteen. His hair is dark blond. It sprouts in many different directions. Round wire-rimmed glasses sit across a round face that's pocked with brown and orange freckles.

'Mom,' he says, sounding agitated as he pats down his disorderly curls, 'you didn't tell me she was *hot*.' Judging by his hushed tone and the way he turns his face away from me when he speaks, I don't believe he meant for me to hear this. But I do.

Heather laughs and ruffles the same hair that Cody has just attempted to smooth. 'What does it matter what she looks like?'

His eyes dart towards me and then away again. 'It *matters*,' he says, his teeth clenched tightly.

'Violet,' she says with a smile, 'this is our son, Cody, who apparently thinks you're "hot".'

'Mom!' His eyes grow wide and his face turns a curious shade of red.

'I feel a normal temperature,' I reply, slightly confused by the exchange.

Heather laughs again. 'Violet still hasn't regained her memories,' she explains delicately. 'She's not familiar with a lot of slang.' She puts her arm around Cody's shoulder. 'Maybe you can teach her the "hip" words teenagers are using. Help her become cool.'

Cody's eyes roll upward. It's an expression I've never seen before but make a mental note to attempt in front of the mirror later. 'First of all, Mom,' he says with a groan, 'no one uses the word *hip* except you, and second of all, I'm the last person in the world anyone should go to for tips on how to be cool.'

'Well, that's just not true,' Heather argues. 'You're cool to me.'

Cody's eyes roll again. 'Oh, great,' he says, his voice sounding hoarse and insincere. 'My *mother* thinks I'm cool. I'm sure the freshman chicks are going to fall all over themselves.'

Heather turns to me. 'Cody is starting high school in a couple of weeks. He's a bit nervous.'

'Mom!' He pushes her arm from his shoulder. '*Stop!*'

I watch him toss the strap of a large backpack over his arm and walk up the stairs. I'm intrigued by how much louder his footsteps are than anyone else's in the house. Particularly in proportion to his size.

'You'll have to excuse him,' Heather says as she finishes emptying the bags of groceries. 'He's at an awkward age.'

Awkward age. I dissect the phrase, trying to make it fit with what I just witnessed. Is she referring to his small size? Or the fact that he changes colour so frequently? I'm about to ask her to elaborate but she does so without prompting.

'Thirteen is hard. You don't know who you are yet. Who your real friends are. Who you can trust. You don't yet know what you're capable of.'

I absorb her definition, mulling it over. 'I suppose I'm at an awkward age too, then.'

She smiles. I like the way it crinkles the skin around her eyes. And slightly softens them. She closes a cabinet door and looks at me. 'Thank you,' she says.

'For what?'

'You have a good heart.'

I think back to the hospital, remembering what Kiyana said about my vitals, and assume that's what Heather is referring to. Although I don't understand how it relates to this conversation.

'Anyway,' she says, rinsing her hands in the sink, 'I suppose it doesn't help that Cody is only interested in math and science. It's been a long time since I was a teenager but I know those kinds of hobbies never help one's social situation in school. Plus, he's a bit on the small side. But his father didn't hit his growth spurt until he was fifteen.'

I listen to everything that Heather is saying even though I don't comprehend the meaning of all of it. I have a feeling, however, she doesn't need me to.

'You're a lucky girl to be so pretty so young,' she says to me. 'I'm sure wherever you're from, you didn't have any trouble getting dates or making friends.'

I wonder if that could be true.

She wipes her hands on a towel. 'Anyway, if Cody acts strangely it's because he gets nervous when he's around pretty girls. Give him some time to get used to you being here. He's a very sweet boy.'

I nod and smile, unsure of what to say next.

Heather suggests I go upstairs and rest, promising to call me when dinner's ready.

I don't argue. I'm anxious to be alone. I climb the steps quietly and retreat to my room, closing the door behind me.

I sit in the rocking chair and sway back and forth. The movement calms me. The range of motion is limited. Confined. It fits in a box.

I like things that fit in boxes. Especially boxes that have labels.

It's the misshapen, unmarked containers with unknown contents that bother me.

Although I tell myself not to, I think about the boy. I can't help it. He fascinates me. And infuriates me at the same time.

What does that mean?

Maybe nothing.

Maybe everything.

He wasn't like Cody. He was tall. Taller than me. His face was long and oval-shaped. His arms were not scrawny, but loosely defined by muscle. I assume this signifies he's already hit his 'growth spurt', as Heather called it. Which means he's older than thirteen. I find myself wishing I had a better frame of reference.

For everything.

Is it possible he really knows things about me? Where I'm from. What I'm like. Who I am.

'Sera. That's your name. It's short for Seraphina.'

Seraphina.

I walk over to the mirror and stare at my reflection while I repeat the name aloud, dissecting it in my mind.

'Sera. Short for Seraphina.'

Seraphina . . . Sera . . . S.

I hurry over to the dresser, pull open the drawer, and snatch up the locket, flipping it over to study the engraving on the back.

S + Z = 1609.

The equation that I can't solve. Despite the fact that math seems to come easy to me.

But perhaps that's the problem. Perhaps the equation has nothing to do with math.

'You're not who you think you are.'

I'm not anyone! I want to scream. I don't even *know* who I am. How can I possibly be someone I'm not?

My head starts to throb. I return to the chair and rock frantically back and forth, waiting for the motion to calm me once more. But this time it does nothing. I close my eyes and concentrate on the boy. On his face.

I watch his demeanour change as soon as he sees Heather approaching us. His face becomes sombre. Earnest.

'Try to remember what really happened . . .'

I create a mental index of everything I know to be true:

I like numbers.

I have a tattoo.

I like grilled cheese sandwiches.

And supermarkets.

I have long brown hair and purple eyes.

I survived a plane crash.

A plane crash I have no memory of.

A glitch in a computer erased me from a list.

'You were never on that plane . . .'

Suddenly my eyes flutter open. I rise from the chair and pace the room. I hate all these unanswered questions. I hate the doubt that he's planted in my mind. I hate that he's made me second-guess everything I know.

And mostly I hate how unforgettable he seems to be.

Somehow every memory in my brain has managed to abandon me and yet his face is the face I can't seem to chase away.

As I walk, I repeat my mantra.

I don't know him. I don't remember him. I can't trust him.

The last line makes me stop. Apprehensively I glance down at the locket in my hand. I draw in a deep breath and pop open the black heart-shaped door, removing the crumpled note and placing it on the dresser.

I ransack the room, searching everywhere until I find what I'm looking for in a nightstand by the bed.

A pen and a blank sheet of paper.

I place the paper next to the yellowed note and slowly, carefully, scrawl out two words.

Trust him.

I glance between the two messages – one yellowed and ragged and faded by lost time and salt water, and the other white and crisp and right now – and I see what I was afraid I would see.

They are exactly the same.

They were both written by my hand.

11
PROOF

Heather and Scott try to make conversation with me during dinner but I'm not really there. My mind is elsewhere.

More specifically, on the note.

The note that I wrote.

But *why*? This is the question that bothers me the most.

Did I intend it for me? Or for someone else?

It had to be for someone else.

Otherwise, doesn't that imply that I *knew* I was going to lose my memory? Why else would I need to remind myself to trust someone? But I know that's impossible. No one can predict a plane crash. No one can predict amnesia. Did I somehow manage to scrawl out the message right as the plane was going down? Just in case?

And who is *him*?

Trust *him*.

I can only think of one person. And he's the last person I want to trust. Because it would mean believing everything he's told me.

That there are people looking for me.

That I'm in danger.

That I was never on the plane.

No. I can't.

There are a million *hims* in the world. It seems far-fetched and completely irrational just to assume *that* boy is the one the note is referring to.

But I suppose if I really am the girl who wrote that note, then I at least owe it to myself – to *her* – to find out for sure.

After dinner I go to my bathroom and wash my face with the cleanser Heather bought for me at the store today. While I was in the hospital, Kiyana taught me how to take care of myself. Teeth need to be brushed, faces need to be washed, fingernails need to be kept clean. I find it annoying that I have to be reminded of these things that seem so basic. So human.

I have started over in so many ways I'm beginning to lose count. And I have a feeling I'm not one who loses count easily.

I notice a light under the door of Cody's bedroom. I can hear voices. Three in total. It sounds like an argument.

Cody told his parents at dinner that his friends from school were coming over.

I unlock the door and open it, revealing Cody and two similar-aged boys crowded around a giant board with a glossy white surface. It's covered in red scribbles. Cody holds a matching red marker in his hand.

The voices quiet immediately and all three boys turn to look at me.

'Haven't you ever heard of knocking?' Cody asks. I can infer from his tone that he's angry with me, although I'm not sure why.

'I have.'

He releases a funny sound from his nose. 'Then why didn't you?'

'I wasn't aware I was supposed to.'

One of the other boys starts to laugh and then covers his mouth with his hand.

'Well, you are,' Cody replies. His tone still has that edge to it. I don't like the way it makes me feel.

'Are you angry with me?' I ask, taking a step towards him, searching his face.

He won't look me in the eye. 'No,' he says, barely audible.

'You seem angry.'

'I'm not. What do you want?'

I look to the other boys, wondering if I can trust them with what I'm about to ask. Wondering if I can even trust Cody. But right now he's my only option. I would go to Heather and Scott, but something tells me that they wouldn't grant my request. And that they would ask me for explanations I'm not ready to give yet.

'I want to go to Los Angeles,' I finally say. 'To the airport, specifically.'

Cody laughs but it doesn't sound genuine. 'Then ask my parents to take you.'

'I can't go with them.'

'Well, good luck with that.'

I understand the phrase but I'm fairly certain he's not really wishing me luck. His tone and body language say otherwise. I find the contradiction frustrating.

'My parents are never going to let you leave this house alone,' he points out.

'Yes, I agree. That's why I'd like you to take me.'

His eyes widen. 'What? Now?'

'No,' I reply. 'In the morning. Before Heather and Scott wake up.'

'This girl has lost her mind,' he says to his friends.

'Yes,' I say again. 'And that's exactly why I need to go. To see if I can find it.'

They all laugh in unison now but I don't understand. Did I make a joke? I would hate to have made one without even realizing it. What a waste that would be.

'So, can you take me?' I repeat, once their amusement has subsided.

'No.' Cody turns his back to me and faces the whiteboard. He continues to write with his red marker.

'Why not?'

'Because I'm busy,' he snaps.

I glance at the whiteboard and review the series of scribbles. On closer inspection, I notice that the board is covered with numbers, letters and mathematical symbols.

'You're busy with this?' I confirm.

He doesn't look at me. 'Yes. If we can solve this problem, we start out freshman year with like zillions of extra credit. Not to mention go down in the math hall of fame. And since school starts in less than two weeks, I don't exactly have time for clandestine journeys to LA.'

'So if you solved it, you'd have time,' I conclude.

He snickers. 'Yeah, sure. If I solved it, then I'd have time to take you.'

'Well, what if I helped you solve it?' I suggest, feeling hopeful.

This makes him laugh again. The two other boys join in. 'Yeah, because someone like *you* is so likely to solve Goldbach's Conjecture, a conjecture that hasn't been proved or disproved in over two hundred and fifty years. Award-winning mathematicians around the world haven't been able to solve it, but *you*, the amnesiac supermodel, you can.'

'And if I do, you'll take me to Los Angeles?'

He finally turns back around and looks at me, replacing the cap on his red marker with a loud *click*. 'Yes.' He's smiling now. It's not the kind of smile I saw on Heather earlier today. His eyes don't crinkle. 'If you can prove or disprove that every even integer greater than two can be expressed as the sum of two primes, then I'll personally escort you to Los Angeles.'

I focus on the whiteboard, expanding my field of vision until I can see it all at once. Then I approach and examine each section individually, noticing where the boys started with the original formula and where they strayed off course. I grab the eraser from the shelf below and wipe out the second half of their markings, eliciting a series of gasps behind me.

'You c-c-can't . . .' I hear one of them stammer. 'She just erased two hours of work!'

I ignore the protests, pluck the red marker from Cody's hand, and continue where the proof leaves off. My hand moves fast. Almost faster than I can follow. I don't remember anything I'm doing and yet the numbers and symbols that are appearing on the whiteboard in front of me are familiar. Familiar in a way I can't explain. They don't come from memory. They come from somewhere else. I know how to form them like I know how to walk. How to speak. How to count items in a shopping cart.

I'm finished less than a minute later. I step back and examine my work. The entire white space is now filled. I circle the final result. 'Proved,' I say.

Cody doesn't reply. His mouth is hanging open at a funny angle. The other boys have similar expressions on their faces. I interpret them as surprise. I'm surprised as well. Not by the fact that I could do it. But by the fact that Cody inferred that it was near impossible. It definitely didn't *feel* impossible.

But I have other things on my mind to think about. Higher priority items on my list of impossibilities.

I hand the marker back to Cody, who is still silent, staring at the whiteboard, his eyes running rapidly across my lines of scribbles, his lips moving as he silently reads what I wrote. If he's checking it for errors, he won't find any.

That much I can be certain of.

It actually feels nice to be certain of something for once.

I make my way back to the bathroom. 'I think we should leave early tomorrow,' I tell him. 'Five a.m.'

Cody nods ever so slightly as I close the door behind me.

12
LINGUAL

It's still dark outside when we leave the house. I've taken the liberty of borrowing Scott's baseball cap again to hide my face from view and I'm dressed in the same clothes I wore yesterday. Heather had planned for us to go shopping today. I guess it will have to wait until I get back.

'I feel funny,' I tell Cody as we walk down the road that leads into town, glancing back at the sleeping house.

'It's called guilt,' he says. 'And I just want you to know that if I get in trouble for this – which I most certainly will – I'm telling them you kidnapped me.'

'Kidnap.' I echo. *'To abduct by force.'*

He makes that strange sound with his nose again. I think it's called a snort. 'So she's a walking dictionary too.'

'I didn't force you.'

'No, you're right,' he concedes. 'You hustled me.'

'Hustle,' I say. 'To be aggressive, especially in business matters.'

'It also means to con someone out of money. Like at pool.'

I frown. 'But I didn't take any money from you.'

'Never mind,' he replies quickly, hitching his backpack further up his shoulder. 'Why don't you just start by telling me how you proved Goldbach's conjecture?'

I shrug. 'I don't know.'

'Well, I don't believe you. I think you found it on the Web or something.'

'The Web,' I repeat with curiosity. 'Like a spiderweb?'

Cody gives me a strange look. 'No, the *World Wide* Web. You know, the Internet. You seriously don't even remember *that*?'

'I don't remember anything.'

'But you can walk and talk and prove unsolvable conjectures.'

I take a deep breath. 'I guess so.'

The road is silent. And very dark. There are no street lamps like the ones I noticed when we were in town yesterday. But I can see Cody's face perfectly. His forehead is crumpled and his lips are twisted to the side.

'So then how could you not know what the Internet is?'

This is the very thing that frustrates me. 'I don't know. I can't explain it. I know certain words but not others. There doesn't seem to be a pattern. Or if there is, I haven't found it yet.'

Cody glances at me out of the corner of his eye. 'That's gotta suck.' Then, upon noticing my puzzlement, he hastily adds, 'I mean, that has to be hard.' He motions towards my left wrist. 'And I suppose you don't remember why you chose to get such a weird tattoo?'

I cover the thin black marking with my other hand, embarrassed by it. 'No.'

Cody pushes my hand away and leans down to get a closer look. Then his eyes light up. 'Whoa, I wonder if it's like a gang symbol or something.'

'Huh?'

He shakes his head. 'Nothing.'

'So what is it?' I ask.

'What?'

'The Internet.'

'Oh. Right. It's . . .' He pauses, wheeling his hand around in a circle. 'Well, it's where you find everything.'

The definition intrigues me. 'Can we go there?'

He laughs. It sounds kinder than the one I heard last night in his bedroom. 'No, you don't *go* there. It's on a computer. Or a phone. Or a mobile device.' He reaches into his pocket and pulls out what I now recognize as a cellphone. It lights up at the press of a button and he begins tapping on it.

'Look,' he says, handing it to me. 'This is the bus schedule. It's posted on the Internet.' He points to a line of text and my gaze follows his finger. 'This is the bus we're taking to LA. It leaves here in twenty minutes and gets into Los Angeles at 9:42 a.m.'

He shows me how you can scroll through the rest of the page and I absorb the information eagerly. 'What else can it tell you?' I say when I reach the bottom.

He shrugs. 'Anything.'

My mind is on fire. The thought of all that data – that information – accessible through a single device, is unbelievable. I want to search for more, but Cody takes the phone back and returns it to his pocket. 'It's faster if you have Wi-Fi.'

We arrive at the bus station five minutes later and Cody leads me to the ticket counter. He speaks to a man sitting behind a clear pane of glass.

'Two round-trip tickets to Los Angeles, please.'

The man taps three times on a screen in front of him. 'That'll be $138.00.'

Cody turns to me. 'I'm guessing you forgot your bank account information too, huh?'

'I . . .' I fumble awkwardly.

'Figures,' he says, and then reaches into his pocket and produces a pile of green bills. 'This is nearly two weeks of allowance. You owe me big time.'

Mounted on the counter is the same kind of card-reading device that I saw at the supermarket yesterday. I point to it. 'Why don't you just use that?' I ask, trying to be helpful.

But once again, I've said the wrong thing. Cody groans as he hands the man two bills. 'Because my parents won't get me a credit card. No matter how many times I ask. But thanks for reminding me.'

'Credit card,' I repeat, dissecting the words. '*Credit: commendation or honour given for some action. Card: a rectangular piece of stiff paper.*'

The man behind the glass gives me an odd look as he hands Cody our tickets. Cody flashes him a hurried smile. 'She's from –' he grabs my arm and leads me away from the ticket counter as he mumbles – 'somewhere else. You're like a small child,' he tells me sharply. 'You really don't know *anything*.'

The comment stings the back of my throat. I have to swallow before speaking. 'I suppose I did at one point.'

Cody shakes his head. 'A credit card is a plastic card that you use instead of cash. It keeps track of what you purchase and then, at the end of every month, you pay the total. I swear I feel like I'm in a bad sci-fi movie. Are you sure you're not from outer space?'

'I don't think so.'

He laughs. 'Well, it would certainly explain a lot. Wouldn't it?'

'How so?'

Cody rubs one of his bushy yellow eyebrows with his finger. 'Never mind. Look, I'm going to use the bathroom. Wait here until I get back and don't go anywhere, OK?'

I nod. 'OK.'

He points to an orange plastic chair behind me. 'Sit there.'

I do.

'Don't move.'

I watch him disappear behind a door marked MEN, and I peer around the room, counting the number of people (eleven) and the number of seats like the one I'm sitting in (forty-eight).

A young brown-haired woman in a blue dress approaches and asks me if I know when the bus to San Francisco stops here.

'Five forty-five,' I tell her.

She seems to be pleasantly surprised by my response. 'Are you going there too?'

'No. I'm going to Los Angeles. But I read the bus schedule.'

'Do you live there?' she asks.

'Maybe,' I say, and then upon seeing her confused expression and not wanting to attract any unnecessary attention to myself, I quickly add, 'My family lives there.'

It's only the second time I've lied. The first was when I told Heather that the boy in the supermarket parking lot merely recognized me from the news. I'm starting to understand the purpose of lying. It's a protection mechanism.

'How nice,' the woman says. 'Are you from Portugal or Brazil?'

I'm confused by the question, unsure of why she would assume these are the only two options. Do I look like I'm from Portugal? Or Brazil? And if so, why has no one else remarked on that before?

'I don't really understand,' I begin. I want to ask her why

she's made this seemingly arbitrary assumption, hoping it might reveal some clue to my identity, but I'm not given the chance. I feel an urgent tug at my arm. Cody pulls me out of the seat and leads me to the other side of the station.

'OK,' he says, his voice serious. 'First of all, don't talk to random people in bus stations. It's sketchy. Especially given your . . . well, celebrity status.'

'She asked me about the bus to San Francisco.'

'And *secondly*,' he continues, ignoring me, 'and probably more important, um, hello? You speak Portuguese?'

'I don't know.'

'How could you not know? I heard you back there.'

'Heard me what?'

'Speaking Portuguese,' he clarifies, sounding exasperated. 'To that woman.'

I glance over his shoulder at the young woman in the blue dress. She's taken the seat I just vacated. I think back to our conversation, suddenly hearing it differently in my memory.

'Você sabe quando o ônibus para São Francisco chega?'

'Cinco e quarenta e cinco.'

'I speak Portuguese?' I repeat Cody's question.

'It would appear so.'

I reflect on what this means. Where I might have learned it. Perhaps I lived there once. Or perhaps I really *am* from Portugal or Brazil, just as the woman speculated. Is that why no one has come for me? Because they live in another country?

'When I was little I had a nanny from Portugal,' Cody says. 'She used to watch Portuguese soaps all the time.'

'Do you think that might be where I'm from?' I ask.

Cody shrugs. 'I guess it's possible. But you don't speak English with an accent so I don't know.'

I don't know either. I index this incident away in my mental file, adding it to the slow-growing list of clues I've collected.

The only problem is, so far the clues don't exactly fit together in any coherent way.

What does Portuguese have to do with the locket? Or with this tattoo on my wrist? Or with the boy who claims to know me?

'I'm learning all sorts of interesting stuff about you,' Cody says, that peculiar distortion suddenly back in his tone.

'Me too.'

A loud voice comes from a speaker above our heads, announcing the arrival of bus 312 to Los Angeles. 'Well, that's us,' Cody says. 'Should we go find that lost mind of yours?'

I gaze out the window at the large silver-and-blue vehicle pulling noisily up to the kerb. There's an illustration of a dog on the side. He's running. To where? I don't know.

I wonder if he does.

There's a sign on the front of the bus that reads LOS ANGELES.

It's a start. I suppose I can't ask for much more at this point.

'Yes,' I reply to Cody, taking a deep breath. 'Let's go.'

13
GRUDGES

The bus isn't smooth like the car we took from the hospital. It's jerky and smells funny. And there are no buttons to make the windows go down. As soon as we sit, Cody takes his phone out of his pocket and I get excited because I think he's going to show me more about the Internet. But instead he holds the phone close to his face and becomes incredibly absorbed in running his fingertip across the screen in rapid motion, causing images of small animals to move around.

I face forward and allow my eyes to drift shut.

But the second they close, he's there. The boy. His mouth is curved in that easy smile. His eyes gaze at me with an undeniable longing.

'So you do remember . . . At least some part of you does.'

My eyes flutter back open. I stare at the seat in front of me. Blue cloth. A fold-up table. A pouch made of string. I try to distract myself by counting the threads in the fabric, but it doesn't work.

My mind still wanders. To him. His smooth, settling voice speaking such jagged, unsettling things.

I wish proving or disproving his claims were as easy as solving Goldbach's conjecture. A few lines of formulas on a whiteboard. A few calculations and it's done. Circled. Disproved. Moving on.

But it's not.

So here I am. On this bus. Travelling one hundred and seventy-five miles to try to refute something I'm unable to refute on my own.

Maybe then it will go away – this feeling I get every time I see his face in my mind. It starts deep in my stomach and spreads quickly. Growing stronger by the second. And if I focus on his eyes, it becomes unbearable. It's like a sickness. A prickle just under my skin. A clenching of muscles.

And the worst part is, I don't know what it is. I can't label it. Is it simply because I'm a girl and he's a boy? Some kind of biological, hormonal reaction to the opposite sex that I have no control over?

But if that's the case, then I should feel the same sensation when I'm around Cody. Who's also a boy. However, when I turn and look at him, his face partially lit by the screen of his phone, the feeling vanishes. I stare longer, harder, waiting for it to return, but it doesn't.

He looks up at me with a displeased expression. 'Can I help you?'

I shake my head. 'I don't think so.'

'What's the matter? Spellbound by my irresistible good looks?'

I'm once again perplexed by his cutting tone. 'What is that?'

He glances down at his screen. 'A game.'

'No, in your voice. Why do you talk like that?'

'Like what?'

'You say things you don't mean.'

He chuckles. 'It's called sarcasm. You don't have that in your little mental dictionary either?'

'I do,' I admit.

'Well, there you go.' He turns his attention back to the phone.

'You don't like me.'

He smiles but I can tell immediately it's not the genuine kind. I'm starting to realize that there's a difference. And it's an important one.

'That's not true. I like you tremendously.'

And there it is again.

'Why are you bitter?' I ask.

'Bitter?'

'Sarcasm: bitterness. Used to convey scorn or insult. Why are you bitter?'

He sighs and places the phone down in his lap. 'I'm not bitter.'

'Then why are you conveying scorn or insult?'

He shifts in his seat. 'OK, I'm not bitter at *you*, specifically. More at . . . I don't know . . . girls *like* you.'

I struggle with this. 'Girls like me?'

His face starts to turn that peculiar shade of red again. 'You know –' he glances out the window – 'girls who *look* like you.'

'What do I look like?'

He groans and peers back at me. 'Are you really going to make me say it?'

I don't reply.

'Pretty!' he finally says, the red deepening. He faces the window again. 'OK? You're very pretty. You should be a model. If you're not already. There you go.'

I process this. 'And you don't like that.'

I can see his reflection in the glass. He's shaking his head and closing his eyes. 'No. I do. It's just that pretty girls don't normally talk to guys like me. Or if they do . . . Well, let's just say they're not very nice.'

'So you're bitter,' I confirm. 'At pretty girls.'

'Yeah,' he says, kicking the seat in front of him. 'But I will admit that you're not like the rest of them.'

This statement makes me feel happy and sad at the same time. 'Why not?'

'Well, for starters, none of the pretty girls I know can prove Goldbach's conjecture. And . . . you know . . . you actually *talk* to me.'

'So maybe then you shouldn't be bitter at *all* pretty girls,' I say.

He laughs. 'You're starting to sound like my mother.'

'Is that good?'

'It's –' he struggles – 'complicated.'

I'm starting to wonder if there's anything that isn't.

'What about you?' he asks, finally facing me again. The scarlet tinge to his skin is gone.

'What about me?'

He digs a bottle of water out of his backpack and unscrews the cap. 'Think you had a boyfriend back home? You know, before your memory went all MIA.' He takes a sip.

I consider the question, attempting to translate the term *boyfriend*. 'You mean a male lover?' I ask.

Water sprays from his mouth, a few droplets landing on me. A woman across the aisle gives us a contemptuous look.

'Sure,' he replies, when he finally stops laughing. 'A male lover. Did you have one of those?'

I think about the locket tucked away in the top drawer of my dresser.

'I'm the one who gave it to you.'

I shake my head. 'I don't remember.'

'I'm sure you had *several*,' he affirms with a nod and another sip of water. This time it stays in his mouth.

'I doubt it,' I say, closing my eyes and resting my head against the seat.

'Well, then, in that case, you're probably better off.'

My eyes open again in surprise. 'Why?'

He shrugs. 'Not that I have any experience in the matter, but from what I've heard love's a total bitch.'

'A what?'

'A pain in the butt,' he rephrases, and then upon seeing my still-confused expression, he tries a third time. 'A real drag. You know, like up and down and back and forth. "I love him, no, I hate him, no I love him again but I think he really likes Claire. Can you *please, please* ask him for me." I don't know, it sounds like a total waste of time to me.'

'Yeah,' I agree wholeheartedly, trying to ignore the warm tingle that has started glowing in the centre of my forehead. 'Definitely not for me.'

14
CONFIRMATION

From the station in downtown Los Angeles, we take a bus to the airport. Cody has navigated the entire journey using his cellphone, further increasing my longing to acquire one of my own.

When we arrive, he asks, 'So what now? Do you like have a plan or something?'

I don't really. I glance around, hoping something will feel the slightest bit familiar. It doesn't. I'm not sure why I keep thinking that eventually *something* will trigger a response – a memory – when so far nothing has. 'I guess I just wanted to talk to anyone who might have seen me get on the plane.'

Cody's forehead crinkles. 'What do you mean?'

'Well, I was supposedly on Freedom Airlines flight 121 to Tokyo. And I want to authenticate that.'

'Whoa, whoa,' he says, hoisting both hands in the air. 'You're telling me you dragged me all the way here to confirm something that the news has already confirmed a thousand times?'

The sidewalk is crowded. People come and go, lugging large bags behind them. I pull the brim of my borrowed cap further down my face.

'How do I know they're telling the truth?' I ask Cody.

'What makes you think they're not?'

I consider telling Cody about the reporter in the crowd and the boy at the supermarket. About the things he said. '*You were never on that plane and you know it*.' But I decide it's not something I want to repeat yet. At least not until I have more evidence.

'It's just a feeling,' I tell him. 'There are still things that don't add up. Why was I not on the passenger manifest?'

This doesn't appear to concern Cody. 'My dad said it was a computer glitch.'

'What if it wasn't?' I challenge. 'What if they're lying?'

Cody takes a moment to ponder this. 'Why would they lie about *that*? If anything they would lie and say that you *were* on the manifest. To cover their own corporate butts.'

I can't decipher that phrase but I let it go. 'I just need to know for sure.'

He hikes his backpack up his shoulder and breathes a heavy sigh. 'Fine. Let's go see if we can find someone to talk to.'

We enter through a set of automatic doors and stand in line at the international ticket counter for Freedom Airlines. I recognize the logo on the wall. It's the same one that was on the piece of plane debris that I watched being pulled from the ocean. I half expect myself to shudder upon seeing it up close, but I don't.

When we get to the front of the line, a woman beckons us forward from behind the counter. I follow Cody as he approaches her, keeping my eyes downcast.

'Good morning,' he says, after clearing his throat. I'm amused at how different his voice sounds. As though he's purposely trying to deepen it.

I'm glad I asked Cody for help. He's proved himself to be a

true asset today. Even if he does claim I hustled him into coming.

'Good morning,' the woman echoes with a welcoming smile. 'Are you checking in?'

Without looking up, I give Cody a nudge and he says, 'No. Actually we were hoping to speak to someone about flight 121. You know, the one that crashed.'

Her smile vanishes instantly. 'I'm sorry. We're not authorized to speak about that.'

Cody turns to me and shrugs. 'You heard her. They can't talk about it. Let's go.'

He starts to leave but I snag his shirt between my fingers and twist him back around. He groans and tries again. 'We were just hoping to talk to someone who maybe was there when the flight boarded or maybe someone who was working the counter that day.'

The woman's face tightens even more. 'I told you. I'm not authorized to talk to anyone about that flight. If you're not checking in or purchasing a ticket, I'm going to have to ask you to leave.'

Cody sighs and reaches over to push up the brim of my hat, exposing my face.

He doesn't have to say anything. The loud gasp tells me the woman clearly recognizes me. 'It's . . . you.' Her voice is hushed. Broken.

I nod.

'What are you doing here?' she asks anxiously.

'I really need to speak to someone about that flight.'

She shakes her head adamantly. 'No. You need to leave. Now.'

'Were you there?' I press on, ignoring her warning. 'Did you happen to see me get on the plane? Can you confirm that I was on the flight?'

'I told you. I can't talk about this. You shouldn't even be here.'

'Please.' My voice starts to quiver. 'I'm just trying to answer *one* of the million questions that are piling up in my head. I'm . . . lost. And frustrated. And I don't know what to believe. I have to talk to someone.'

The woman grabs a nearby phone and starts punching buttons. 'I'm calling Security.'

'And *that* would be our cue to leave,' Cody says, wrapping his fingers around my elbow and tugging me away from the counter.

'No,' I protest, yanking my arm free. I turn back to the woman at the counter. 'Will someone just talk to me? Please?'

She ignores me, speaking brusquely into the phone. 'We have a situation at position 12. Requesting assistance immediately.'

Cody gives me a grave look. 'We either leave, or we get thrown out. And trust me, option two is going to cause a much bigger scene than option one. So unless you want your face all over the news again, I suggest we get the hell out of here.'

I really don't want to deal with another media circus so I surrender with a sigh, pull my cap down over my eyebrows again, and follow Cody out the door until we're back on the busy kerb.

I collapse on to a metal bench and clutch my head in my hands.

Cody slowly lowers down next to me. He pats me awkwardly on the back three times before folding his hands in his lap. 'Sorry,' he offers.

I lift my head. 'What do we do now?'

'I don't think we have much of a choice. We should probably just head home.'

'But I have to know.'

'Violet,' he says gently, 'I don't think there's anything to know. Are you sure you're not simply in denial or something?'

I wish I was. I wish I could deny everything that boy said to me. Every doubt in my mind. But I can't.

'Excuse me?' I hear a delicate voice say. Cody and I both look up to see a petite blonde woman standing next to us. She's dressed in the same navy-blue uniform that the woman at the Freedom Airlines ticket counter was wearing.

Upon seeing my half-shadowed face, she sucks in a large gulp of air. 'Wow, it really is you.'

'Can we help you?' Cody asks defensively.

She glances surreptitiously over both shoulders. 'I overheard you. At the ticket counter.'

'Yeah, what of it?' Cody demands.

She seems oblivious to his petulant tone. 'I'm Brittany,' she says, sounding anxious. She touches her hairline. Then her ear. Then her mouth. She chews on a fingernail. Finally, after another peek over her shoulder, she whispers, 'I was the gate agent for flight 121. I scanned all the boarding passes of the passengers getting on the plane.'

My eyes open wide and I launch to my feet. 'So you saw me get on? You can confirm that I was on the plane when it went down?'

Cody stands up and offers Brittany an apologetic glance. 'She's a little paranoid,' he explains. 'I imagine it's typical of amnesiacs. Her memory is completely gone and for some reason she's come up with this crazy idea that maybe possibly somehow for whatever far-fetched reason, she was never on the plane. I tried to tell her, of course, that this is ludicrous. But she needs to hear it from someone else, I guess. So if you could put her mind at ease and tell her that—'

'That's the thing,' Brittany says, closing her eyes for a moment. 'I can't.'

'I know, I know,' Cody continues, waving his hand in the air. 'You've been given strict orders by your supervisor to keep quiet and not talk about—'

'I mean,' she interrupts again, her voice barely audible, 'I can't confirm that you were on the plane.'

'What?' Cody blurts out.

'Shh, *please*,' she urges, glancing nervously at a group of travellers who are hurrying past. 'I'm . . . I could get in serious trouble for talking to you. I haven't told anyone about this because it doesn't make any sense. I know that. So I've been trying to forget about it. But then I saw you there at the ticket counter. I heard what you were asking . . .'

A knot forms in my stomach.

'I don't remember you,' she says heavily. 'I've *tried* to remember you, I swear. Every night I think about it. I play back the whole day in my mind. Over and over again. But you're just not there.' She pauses to suck in a juddering breath. 'I'm sorry but I – I don't remember seeing you board the plane.'

'Well, yeah,' Cody argues, clearly unconvinced. 'But there were probably like two hundred people on that plane. Not to mention all the other flights you board every day. You can't be expected to remember *everyone*.'

Brittany shifts her weight. She reaches up to touch her hair again and I now notice that her hands are shaking. 'Yes, but when they showed your photo on the news, you were so . . . beautiful . . . I mean, simply *breathtaking*. And your eyes . . . I – I . . .' Her voice trails off as her gaze flickers nervously to mine. The longer she waits in silence, the more I worry she won't ever finish her sentence.

But then, finally, she bites her lip and leans towards me. Her eyes are watery and full of fear when she whispers, 'I just *know* I would have remembered a face like that.'

PART 2

THE RETURN

15 RATIONALIZATIONS

Cody has not stopped talking since we left the airport. I think the gate agent upset him. Or rather, what she said. His speech has changed. It's faster. His voice is higher. He's using his hands a lot more than he normally does. His eyes are dilated.

'There are probably five hundred reasons why that woman doesn't remember you,' he says as we ride the bus back to the station. 'All of which, might I add, are a thousand times more believable than the completely implausible idea that you weren't on the plane.'

I'm feeling just as anxious and confused as Cody is but I keep my reaction on the inside. Along with my thoughts. So I can try to sort through them and make sense of this.

'For instance,' Cody continues passionately, 'she could have been called away for a moment while the plane was boarding. And another gate agent stepped in. And *that's* when you boarded the plane. You could have been wearing another hat.' He flicks the one on my head. 'Like this. You could have been looking down when you boarded. I mean, really, who looks the gate agent right in the eye when they get on a plane? I certainly don't. And she's been through *a lot* this past week. One of the flights she boarded *crashed* into the Pacific Ocean. And everyone died!' He glances briefly at me. 'Sorry. I mean, *almost* everyone. But that has to affect a person's memory a little. I mean, she's not exactly the most reliable witness.'

Cody is right. Just because that gate agent never saw me get on the plane doesn't mean I wasn't on it.

It doesn't mean the boy in the parking lot was right.

Although that would certainly explain a lot.

Why I survived when no one else did.

Why I wasn't on the passenger manifest.

If it's true that I was never on the plane, then that would mean there was no glitch. Except the one that still holds my memories captive.

'Here's another plausible explanation,' Cody says, oblivious to my silence. 'You're actually a terrorist. You snuck into the baggage compartment and were planning to blow up the plane. She never saw you *board* the plane because you never did. You were a stowaway. And the airline is blaming a computer glitch to keep the whole thing hush-hush.'

The baggage compartment?

Is that where I was? Did I sneak on to the plane? Am I a terrorist?

My mind struggles to process the barrage of new questions piling up on top of all the still-unanswered ones that have already amassed in my brain.

Did the boy at the supermarket *know* that the gate agent wouldn't remember me? Does he work for the airline? Is that who he claims is looking for me?

'Seriously, what is she implying?' Cody asks. 'That you just happened to be floating in the middle of the ocean in the *exact* same spot that a plane crashed down? Or that maybe the plane crashed right on top of a boat – or raft – that you just *happened* to have been riding on.'

I can tell from the scornful quality of his voice that he's doing that sarcasm thing again.

'Oh! Oh! I've got it!' Cody says, clapping his hands together. A few other passengers on the bus look up. I glimpse nervously behind me and take notice of a tall, thin, middle-aged man with fiery red hair and a matching beard. He gazes at me intensely with his head cocked to one side. It's making me nervous. I pull my cap further down, bow my head and turn back around.

'The plane crashed *and*, at the exact same time, you magically just . . . *fell* from the sky!' Cody rants. 'You're a fallen angel, that's it. Why didn't I think of it before?' He slaps himself on the forehead. 'That would certainly explain the face.'

I'm not sure he's even talking to me any more. He's not looking at me. He appears to be speaking more to himself at this point. But as jumbled as Cody's chatter may be, he's touched upon a very important point.

If I wasn't on the plane, why was I found near the crash site?

The odds that I just happened to be at the same place at the same time are too slim to even calculate. Which means there's another explanation.

One that I'm determined to find.

'Uh-oh,' I hear Cody say. His voice has shifted. It sounds normal again. I glance over to see him frowning at his cellphone.

'What's wrong?' I ask. They're the first words I've said aloud since we left the airport.

'The parental inquisition. They're calling.' He shows me the phone and I read the screen.

Call from Home.

And it looks like they've already called six times.' He winces. 'Obviously they've noticed that we're gone. Should I answer it?'

'Yes.'

His face contorts. 'Are you crazy? That was a rhetorical question. I'm not answering it.'

'They'll be worried.'

'Yeah. And *pissed.*' He makes a hissing sound with his teeth. 'If I'm going to get totally reamed out, I'd rather it only happened once.'

'What do you mean?'

He sighs. 'If I answer it, they're going to yell at me for taking you out of town. Then when we get home, they're going to yell at me *again.* So if I don't answer and just take you home, I'll only receive one scream fest. Get it?'

The phone has stopped ringing.

That funny feeling punches me in the stomach again. The one Cody earlier identified as guilt.

'Maybe you should tell them that we're OK?' I suggest. 'So they don't worry.'

Cody settles into his seat and gazes out the window. 'Nah. We're almost at the bus station. We'll be home in a few hours. They can just chill until then.'

16
PROMISES

'ARE YOU OUT OF YOUR MIND?' Heather's voice screams from the balcony as Cody and I scamper down the driveway of the house four hours later. 'YOU DISAPPEAR WITH NO NOTE. AND NO PHONE CALL. AND YOU TAKE A POOR, HELPLESS AMNESIAC GIRL WITH YOU? DO YOU NOT SEE WHAT'S WRONG WITH THIS PICTURE, CODY?'

Cody shoots me a sideways glance as Heather hurries down the stairs and starts to stomp towards us.

'Your father was about to call the police! Do you have any idea what would happen if the authorities found out that we *lost* a foster-child on her *third* day of staying with us?'

She grabs Cody by the elbow and he whimpers as though he's in pain. I know that I have to say something. I have a responsibility to Cody. To deflect Heather's anger.

'Heather, this is not Cody's fault,' I say quickly. 'It's mine. I forced him to take me. He didn't want to go but I made him.'

I notice Heather's grip on Cody's arm loosen. 'Take you where?' she asks. Her voice softens when she addresses me and

I immediately feel regret for getting Cody involved. Especially when he didn't want to go in the first place. I probably should have tried to figure it out on my own.

'To Los Angeles,' I tell her.

'YOU TOOK HER TO LOS ANGELES?' Heather's voice is back to a roar and her fingers retighten around Cody's biceps.

'Please,' I implore. 'Please don't be angry with him. He tried to stop me. But I was determined to go.'

'What on earth were you doing back in Los Angeles?'

Cody's eyes flicker to me. I immediately know what he's thinking. He's wondering if I'm going to tell Heather the truth. About what we did. About who we talked to. About what she told us.

'I . . .' I begin with hesitation.

Lying protects people.

'I wanted to go to the airport,' I finish. 'I thought it might trigger a memory. I thought it would help.'

Heather exhales a heavy sigh and releases Cody's arm. I hear myself sigh as well. 'Violet,' she begins, her voice once again gentle. Patient. It's the Heather from yesterday and the day before. The one who picked me up from the hospital and made me a grilled cheese sandwich. 'You can't just sneak out of the house. You're our responsibility now. It's our job to make sure you're safe. And we can't do that unless we know where you are at all times.'

'I'm sorry,' I say. 'I shouldn't have left.'

'No, you shouldn't have,' she says, and then she turns her attention back to Cody. 'And *you*,' she says, her voice sharpening. 'You shouldn't have taken her. You're grounded until school starts.'

'Mom! That's so not fair! You heard her! She basically kidnapped me.'

'I don't care,' Heather says. 'You're still grounded.'

Cody kicks at a pebble on the driveway. 'This sucks!'

I want to ask what *grounded* means but I suspect it's not the right time. Regardless of the definition, I can read Cody's body language well enough to know that the word doesn't have a positive association. I reach out and gently touch Cody's hair. It's something Kiyana used to do to me in the hospital when I was upset and somehow it always made me feel better. 'I'm sorry, Cody.'

His face reddens and he ducks out from under my reach. Then he lumbers towards the house, mumbling, 'Whatever.'

Heather looks at me again. 'Violet, honey. You know if you want to go someplace you can come to us.'

'I didn't think you would take me.'

My first piece of truth.

Heather reaches out and rubs my arm. 'Of course we'll take you. Anywhere you want to go. Just promise me, in the future, if you want to go somewhere, you'll ask us.'

And apparently my last piece as well. Because before I even open my mouth, I know my answer will be another lie. 'I promise.'

'Good.' She smiles. The first one I've seen since we arrived home. 'So, did it work?'

'Did what work?' I ask.

'Going to the airport. Did it trigger any memories?'

In a flash I see everything: Brittany, the gate agent. The ocean. My locket. The engraving. The boy.

'Try to remember what really happened. Try to remember me.'

'No,' I say.

She puts an arm around my shoulder and squeezes. 'Don't worry. It will all come back to you eventually.'

I nod, as though I agree, and barely muster a smile.

'And first thing tomorrow,' she says brightly, 'I'm taking you somewhere that's guaranteed to get your mind off things for a while.'

I glance over at her, genuinely curious. 'Where?'

She flashes me a wide grin and a wink. 'The mall.'

17
EXPOSED

The mall is a crazy place. Massive and full of people and activity.

Heather does most of the shopping. As we walk through something called a department store, she plucks items from the racks and expresses her enthusiasm with phrases like, 'Oh, this is adorable!' and 'You would look so cute in this!' and 'If I had your tiny figure, I would wear this!'

A friendly lady named Irina shows us into a small room in the back where I'm supposed to put on the clothes to see if they fit right.

'Do you want me to come in with you?' Heather asks. 'Or I can wait out here and you can come out and show me the stuff you like.'

I shrug. I don't really have a preference. 'Whatever you prefer.'

She opts for entering the dressing room with me. 'Just in case you need help putting anything on,' she explains. 'Some of those zippers can be hard to reach.'

Heather sits on a bench and watches as one by one I try on all the clothes she selected for me. Since I don't seem to have an opinion about anything she makes the final decisions on what is working and what is not.

'Isn't this fun?' she asks as I slide a purple dress over my head. Heather pulls it down around my knees.

I nod to appease her. 'Yes. It's fun.' Even though I actually find the process quite tedious.

'Oh,' she breathes, her eyes lighting up as she admires the dress. 'That is just stunning on you!' She stands up and motions eagerly towards the door. 'Let's take a look in the big mirror.'

She leads me out into the hallway and towards a platform with three mirrors forming a semicircle around it. 'Go ahead, step up there so you can see it from the back.'

I do as I'm told, turning from side to side to view the dress from every angle. I admit, it is a nice dress. The fabric is lightweight and soft. The colour matches my eyes. And it seems to fit me well. But beyond that, I'm not really sure what Heather is getting so excited about.

I hear a trample of footsteps behind us and four girls prance into the dressing room, giggling.

'OMG, Lacey!' one of them exclaims. 'That skirt is going to look so good on you. Trevor is going to fall madly in love with you the moment you walk into that party tonight.'

I look at the girl holding the hanger with the skirt on it – Lacey, I presume – and our eyes meet for a brief second. She offers me a tight-lipped smile before slipping into one of the dressing rooms with her friends and closing the door.

'You totally have to get it,' another girl chimes in. 'It'll go perfectly with that white belt you bought last week.'

I continue to listen in on their conversation as Heather leads me back into our stall and helps me out of the dress.

'They sound about your age,' she remarks as she hands me another one to try. 'Do you want to go talk to them? Maybe ask them for an opinion on what we picked out?'

I slip my arms through the sleeves and shake my head. I can't think of one thing to say to those girls. It's not as though we have anything in common. I'm an amnesiac who likes to count things, and they seem to be most focused on whether or not a belt will make someone named Trevor fall in love faster.

Plus, after observing their excitement, I'm starting to think that my disinterest in trying on clothes is not normal. I wonder if I used to be as enthusiastic about shopping as they are. Before my life became one giant black void and all I had left was an empty locket, a cryptic note and a mountain of unanswered questions.

Somehow I doubt it.

I'm starting to get the feeling my life was *never* normal.

'That one's nice too,' Heather comments. 'Let's add it to the pile.'

I slide it over my head and hand it back to Heather.

There's a knock on the door. 'How's it going in there?' Irina asks.

Heather takes inventory of the items she's placed in her collection. 'We're almost done.' She holds up the purple dress to me. 'I think you should wear this one out. It looks so pretty on you.'

'If you hand me the tag, I'll ring it up,' Irina offers from the other side of the door.

'Great.' Heather pulls the price tag from the dress and places the hanger on the hook. Then she scoops her selections into her arms. 'I'll pick out a few accessories and meet you by the cash register.'

'OK.'

She slips out the dressing-room door and I'm left alone with my reflection.

Lacey and her giggling cohort exit a few moments later and the room falls silent. I stare at the girl in the mirror wearing nothing but her underwear. I take in her smooth honey-coloured skin, long lean legs, glossy chestnut hair and violet eyes. Despite everything that's happened – despite the efforts I've made – she's still just another unfamiliar thing that I hope to recognize one day.

Heather said I was beautiful. The nurses at the hospital said I was beautiful. Even Irina said I was beautiful when she showed us into this dressing room. But I can't see it.

I don't know what beautiful looks like.

And suddenly I find myself wondering if that boy from the supermarket thinks I'm beautiful too.

That spot in the centre of my forehead begins to glow with heat again. Like it did when he stood before me in the parking lot. I try to push the thought from my mind, feeling embarrassed for even entertaining it.

Just then, I hear Irina's voice through the closed door. She's whispering but I hear every word.

'No. It's her. I swear,' she says. 'She has those same purple eyes. It's the girl. The one from the news, who survived that crash. She's here buying clothes.'

My whole body turns to ice and I yank the door open and see that she's speaking into her cellphone. 'Please don't,' I plead. 'Don't tell anyone that I'm here. I can't handle any more media circuses. I can't go through that again.'

Irina's mouth falls open and her cellphone slips from her hand. She barely manages to catch it and fumble it back to her ear. 'I'll call you back,' she says hurriedly, and tucks the phone into her pocket.

'I'm so s-s-sorry,' she stammers, her eyes wide. 'It was my

sister. She won't tell anyone. I was simply so excited to meet you. We never get celebrities in the store.'

'I'm not a celebrity,' I insist. 'I'm just a girl trying to figure out who she is and where she came from.'

Truth.

It feels good.

She nods and gestures quickly between the two of us. 'Well, this has to be some kind of clue, right?'

'What?'

'The fact that you speak Russian, of course. And so flawlessly! Not even an accent!'

I blink. 'What are you talking ab—' But before I can finish the question, I hear it. The words. The unfamiliar, sharp sounds. They're not Portuguese. And they're certainly not English.

'They did not mention that on the news,' she says. And I now hear it in her voice too. The same language.

Russian.

I speak Russian.

On top of everything else.

'There must be some mistake,' I say, switching to English and going back into my dressing room. I close the door and lock it, falling on to the small stool and burying my head in my hands.

I haven't cried since the day Kiyana showed me my own face in the hospital. But I can't help it. The tears form on their own. I have no control over them. They stream down my face. I sniffle and try to wipe them away but it's an endless task. They just keep coming.

'Are you all right, dear?' Irina calls through the door, thankfully in English.

'Yes,' I lie, although I can't imagine it's very convincing.

'I'm . . . going to help your . . . moth– um . . . the woman you came in with.' I hear Irina's footsteps retreat and I start to sob again.

Mother. That's what she was about to say.

My mother.

Even *she* knows Heather's not my mother. Even she knows I have no family. At least not one that cares enough to come claim me. Who is my mother? Does she speak Russian? Portuguese? Both?

Is she good at math like I am?

Does she hate to shop too?

Is she so busy that she doesn't have time to watch the news and see that her daughter is lost and alone and in desperate need of some answers that make sense?

I hear a faint knock on the dressing-room door. Irina must have told Heather that I was upset. And Heather, being the kind, caring replacement mother that she is, came running to help.

I sniffle, rub the moisture from my cheeks and pull myself to my feet.

When I open the door, however, I'm startled to see the boy standing in front of me. His wavy dark hair is swept back. His forehead is creased in concern as his soft chocolate eyes take me in. Then he tilts his head to the side, studying my current predicament.

Tears.

Snot.

No clothes.

It's only then I realize I haven't yet gotten dressed. Logic tells me that I should care. If people were meant to be seen in their underwear they wouldn't have these dressing rooms with locks on the doors.

But I don't care.

The only thing that bothers me about this situation is the fact that it doesn't seem to bother me. Not in the slightest.

Another item to add to my list of abnormalities.

But I grab the purple dress from the hanger and hold it over my exposed body anyway. Just for show.

He smiles at my attempt. As though he *knows* it's an act. 'I've seen it all before,' he says. His smile quickly fades and is replaced with a look of sincerity. 'And it's still beautiful.'

I don't know what to say. I don't even know if I want to talk to him. I can't deal with this right now.

I have to get out of here.

I throw the dress over my head and pull the hem down to my knees.

He watches the fabric fall around my legs. And his endearing smile returns. 'It's nice to see you in *something* other than those boring grey things you always wore.'

The clothes I was wearing when they found me. The ones Kiyana packed up for me in a brown paper bag.

He knows about them.

But I don't care. Regardless of what the note says, regardless of what the gate agent told me, regardless of the way his eyes seem to heat my skin and melt my insides, I don't want to do this. I don't *want* to trust him. I don't want to believe anything he has to say. I just want to buy some normal clothes, go home to a normal, loving family and try to live a normal life.

I reach for the door. He doesn't try to stop me. He simply says, 'You went to the airport.' As though it's a well-known fact.

'So?' I mutter, pushing past him.

'So now you know that I was telling you the truth. That you weren't on the plane.'

'No. I *don't* know that.' I move up the row of empty stalls, determined to get out of here. But something stops me. I turn around. 'Wait a minute. How did you know I went to the airport?' My eyes widen in horror. 'Have you been *following* me?'

He shrugs as though this is not important. 'I had to make sure you were safe. It's my job to protect you.'

'Your *job*?'

'Well,' he says, 'it's not an official title. Just something I swore to do once. Even if you don't remember it, I'm still determined to keep that promise.'

I run my tongue over my front teeth as I try to control my temper. This boy, despite his ability to crawl into the deep back pockets of my mind and stay there, is really getting on my nerves. I sigh. 'Protect me from *who*? These people who are supposedly looking for me but whom I've yet to see?'

'Yes.' His face turns solemn. Like a cloud has passed over it. He gestures towards my left wrist. 'The same people who gave you that.'

With a sharp inhale, I glance down at the razor-thin black line and try to conceal it with my other hand. 'Just because you know about my tattoo doesn't mean—'

'It's not a tattoo.'

I'm fairly certain I already knew that.

'It's a tracking device,' he continues.

I shake my head. I know I should keep walking. Turn my back on this boy forever and keep trying to forget he even exists. But something compels me to ask, 'Who are you?'

'My name is Lyzender.'

Just as I suspected. This means nothing to me. 'I don't recognize that name,' I say flatly.

I expect his face to drop. I expect to see disappointment in his eyes.

But I don't.

He appears as determined as ever. He moves towards me, takes my hand, holds it, squeezes it. Despite my impulse to flee, I don't pull away. His touch is warm. Comforting. Almost . . . *familiar*.

'You *wouldn't* recognize that name,' he consents. 'You always called me Zen. You said it was because I brought you peace.'

A shiver runs up my legs. It weakens my spine. My body starts to crumple. I fight to stand upright.

Lyzender. Zen. Z.

Seraphina. Sera. S.

S + Z = 1609.

My breath quickens. I try to speak but no words seem able to take shape. My mouth feels dry. Rough. I rub my tongue against the roof until I feel saliva start to form again.

I think of my conversation with Cody – the one we had on the bus to Los Angeles – and I manage to ask, 'Are you . . . uh . . . were you my boyfriend?'

His almond-shaped eyes squint as he smiles. He squeezes my hand again. 'I'd like to think I was more than that.'

'What do you mean?'

I watch the colour of his face change. It doesn't turn the same shade of red that I've witnessed on Cody's skin so many times, but there is a clear tint of scarlet flushing his cheeks. He casts his eyes downward. 'You told me I was your soulmate.'

The way he says *soulmate*, I realize it means something. Something important.

Mate: one member of a pair.

Soul: the principle of life, feeling, thought and actions in humans; regarded as a distinct entity separate from the body.

I glance anxiously down at his hand on mine. 'I don't know what that is.'

He chuckles softly. Knowingly. 'I had to teach it to you the first time too.'

The first time?

Has this happened to me before?

My mind flashes to the note. The one currently stuffed inside my top dresser drawer.

Trust him.

'You had to teach me a word?' I ask.

'I've had to teach you a lot of things.'

'Why?'

'Sera,' he urges, tugging faintly on my hand, 'come with me. Right now. I promise to answer your questions. But it's not safe here.'

'*Why?*' I repeat adamantly, ignoring his request. 'Why did you have to teach me things?'

He rubs at his chin and looks over his shoulder. Then finally he sighs deeply. 'They were very selective about what vocabulary you knew. I think it was how they attempted to control you.'

'*Who?*' I demand, ripping my hand from his grip. My rage has finally boiled over. It's taken control now. 'Who are you talking about?'

He seems to have lost control of his emotions too. Because when he answers, his voice is much sharper. Commanding. Not to mention louder. 'I'm talking about the people who made you like this!' He gestures to all of me.

'Like what?'

'Don't tell me you haven't noticed. Because I know you have. You're not like everyone else. You're different, Sera. Special. You have unique abilities that other people don't have. Does any of that sound familiar?'

It does. It sounds *way* too familiar.

But right now it's the last thing I want to think about.

My brain feels as though it's on fire. I close my eyes and rub my temples in small circles with the tips of my fingers. 'I don't want to be different,' I whisper. 'I just want to be normal. I just want to find my family.'

'But you're *not* normal,' he maintains, his voice soothing once again. 'I think you've figured that out by now. And as far as I know, you don't *have* a family.'

I open my eyes and take two large steps back. 'What are you talking about?' I ask in a measured tone.

'Sera,' he begins, closing the gap between us. He places his hands on my shoulders. His touch is urgent. Heavy. 'When I first met you, you were living in a *lab*.'

Lab: short for laboratory.

Laboratory: a building, part of a building or other place equipped to conduct scientific experiments, tests and investigations.

He keeps talking. 'On a compound for a company called Diotech. They're a massive technology conglomerate. You were involved in one of their research projects. They do everything from aeronautics to experimental science to . . .' He pauses and nods ambiguously in my direction. Then he seems to change his mind about continuing and instead says, 'Listen. I'm staying at 1952 Bradbury Drive, room 302. Meet me there and I will explain it all to you.'

I shake my head and cover my ears but it does nothing to block the sound of his voice. I look for something to count. Tiles on the floor. But there aren't enough.

'No,' I resolve fervently. 'You're lying. This is all a lie!'

He reaches for my hand again but I pull it away so fast – so *unnaturally* fast – it blurs in front of my eyes.

'Sera, please,' he urges.

'Don't call me that!' I roar. 'That's not my name! And you are not my . . . my . . . *soulmate*. You aren't anything! I don't *know* you! And I don't know why you keep telling me these awful things that aren't true but I don't want to hear any more. Please, just leave me alone!'

I whirl around and stomp towards the doorway, determined to find Heather and get out of here as fast as I can. I expect to hear footsteps behind me but all is silent. I fight the urge to turn back and study his reaction.

Then, out of the stillness, comes his voice. Passionate and earnest. '"Let me not to the marriage of true minds admit impediments."'

And before I can process what he's saying – before I can even fathom what is happening – I feel my lips start to move. I hear my own voice speak. Almost as though it's coming from someplace else. An entity distinct from my body. *Separate.*

'"Love is not love which alters when it alteration finds, or bends with the remover to remove."'

I skid to a halt, playing the words over and over in my mind. What do they mean? Where did they come from? How do I know them?

Did I recite that from . . . *memory*?

I turn and look at the boy again. The one who calls himself Zen. The one who calls himself my soulmate.

His eyes illuminate. His lips part. 'Welcome back, Seraphina.'

18
FICTION

My instincts take over and I do the first thing that comes to mind.

I run.

I bolt through the doorway and zigzag frantically through the racks of clothing until I find Heather, standing at the cash register. 'I need to go. Now.'

She peers at me in alarm. 'Why? What happened? Is everything OK?'

No. It's definitely not.

I nod. 'Yes. I just want to go.'

Irina hands Heather three large bags and a receipt. Heather thanks her and then turns back to me. 'OK. Let's go.'

I follow close behind her as we head for the exit. I can see the boy watching me from the doorway where I left him. His eyes track my every footstep. My every move.

I feel my face grow hot with rage. My teeth clench.

I'm angry at him for lying to me. For clearly trying to take advantage of my memory loss, preying on my naivety. And I'm angry at myself for believing him. Even for a second.

'I think we got some really cute stuff,' Heather says as she starts the car and reverses out of the parking spot.

'Yes.' I stare vacantly out the window, trying to backtrack through all the things he's told me and discount them one by one.

You were never on that plane. Lie.

Your name is Seraphina. Lie.

I gave you the locket. Lie.

You're some kind of human science experiment for a company called Diotech.

Even I, the dysfunctional amnesiac, can recognize how ludicrous that sounds.

Heather peers at me. I must be clenching my teeth again because she puts a tender hand on my arm and asks, 'Did something happen in the dressing room while I was gone?'

I cringe at the memory. 'No.'

'Was it those girls?' She takes a guess. 'Did they say something to upset you?'

If only it was as simple as that. If only I was a normal human being who couldn't speak in foreign languages without knowing I was speaking them and solve unsolvable math problems without remembering how. If only I didn't have boys following me around, feeding me blatant insulting falsities. Then maybe my only problem would be girls in a dressing room.

But my life is not as simple as Heather would like it to be. I'm learning that far too quickly.

And now I just want her to stop asking questions.

I want to forget the boy and all the inexplicable things that have happened to me.

'No,' I assert again. 'I'm fine. Nothing happened.'

I can sense Heather struggling. She wants to press on and

investigate further but she can sense that I'm not willing to talk. I'm grateful when she remains quiet and leaves me alone.

I feel desolate and lost. Without an identity. Without a home. Without anything.

I don't know who I am or what I am.

I'm certainly not like those girls in the dressing room.

I'm not like the Carlsons.

And even Cody admitted I'm not like the other girls he knows.

So what am I like? Where do I fit in?

And the question that is truly beginning to plague me: if that boy – the one who calls himself Zen – is really lying, why do all his answers make sense?

As soon as we get home, I go straight to Cody's room. When I open the door, he's sitting on his bed reading a magazine.

'I really have to install a lock on *this* side of the door,' he mumbles. He's clearly not happy with me. I suppose I can understand that.

'I'm . . .' I fumble with an apology but it's apparent from the stilted nature of my voice that unlike math problems and foreign languages, apologies are not something I'm inherently good at. 'I'm . . . sorry . . . about—'

'Yeah, yeah,' he snarls. 'Save it. What do you want now?'

'I need your help.'

He snorts. 'Forget it.'

'Please, Cody.'

'In case you haven't heard,' he begins, his tone more venomous than I've ever heard it, 'in case you happen to have already *forgotten* the conversation that happened outside yesterday, I'm grounded. Like for life. All thanks to you. So if you think I'm going to help you again—'

'I just need to use the Internet,' I interrupt.

His eyes narrow suspiciously. 'The Internet?'

'Yes.'

'That's it?'

'Yes.'

'You're not going to ask me to take you to Guam or something.'

'No.' I pause, considering. 'Unless the Internet is better there.'

Cody is silent for a brief moment and then he breaks into laughter. 'Was that a joke? Did the infamous amnesiac supermodel actually make a *joke?*'

It wasn't a joke. But I know better than to admit that because whatever I said clearly seems to have lightened his dark mood. So I smile and shrug my shoulders.

Cody closes his magazine, which I can now see is titled *Popular Science*, and slides off his bed. 'Fine,' he says with a heavy sigh. 'You can borrow my laptop.' He grabs a thin, rectangular metal device from the desk in the corner, tucks it under his arm, and motions for me to follow him. 'C'mon. I'll set it up in your room and teach you how to use it. But don't go looking at any porn on here. My parents have one of those cyber-nanny tracking services set up and they can see everything I look at.' He cringes. 'I learned that one the hard way.'

He steps through the bathroom and into my room. I follow closely behind. 'What is porn?' I ask.

He chuckles and sets the laptop on my bed. 'It's . . . You know what? Never mind.'

He sits down and I stand over him as he flips open the device, revealing a dark screen and a black-and-silver keyboard.

'Is this a computer?' I ask, watching with fascination as he presses a small round button and the entire machine illuminates.

Cody flashes me a funny look. 'Yeah.'

We wait as the screen cycles through a series of images and text. Cody's eyes dart nervously up at me, taking in my new dress. 'You look . . . nice, by the way.'

I smile and say thank you because it seems like the appropriate response.

He steals another peek. 'That dress is . . .' he starts, but his face colours and he looks away. 'Well . . . it fits. Which is a nice change. That's all.'

I smooth the soft purple fabric with my hands. 'Yes,' I agree. 'It fits very well.'

Cody clears his throat. 'So anyway, you type whatever you want into this little box,' he explains hastily, pointing to the screen, 'and Google will show you everything there is to know about the subject.'

He pulls the computer towards him. 'Like this for example.' He types in:

Freedom Airlines flight 121, survivor

He presses a key marked 'Enter'. Instantly the screen morphs into a list of results. Halfway down the page there's a row of photographs. Of me. I recognize one as the picture they showed on the news, and the rest appear to have been taken when I was walking from the hospital to the car the day I was released.

The day I saw the boy in the crowd.

'Change it,' I tell Cody urgently. 'Put in something else. Please.'

He studies my face curiously for a moment before finally yielding. 'OK,' he says. 'What did you want to look up?'

I lower my gaze. 'Something I think I might have remembered but I'm not sure what it is.'

His eyebrows rise in interest. 'No kidding? What was it?'

I take a deep breath and let my mind drift back to the

dressing room. Although I don't want to repeat it, I have to know what it means.

'"Let me not to the marriage of true minds admit impediments,"' I recite, fully expecting Cody to display the same befuddled expression that I had when I first heard the words, and to confirm what I've believed since then: that they don't mean anything.

But he doesn't.

Instead he laughs.

'What?' I ask, affronted.

'That's the first memory you've had!?' He laughs harder.

I don't understand why this is humorous. And I don't appreciate his amusement either. 'Yes. Why are you laughing?'

He wipes his eyes. 'Sorry. I just find it totally messed up that you can't remember what the Internet is but you know the words to Shakespeare's Sonnet 116.'

My eyes widen in surprise. 'Shakespeare's what?'

'It's a famous poem.'

I feel somewhat disappointed. A *poem*. Why would I remember a poem? Of all things? 'Well, what does it mean?' I ask impatiently.

Cody rolls his eyes. 'It's some sappy crap about eternal love or something.' He sticks his finger in his mouth and makes a gagging sound with his throat.

Eternal love?

I think of the locket sitting in the top drawer of my dresser. Two hearts, intersecting at their cores.

'How do you know it?' I ask.

'We studied Shakespeare in school last year.'

'So it's possible that's where I learned it too?' I ask, my hopes instantly rising. 'In school?'

Not in some sinister lab.

Just a regular, everyday school.

He shrugs. 'Probably. Girls totally dig that mushy stuff. So I guess I'm not surprised you remember it.' He contemplates for a second. 'Or you could have been a serious history buff or something.'

This piques my interest. 'History?'

'Yeah,' Cody says, as though it was obvious. 'That poem was written like four hundred years ago.'

My blood starts to pump faster as my mind automatically does the math. 'Four hundred years ago,' I repeat. 'In what year?'

He shrugs again. 'I don't know. Sixteen something.'

'Sixteen *what*?' I demand, surprised by the intensity in my own voice.

Cody shoots me a look of contempt. 'Chill out. I don't know.'

Exasperated, I gesture towards the computer. 'Well, can you look it up?'

He throws his hands in the air. 'Fine, fine. Calm down.'

As he starts typing, my leg bounces nervously. Cody shoots me another strange look.

The screen morphs into a page of text. An illustration of a man with puffy black hair and a white collared shirt appears under the name 'William Shakespeare'.

'OK, let's see.' Cody leans in. 'Sonnet 116. It says here, first published in –' his eyes quickly scan the page – '1609.'

19

VISITOR

Heather says Scott wants us to meet him in town for dinner. We're going to go to something called a restaurant. Cody explains from the back seat of the car that it's what people do when they don't want to cook at home. Or when they want better food than what their mother can make.

Heather gives him a bitter look in the rear-view mirror. 'Just be grateful we're bringing you at all, Cody.'

He crosses his arms and makes a *pff* sound with his lips.

'Your father and I are still extremely disappointed in you.'

'Whatever,' is his reply.

At the restaurant, Heather shows me how to order from a menu and recommends a few items she thinks I would like. I finally decide on something called baked ziti because Heather says it shares an ingredient with the delicious sandwich she made for me a few days ago.

And although the dish is very good – unbelievably good – I can't fully enjoy it. My mind is distracted. The events of the day are replaying on an endless loop.

'Did you have fun shopping today?' Scott asks me after he sucks a long noodle into his mouth.

'Yes,' I lie.

I seem to be doing a lot of that lately. I wonder if it's somehow indicative of who I used to be.

'We got some really adorable stuff,' Heather adds. 'It was so much fun to be able to shop for a girl for a change.'

Across the table, I see Cody roll his eyes. He's fully engaged with something on his phone.

I'm not very talkative and soon the conversation shifts to the topic of Scott's work. I'm grateful to have the time to myself to think.

Why am I reciting poetry from the year 1609?

Why do I have a locket with that very year engraved on the back?

Why is it the first thing I said when they pulled me from the ocean?

And why is that boy – Zen – the only one who seems to know anything about any of it?

I don't know what to believe. I don't know who to trust. I can't even trust my own mind. I want to crawl under this table and never resurface. I want to swim into the sea and never turn around. I just want to escape.

After dinner, we step out into the warm summer-night air. It feels fresh and rejuvenating on my skin. The sun has already set and I can smell the faint traces of the ocean a few miles away. Scott takes Cody in his car, saying something about making a quick stop at the drugstore, and I go with Heather.

She navigates the twisty dark road that leads to the house, the headlights illuminating only a few feet of the way ahead of us. As we near the driveway, I notice a man walking up the hill from the other direction. Heather spots him a good five seconds later and slows the car.

I find it odd for someone to be walking alone in the dark but it doesn't seem to bother her. She simply smiles and waves. The same way she always does when she passes pedestrians. On the way to the supermarket the other day she explained that it's something people do in small towns: they wave to each other.

But the man doesn't wave back.

As the car comes closer, his eyes lock on me and my heart leaps into my throat.

I recognize him.

He's tall, with bright auburn hair and a matching beard.

I saw him yesterday. He was on the bus Cody and I rode from the airport to the bus station.

In *Los Angeles*.

Nearly two hundred miles away.

So what is he doing *here*? In *this* town? On *this* street?

Heather seems completely oblivious to my reaction and the strangeness of the situation. Meanwhile my brain is scrambling for an explanation. When I saw him staring at me on the bus, I assumed he recognized me from the news. So I lowered my baseball cap and turned around.

But I can't do that now.

I can't just turn away and ignore him.

I observe him carefully until we pass and then I whip my head around and continue to study him through the back window. He's stopped walking. He stands in the middle of the road, watching Heather's car as it turns into the driveway.

I fumble with the ramifications. Whoever this man is now knows where the Carlsons live. Where I live.

Chances are, he's just another one of those media-hungry people that Kiyana warned me about in the hospital. Chances are, he just wants a photograph of the girl who fell from the sky and lived to tell the tale.

But it's not *these* options that cause my stomach to tie in knots.

It's those *other* options. The ones I don't know about. The ones my imagination creates.

'There are people looking for you, and trust me when I say, you do not *want them to find you.'*

A strange sensation floods through my body. My muscles are tingling. Almost as though they're warming up for something. *Anticipating*. My arms and legs vibrate. My head feels light. Almost dizzy. My fingers twitch.

I eye the car door, feeling a sudden urge to shove it open, leap from the moving vehicle and run. Run until I'm far away from here.

I grow antsy. Jittery. My legs burn. Like there's a fire lashing inside them. I can't make sense of what I'm feeling. I can't think. All I know is I have to get out of here. I have to get out of this car. *Now!*

My breathing has become ragged and fast. But Heather doesn't seem to notice. She continues to steer the car down the long driveway towards the house. We're almost there. Only a few more seconds. My whole body is trembling now. I rest my shaking hand on the door.

When the car finally pulls to a stop, I yank swiftly on the handle and kick open the door, readying myself to run. But I'm stopped by a startling noise. A horrible crunching, grating sound. Like metal ripping and glass shattering.

Heather gasps and drops the box of leftovers she brought home from the restaurant, splattering red pasta sauce everywhere.

I glance down. The entire car door is lying on the asphalt driveway.

20

DEPARTURE

Night has long since fallen but the house is still awake.

Cody is in his room. I hear the soft patter of his fingertips. I believe he's playing another game on his cellphone. Heather and Scott are having a heated conversation in their bedroom one floor below.

And I lie on my bed . . . listening.

I can tell by their hushed whispers that they don't want anyone to overhear their discussion. But I don't seem to have a problem. I hear it as easily as if they were standing at the foot of my bed.

Heather is really upset about the car-door incident. She hasn't said as much to me but I can tell. She acts differently around me now. Almost skittish. And as soon as Scott returned home from the drugstore, she ushered him into their bedroom and closed the door. I haven't seen either of them since.

Even if I couldn't hear them right now, it wouldn't be difficult to surmise that they're talking about me.

But fortunately (or perhaps unfortunately) I can.

'You should have seen it, Scott,' Heather is saying. 'One minute the door was there. The next it was lying on the ground. She kicked the whole thing off like it was made of tinfoil. Don't you find that just a little bit odd?'

'I think you're blowing this whole thing out of proportion,' Scott tells her. 'There's obviously an explanation for it. Did you ever stop to think that maybe the door was already loose? That something was wrong with the hinge and it just happened to fall off at the same time that she opened it.'

I don't believe this explanation and I don't expect Heather to either.

I close my eyes and imagine Heather shaking her head. 'No. There was nothing wrong with the door, Scott. Car doors don't fall off for no reason. I'm starting to think there's something strange about that girl.'

'Yes,' Scott says gently. 'She lost all her memories in a plane crash. She's not going to act like you and me.'

'A plane crash she mysteriously survived!' Heather's voice rises and Scott immediately shushes her. When she speaks again, she's back to an intense whisper. 'When no one else survived. I can't put my finger on it but something is not right.'

Cody's laptop is still sitting on my bed. I eye it hesitantly and then finally pull myself up and turn it on. Once it has fully booted up, I follow Cody's instructions until I find myself staring at a little white search box.

A short vertical black line blinks expectantly at me. It's waiting for me to point it in a direction.

I sigh and start to poke at the keys with my index finger, one letter at a time, until a word forms:

Diotech.

The company Zen told me about. The people he claimed are looking for me.

I stare down at the razor-thin black tattoo on my wrist,

trying to imagine how this tiny mark could possibly be used to track me.

I click Search.

The page reloads but the results are extremely disappointing. Nothing seems to be even remotely related to the company Zen described.

And apparently even Google is discouraged with the outcome of the search because it asks me if I really meant to search *Biotech* instead of *Diotech*, clearly assuming that I must have made a mistake since there's so little information to be found.

If this is such a massive and powerful corporation, why is there absolutely no mention of it on the Web? Cody said the Internet is where you go to find everything. But there's not even a single reference to a technology conglomerate called Diotech.

More proof that the boy was lying.

I grunt and lean against the headrest, glaring at the unhelpful screen. I think back to the conversation I had in the dressing room. With the boy who calls himself Zen.

'When I first met you, you were living in a lab *. . . On a compound for a company called Diotech. They're a massive technology conglomerate. You were involved in one of their research projects.'*

I screw my mouth to the side and then slowly sit up straight again. I pull the laptop towards me and enter a new search. This time I throw in every halfway-relevant word I can think of:

Diotech + compound + technology conglomerate + research project

And then, as a final afterthought, I quickly add:

Seraphina + Zen

I'm highly doubtful that anything will result, but I click Search anyway, and wait.

The screen refreshes, revealing one result.

I hurriedly click on it and am sent to a website called Beyond Top Secret: A Common Ground for Conspiracy Theorists.

It appears the search has brought me to something called a message board. In the centre of the page is a grey box with white text. It reads:

> The rise of Diotech will be the fall of humankind. This massive corporation will fascinate some and infuriate many. Citizens will willingly fall prey to its allure. Governments will crumble under the weight of its sovereignty. In only a few short years, Diotech will change the world as it is known. We will never be the same.

My hopes crash to the ground as I frown at the screen. What does that even *mean*?

I scan further down the page and find that the post was submitted by someone who calls himself Maxxer. Next to his name is a photograph of a man with a long face and silky snow-white hair that falls to his shoulders. One of his eyes is dark brown while the other appears to be made out of blue glass.

The image unnerves me.

Just underneath the post is a line that says *Tags*. I flinch when I read it:

Diotech, compound, technology conglomerate, research project, Seraphina, Zen

These are my exact search terms. Word for word. In the same order I entered them into the search box. As though whoever wrote this knew exactly what I would search for.

As though whoever wrote this . . . wrote this for me.

The thought makes me shudder.

I hastily close the lid of the laptop and push it aside. I return to lying on my back and close my eyes. One storey below me,

Scott and Heather are still arguing in hushed tones.

Scott exhales a heavy sigh. 'We knew when we signed up to do this that it would be difficult. But we need to try to be supportive. We're all she has right now.'

'I *am* trying,' Heather insists. 'I really am. Sometimes she's sweet. And I can see a normal human being in there. Then other times, she opens her mouth and it's like she's a . . . she's a –' her voice gets very quiet – 'a robot.'

I open my eyes and stare at the ceiling.

I'm not angry. I don't blame Heather for feeling the way she does. For being afraid of me. I'm afraid of me too right now.

With all the surprises and strange discoveries, no one ever knows what will surface next . . . including me.

I think about the car door lying on the ground and how it got there. Regardless of the more realistic explanations Scott tries to come up with, I know the truth. That door was on the ground because of me. Because I kicked it. I kicked it so hard it tore right off the hinges.

Without even trying.

And I also know that, like so many things about me, the ability to kick car doors off hinges is not normal.

Which leaves me with only one solid conclusion: whoever I am, I'm not safe.

I'm volatile and unpredictable. Something came over me when I saw that redheaded man. Something I can't explain. Nor could I control it. It was . . . instinctual. An impulsive reaction.

Not to mention, if there *are* people out there looking for me, I can't lead them here. I have to go. I can't risk something happening to Heather or Cody or Scott.

I stand up and walk over to the dresser, opening the top

drawer and retrieving the only two possessions I have. My locket and the yellowed piece of paper with my handwriting on it.

Trust him.

I walk back to the computer, flip open the lid, and enter a new search term:

1952 Bradbury Drive

'Meet me there and I will explain it all to you.'

I hit Enter. Then I chew on my fingernail. Just like I saw Brittany, the gate agent, do. And now I know why. It has a sort of calming effect.

The search results begin to generate, but before the page can fully load, I slam the laptop shut again.

It's better that I don't know. It's not like I'm ever going to go there anyway.

Come to think of it, maybe it was that boy who posted the thing on the Internet about Diotech. Using some fake picture and some fake name. Because he knew that I'd look for it. Maybe he did it to try to prove his crazy lies. To gain my trust.

But it won't work.

I crumple up the note and toss it in the trash in the bathroom. As soon as I do, I feel a pang in my chest and my forehead starts to heat up again. I turn on the faucet and splash cold water on my face until the sensation goes away.

I change out of my purple dress and pull a tank top and a pair of pants from one of the shopping bags Heather and I brought home from the mall. The top is white with blue trim and the pants are sort of a light brownish colour with lots of pockets down the legs. Very functional. I like them.

I fasten the locket around my neck, then sit on the edge of the bed and wait.

As the minutes tick by on the clock, the house finally begins to go to sleep. Heather and Scott finish their discussion and soon I hear the gentle sound of their steady, rhythmic breathing. Cody's pattering fingertips silence. The light underneath the bathroom door is extinguished. I wait for his soft snores.

Then I tiptoe down the stairs, carefully ease open the front door and exit into the night.

21
BROKE

I don't know where to go so I just start down the road that Cody and I took to the bus station yesterday morning and Heather drove to get to the supermarket and to the mall. As far as I can tell, it's the only way into town. Wells Creek is completely shut down except for a diner at the end of the main street. I didn't eat much at dinner and it's only now I realize how hungry I am so I step inside.

The place is mostly deserted apart from a few customers who sip coffee at a counter. A woman in a blue apron sees me come in and shuffles over.

'Well, aren't you a pretty thing?' she says. It's evidently loud enough for all the customers to hear because they glance up to confirm her assessment.

I flash a quick smile and bow my head, scolding myself for not taking Scott's hat with me when I left.

'Just one?' she asks, glancing behind me.

I nod. 'Yes.'

'Counter or table?'

I peer once again at the people lining the counter. All of them are still giving me a once-over. The man closest to us is doing a more thorough job than the others. 'Table,' I decide.

She nods, grabs a menu and beckons for me to follow her. I do. But it's not until we reach my designated table at the back of the diner that I notice the man sitting at the other end of the counter.

Tall.

Red hair.

Matching beard.

It's the same man I saw on the bus yesterday in Los Angeles and again near Heather and Scott's house on the way back from the restaurant. His face is buried in a newspaper. He looks up momentarily and gives me a half-smile. My whole body freezes and I consider running again. Maybe I should just get out of this town as fast as possible and stop to eat later.

But then he goes back to his reading, seemingly unconcerned with me, and I remind myself to stop being so paranoid. He's probably a harmless local resident.

Who happened to be in Los Angeles yesterday.

It doesn't necessarily mean anything.

Or maybe I'm simply confusing him with someone else.

I choose the side of the booth with the best view of the counter so I can keep an eye on him – just in case – and slide in. The woman places the menu down in front of me and I scan it in one glance. 'Grilled cheese sandwich, please,' I say as she's about to walk away.

She smiles, nods and takes the menu back. 'You got it.'

Then I wait. I rest my chin on the palm of my hand and gaze out the window. There's not much to see but the dark parking lot. I think about where I'm going to go. I have no plan. Except to figure out who I am. But I have no idea where to start. I suppose I should go back to Los Angeles. Maybe talk to Brittany again. Or see if I can find someone who can tell me more about the locket.

I feel its weight against my collarbone. I reach up and touch it, sliding my fingertips over the curious raised symbol. The endless knot.

'I'm the one who gave it to you . . .'

I blink and look away from the window, choosing to focus on the tabletop instead. If I'm going to have any chance of figuring out who I am, I have to start over.

I have to toss out any clue or piece of information that came from that boy.

I have to figure this out on my own.

'I know you,' comes a deep male voice, interrupting my thoughts. When I look up I fully expect to see the redheaded man addressing me. But his face is still buried in his newspaper. Instead, it's the man who was sitting at the front of the diner – the one who seemed the most interested in me when I walked in.

He's out of his seat now and stalking towards me.

I don't know what to do or where to look so I just pretend I didn't hear him. But the closer he gets, the harder that is to do.

'Yeah,' he says almost ominously. 'I know you. Hard to forget those purple eyes. I've never seen eyes that colour. Have to be contacts, right?'

I shake my head ever so slightly. I don't know what contacts are, but I don't exactly want to let him know that.

'Don't try to tell me they're real!' he says with a loud snort. 'God don't make eyes that colour. It's not natural.'

He slides into the booth across from me and I feel my whole body stiffen again. I also notice the redheaded man look up from his newspaper and watch us with curiosity.

'You're that girl they pulled outta the ocean,' the man continues. He has a large, bulky build and light brown hair that only covers half of his head. The rest is skin.

'The one who survived that plane crash.' He keeps talking. 'A regular celebrity. We don't get many of those round here. You really don't remember anything, huh?'

I grip the edge of my seat and shake my head again.

'What a shame.' He makes a clicking sound with his tongue and drums his fingers on the tabletop. His hands are large, rough and covered in unsightly calluses.

'What you doing up here in Wells Creek, of all places?' he asks me.

I keep silent. There's no way I'm going to tell him the real reason I'm here. The last thing I want to do is draw attention to the Carlsons.

'What's the matter?' he asks. 'Did you forget how to speak too?' He starts to laugh. It's a horrible cackling that sends tremors through my arms and legs.

'Leave her alone,' comes another voice. This time it *is* the redheaded man. His newspaper has been folded and placed on the counter and he's rising up from his seat. He walks over to us and stands tall in front of the table. 'She clearly doesn't want to be bothered.'

The balding man throws his hands up in the air. 'Whoa-ho!' he calls out in a rugged voice. 'I didn't know her *daddy* was here with her.' The cackling starts again and the muscles in my legs tighten, like loaded springs. I can feel my whole body preparing to leap. Almost as though it's not even my choice. The reaction is automatic.

Exactly like what happened in the car – I feel the sudden unyielding urge to run.

I eye the window to my left, considering crashing right through it. Whatever it takes to get out of this place. Out of this booth. Away from *him*.

The redheaded man shoots me a look. A look I can only interpret as 'Don't worry. You're safe'. But it's not until I see the balding man rise from his seat that the muscles in my legs start to relax.

'Sorry to bother you, young lady,' he says in that same sarcastic tone that Cody always uses. He slowly saunters back to his stool on the other side of the diner. I watch him sit down and pull a cellphone out of his pocket. 'The boys from the lumberyard are gonna crap their pants when they hear about this.'

The redheaded man slips back into his seat at the counter without another glance in my direction.

It was a mistake to come here. I realize that now.

I should go.

I start to rise but the woman in the apron approaches with my grilled cheese sandwich on a yellow plastic plate. She sets it on the table and the smell sends my taste buds into a frenzy.

I sit back down and gobble the whole thing in a matter of seconds. It's just as delicious as Heather's was. Maybe even more. I decide that whoever I was before I lost my memories, I definitely liked grilled cheese sandwiches.

I wonder if that's a useful clue.

I pull a napkin from the metal dispenser on the table and hastily wipe my mouth. Then I crumple it up, toss it on the empty plate, and dash for the exit.

'Hang on a minute!' the woman calls, stopping me. 'You may be just about the prettiest thing I've ever seen come in here but it doesn't mean you don't have to pay like everyone else.'

Pay?

Vivid memories flash through my head. Cody handing a stack of cash to the man at the bus station in exchange for our tickets. Heather swiping her credit card at the supermarket and again at the mall. Scott throwing down several bills on the table of the restaurant.

I stare back at the woman with panicked eyes.

She sighs and releases my arm. 'Let me guess. You don't have any money?'

'I—' I start to say but my mind drifts. How am I going to get *anywhere* without being able to pay for things?

She groans.

'Don't worry. I'll take care of her tab,' a male voice says.

We both glance up to see the redheaded man standing next to us. He reaches into his pocket and pulls out a few of the same green bills that Cody and his father had.

The woman in the apron shrugs and takes the money. 'I don't care who pays, as long as it's done.'

She presses a few buttons on the register. A *ding* chimes through the diner, followed by the *slam* of the drawer closing.

I look perplexedly between her and the man, unable to fully comprehend what just happened. All I know is that the woman has already gone back to pouring coffee into mugs.

I look the redheaded man in the eye and say, 'Thank you.'

He meets my gaze and I notice his lips curve into a broad grin underneath his stubbly beard. His smile reminds me of Heather's. It's the kind that reaches the eyes. I find myself smiling back.

A sudden jolt of familiarity runs through me. It's something about his eyes. They look so . . .

Tired.

'You should get some sleep,' I hear myself say. Although I have no idea where the remark came from. My lips just opened spontaneously and the words tumbled out.

I laugh to cover my embarrassment. 'I'm sorry,' I say quickly. 'I didn't mean to—'

But the man's smile never falters. In fact, it only grows bigger. 'It's OK, Sera. You're right. I *do* need to get some sleep.'

'Well,' I say, feeling uncomfortable about the entire exchange, 'thank you again.' I turn and head for the exit, anxious to get out of there.

It isn't until I'm already out the door and halfway through the parking lot that his response finally catches up with me.

'It's OK, Sera.'

Sera.

That's exactly what the boy called me.

'It's short for Seraphina.'

I immediately spin around and head back towards the diner. But I'm stopped by a bright light that flashes over my left shoulder. It's followed quickly by another. And another.

'Violet! Violet!' someone calls. 'Over here!'

I slowly turn to assess the damage. There are only a few press people here but more are arriving by the second. A white van with 9 NEWS on the side screeches to a halt and a man with a camera strapped to his shoulder hops out and scrambles towards me.

'Have you gotten any of your memories back?' a reporter asks.

'Are you satisfied with the way the airline is handling the investigation?'

'Do you plan on suing?'

A giant light mounted to a large pole flickers on, illuminating the entire parking lot and blinding me.

I blink, shielding my eyes until the tiny white stars clear from my vision.

I search for an escape.

The wall of press is growing in front of me and there's a thick forest of trees to my left. My best choice is to go right and get back on the main road. I turn and ready myself to run but skid to a halt when I feel a strange tingling sensation on the inside of my left wrist. The skin is pulsating and it's hot to the touch. Just like it was in the supermarket when I accidentally swiped my tattoo in front of the scanner.

'It's not a tattoo,' I hear the boy's voice say. *'It's a tracking device.'*

When I look up, I see a large muscular man standing on the sidewalk in front of me. His features are weathered and worn. Like the yellowed note that sits at the bottom of my trash. He's dressed entirely in black – black turtleneck and loose black pants tucked into tall black leather lace-up boots. He almost blends completely into the night. His hair is cut very short, a layer of black fuzz. An unsettling scar runs down the entire left side of his face, beginning at his forehead, crossing his eye and dripping down his cheek. The sight of it sends a shiver along my spine.

His dark, shallow eyes drift from my head to my feet. Assessing. Calculating.

My wrist prickles again and a small contraption in his hand lets out a soft beep. He peers down at it briefly before returning his gaze to me and I watch the disfigured dark pink tissue of his scar contort as his lips curl into a triumphant smile.

22
DARKNESS

I hear a voice. It's telling me to run. Actually it's screaming it. I don't wait around to figure out who it belongs to. I just obey.

With the swarm of people accumulating to my left, and the man in front me, I turn one hundred and eighty degrees and make a dash for the trees. My legs move faster than I've ever felt them move. They rejoice. As though this is what they were meant to do. As though someone has released them from lifelong bondage.

I duck and weave through the trees easily. My body knows where they are before my mind does.

I hear the footsteps behind me. I don't have to look back to know who's following me. I can sense him there. But his footsteps seem to be growing fainter with each passing second. As though he's struggling to keep pace with me.

I don't feel tired, but I know I can't keep running forever. I have to do something.

I see a clearing up ahead. About a mile away. The forest is

broken by the highway. I can hear the soft roar of car engines as they pass. I lower my head and try to pick up my speed.

The wind whips my face. Branches scratch at my arms. Dried leaves crunch under my feet.

Less than two minutes later, I reach a road. It's wider than the street I walked to the diner. I think this is what Heather called the highway. My body urges me to keep going but my mind is telling me to stop and take a moment to assess the traffic. In the end, my body wins and I plough forward. My feet hit the concrete just as a giant eighteen-wheel truck appears over the top of the hill to my right. I dash in front of it, willing myself to run even faster. The front end of the truck misses me by an inch. I can feel the *whizz* of air on my back as it barely skims past me.

The driver reacts to my blur. Slamming on the brakes. There's a horrible screeching sound as the wheels skid. I stop running and turn around in time to see the entire cargo area of the truck swing out. The torque is too much for the truck to handle. It tips on to its side and continues to skid along the road, sparks flying off the pavement, before finally coming to a rest horizontally across the two-lane highway.

Another car approaches from the opposite direction but isn't able to stop in time. It collides right into the bed of the truck. The drivers are able to scramble out right before both vehicles burst into flames. And soon three more cars have swerved around the wreck.

I stumble up the small hill and stand petrified as I take in the scope of the accident. It looks horrific.

Oh no. Please let this be another dream.

Please let me wake up.

But I don't. Because I am already awake. It's real.

That guilty feeling starts to gurgle in my stomach. It's much stronger than last time, when the only thing I did was sneak out of the house at five in the morning. The bitter sensation rises up, singeing my throat until I can't hold back. I gag and bend over. An acidy liquid spews from my mouth on to the grassy ground.

It tastes like grilled cheese sandwiches.

After it's over, I quickly look up and scan the horizon once again. I see my pursuer emerge from the forest on the other side of the highway. He stops abruptly at the sight of the accident and takes a moment to survey the damage.

The tattoo on my wrist starts to tingle again. A faint buzzing sensation.

I glance down at it and then back at him. His eyes slowly start to climb – up over the wreckage, ascending the hill – until they land on me. And even from this great distance, even in the moonlit night, our eyes lock.

I watch his chilling grey eyes narrow ever so slightly as he zeroes in on his target.

Me.

He starts running again, manoeuvring around the rubble and debris. He disappears momentarily in the smoke, only to emerge a split second later on the other side. I watch him pause to cough before pushing himself forward and running up the hill in my direction.

I let out a small whimper and then take off again.

I can't make sense of anything that's happening. My speed. My dexterity.

None of this is normal. Amnesia or not, *this* I know.

I reach a large open field. Through the blackness I can see a structure at the other end of it. If I can make it there, perhaps I can hide. For at least long enough to gather my thoughts.

I let my legs carry me as fast as they can go. The dark field passes by in a dizzying blur. I reach the building, which I can now see is an abandoned barn that looks partially burned down. I slip inside, ignoring the pungent odour of dead animals.

The ceiling is half gone. Only a few charred rafters remain. There are several broken, rusty metal contraptions scattered throughout the large, dank space. I walk slowly, finding my footing on the uneven ground as my eyes search for somewhere to conceal myself.

I hear a *snap*.

I freeze, holding my breath. I turn back towards the doorway but see nothing.

My adrenalin is pumping but I feel alarmingly calm. I just have to figure out my next move. I just have to—

A shadowy figure suddenly drops from the large gap in the destroyed ceiling. It falls to the ground and lands deftly on its feet. This man is also dressed entirely in black. Although he has the same large, burly build as the other, his skin is darker. Rough. Like the walls of this dilapidated barn. He doesn't have an eerie scar oozing down his face but it doesn't make him any less terrifying.

I should have known, I think, as he lunges towards me. *There are more than one.*

I want to fight him. I want to stand my ground and protect myself. I feel the urge to lash out with my arms and legs and throw myself on top of him, but something is keeping me from taking action. As if there's a strange force embedded inside of me. No matter what directive my brain tries to give my body, the only thing my body wants to do is flee.

But I'm not even given the chance to do that.

As soon as I turn to run, a thick arm clamps around my neck, tightening against my throat. I struggle but it doesn't seem to be making any difference. Out of the corner of my eye I see someone enter the barn, strolling towards us.

'Nice work,' he says smoothly, giving a curt nod to the man behind me, whose hold is like a noose.

I manage to rotate my head far enough to identify the newcomer. And when I do, my stomach lurches.

It's the redheaded man. The one from the diner. Who so graciously paid for my sandwich.

I open my mouth to scream but no sound comes out. Something jabs against the back of my neck. Cold and smooth, like metal. I hear a low fizzing sound. My body starts to crumple and then everything goes dark.

23
HUMANITY

I wake to the sound of clanking metal. I'm sitting upright on a chair. I feel drowsy. Like that morning in the hospital after Kiyana gave me drugs to help me sleep. My eyelids droop but finally I'm able to open them.

There's someone kneeling at my feet. I feel cold steel brushing against the skin of my ankles and wrists. I try to move but my left foot is attached to something – the chair perhaps? – and my hands are bound together.

I'm too tired and confused to struggle. Plus, I have a feeling it's not worth the fight. I'm not going anywhere.

The man beside me stands up and I can see that it's the redheaded man.

Now I struggle. Pushing violently against my metal restraints. But I'm surprised to feel that my right leg is free. It swings so high as a result of my effort that I nearly kick him in the face. He ducks and lets out an amused chuckle before moving to my left side and kneeling again.

'What are you doing?'

'Taking these off,' he says casually.

I look down and see a thick metal cuff lying idly on the ground next to my feet.

'But—' I scan the room for signs of my attacker. Or attackers, rather.

I see the two large men collapsed on the ground on the other side of the barn.

'Are they –' I swallow hard – 'dead?'

'Nah,' the redheaded man responds as he releases the second shackle. I move my left ankle in a circle. 'Just deactivated.'

He holds up a small black gadget, cylindrical in shape, with a single silver prong protruding from the end. 'It's the same one they used on you, actually.'

'Deactivated,' I repeat, silently remarking on the peculiar word choice.

The redheaded man rises to his feet. 'The human brain is a complicated thing. We've learned a lot about it in the past hundred years. Mainly about how to manipulate it.' He grips the device between his thumb and forefinger and brandishes it towards me. 'This is called a Modifier. You see, the brain functions on electricity. The Modifier sends electrical currents to the centre of the nervous system, essentially putting the brain into sleep mode.' He nods towards the unconscious bodies on the ground. One of them lies on his side, one leg twisted awkwardly around the other, his left arm sprawled perpendicular to his torso. 'They'll be awake and good as new in less than half an hour. They won't even know what happened.'

'But why?' I ask him. 'I thought – I mean, aren't you with them?'

He bobbles his head from side to side, returning the strange brain-scrambling device to his pocket. 'Yes and no. It's . . . complicated. I guess you could say we are here for the same reason.'

'What reason is that?'

He laughs as though it's a ridiculous question. 'You, of course.'

Even though this is the very answer I was expecting, I still find myself wishing he had said something else. *Anything* else.

I glance over at the bodies, focusing on the one with the darker skin. Who jumped down from the hole in the ceiling and grabbed me. 'I wanted to fight him,' I say pensively, almost to myself. 'I really did. But I couldn't. It was like . . . I didn't know how or . . . I wouldn't let myself.'

He sighs. 'I'm afraid that's my fault.'

I blink. '*Your* fault?'

'Your DNA is imprinted with the instinct to run. Not fight.'

I squint at him. 'What?'

'I wanted to give you both, so you could at least defend yourself, but my request was denied. It was believed that if you had any fighting impulses in you, given your strength, it might cause problems further down the road if you were ever to . . . well –' he chuckles – 'rebel.'

I stare at him in complete disbelief, hardly able to process what he's saying.

'So,' he goes on, seemingly oblivious to my reaction, 'I decided, for your own protection, I would at least give you a flight instinct. So you could safely escape any danger. That's why you probably feel a very strong desire to flee the moment you encounter any perceived threats.'

Speech doesn't come easy. My tongue feels as though it's too big for my mouth, but finally, in a barely audible voice, I'm able to ask, 'Who *are* you?'

He bows his head, almost looking ashamed. Then he takes a deep breath. 'I'm the person who made you what you are.'

What I am.

Not *who* I am.

The grim disparity between those simple little words makes me shudder.

'And *what* am I exactly?' I immediately flash back on the conversation I overheard between Heather and Scott before I left.

'It's like she's a . . . she's a . . . a robot.'

'Am I human?' I add, the words barely managing to escape my rapidly contracting windpipe.

He sighs, as though this, of all the questions in the world, was the one he dreaded the most. 'The short answer is yes.'

'The short answer?' I repeat dubiously.

He bends down and frees my hands, then leans back on one of the rusty metal contraptions that looks like it hasn't been touched in years. 'You see,' he says reluctantly, 'it's not as straightforward a question as you might think.'

I frown and shake my head. 'I don't understand. It seems like a pretty straightforward question to me.'

'Let me ask you this,' he begins pensively, folding his arms across his chest. 'If a human being – a man – were to lose his arm or his leg in an accident and it was replaced with a prosthetic – an artificial limb – would he still be human?'

I rub my left wrist with my right hand. The shackles left a reddish mark around my tattoo that quickly starts to fade. 'Yes, of course.'

He nods. 'And what if he lost all his limbs and had *four* prosthetics – two arms and two legs – would he still be human then?'

I shrug. 'Yes.'

He twists his mouth, causing his red beard to ripple. 'OK. Now he goes blind. And his eyes are replaced with small cameras that send signals to his brain to tell him what they're seeing. Is he human?'

I nod hesitantly but don't reply.

'*And* he needs a heart transplant. So doctors give him a synthetic heart. It's manufactured in a lab but it works the same way as an organic heart. Is he still human then?'

I shift uneasily in my seat, not liking where this is going. 'I suppose so.'

'And then his brain melts down but doctors are able to download and copy *all* of his memories and experiences on to a computer. They build him a synthetic brain that will function exactly like his old one.'

'Are you talking about me?' My voice is quivering and my eyes are misting with tears. 'Are you saying I have a synthetic brain and heart and cameras for eyes and prosthetic limbs?'

'Shh,' he soothes, pushing himself off the contraption and hurrying towards me. He kneels down again at my feet, looking up at me. And once again I can't help but remark upon the kindness of his eyes. 'No, Sera. I'm simply giving you a very extreme example to show you how complicated a question it is.'

I feel my whole body deflate with relief.

'What makes us human?' he asks. 'Is it our hearts? Our brains? Our senses? Our limbs? Ask a hundred people and you'll get a hundred different answers.'

I peer down at my legs, remembering how fast they carried me through the trees. So fast my pursuer couldn't keep up.

'What are you saying?' I ask hoarsely. 'How does this apply to *me*?'

'Sera,' he begins gently, 'you are so special. Unlike anyone. My greatest creation of all time.'

'Creation?' I repeat. My lips feel numb as the word stumbles out of them. 'What did you do to me?'

He takes hold of one of my hands, rubbing a rough thumb over my skin. 'I made you perfect.'

My mouth goes dry. I try to swallow but it only makes me

gag. I try to speak but words won't form. It's probably for the best. I'm not sure what I would say anyway.

'You are the first human being in the history of the world to be created entirely by science. The most flawless sequence of genetic code in existence. Everything that our species has been craving – beauty, strength, intelligence, resistance to disease – has been engineered in you.'

His words haunt me, causing my lips and fingers to tremble. I shake my head, wishing I could scream at him to stop talking but I can't. And so he goes on.

'Researchers have been working on the science of synthetic biology for years now. It's the creation of life from scratch. Synthesizing in a lab what Mother Nature has been making in her backyard for aeons, and then improving upon it. But no one had ever progressed further than a few single-celled organisms. That is, until us. Until . . . *you*. You are one of a kind. A scientific miracle.'

Infuriation rises in my chest. I don't want to be a scientific miracle. I don't want any of this.

It's the anger that finally revives my voice. I open my mouth to express my grievances aloud but I never get the opportunity.

A booming voice echoes from the entrance of the barn, startling both of us.

'GET AWAY FROM HER!'

I turn to see Zen walking slowly towards us, a heavy determination in his step. His arms are stretched out in front of him and cradled in his fingers is a device I've never seen before. It looks to be made out of some kind of black metal and it's shaped like an upside-down L. There's a round barrel with grooves in it that sits in the middle.

The redheaded man rises quickly to his feet. 'Lyzender,' he states calmly, as though he expected this encounter.

Zen continues to approach us, stealing a curious glance at

the unconscious men on the ground while keeping the device pointed firmly at the redheaded man's face. 'Step away from her, Rio.'

I glance between them, confused by their exchange. 'You two know each other?'

They both ignore me.

'This isn't necessary,' says the man Zen addressed as Rio. 'You can put the gun down. We're both on the same team here.'

'Like hell we are!' Zen shouts. He takes a step closer to the man and shoves the black object in his face.

Gun.

Gun.

I rack my brain for a definition but find nothing.

'What is that?' I ask, standing up and walking towards Zen, my eyes glued to the object in his hand.

'Sera, be careful!' the redheaded man warns me, reaching for me. But Zen forces him back with another wave of whatever is in his hand.

I freeze in place. 'What is it?' I ask again.

'It's a gun,' the man identified as Rio explains. 'It's a weapon that can be used to kill or severely injure someone.'

'Oh!' Zen cries out, rolling his eyes. 'So suddenly you're willing to teach her things.' I can hear the sarcasm on his tongue. It's bitter. I now understand the definition.

'I taught her everything she knows,' Rio argues back.

Zen shakes the gun. 'No! I taught her everything she knows. *You* ruined her life.'

Rio holds his hands up in a surrendering gesture. 'I can see how you would view it that way, Lyzender, but I assure you—'

'Shut up!' Zen screams, transferring the gun to one hand and beckoning me forward with the other. 'Sera, we're getting out of here. Why don't you wait outside while I take care of *him*.' He pronounces the word with an air of disgust.

I glance between them again, the seriousness of the situation starting to sink in. 'No.'

'Sera,' Zen says, losing his patience, 'this is not the time for you to argue with me. Please, just step outside.'

'I don't think you should hurt him,' I say. I have nothing to back up my plea except for a nagging feeling in my chest.

Zen closes his eyes for a brief moment. 'Sera, you've lost all your memories. You don't know what I know. He's evil. And selfish. He doesn't have your best interests at heart. He has only his own.' He sighs. 'Sera, he does *not* love you.'

Love?

The word takes hold inside my brain and doesn't seem to want to let go.

'He released me,' I hear myself argue in response.

'Because he wants to take you back there!' Zen argues passionately. 'And continue to destroy your life.'

'That's where you're wrong, Lyzender,' Rio interjects. 'I only want to—'

Zen takes another step towards Rio, the gun now a mere foot away from his head. 'I said SHUT UP!' he yells. 'Don't try to confuse her again. It won't work any more.'

'Stop!' I shout desperately, holding my head in my hands. 'Please. I need to think.'

Zen falls quiet and they both look at me. I massage my aching temples with my fingertips. This is too much information to absorb at once. I can't process it all. I don't know how to make sense of it. I need to sort through it one thing at a time.

I begin with 'How do you know each other?'

'My mother works with him,' Zen says, disdain dripping from his tone.

'And where do you work?' I ask Rio, but Zen is the one who answers.

'At an evil corporation that has zero respect for human life. Something I didn't realize until it was too late.'

Diotech.

Rio closes his mouth and juts his chin forward.

'What do you do for them?' I ask Rio, but again Zen is the one who responds.

'This!' Zen motions to me. 'This is what he does! He toys with people's minds. He manipulates reality. He plays *God*. He turns human beings into . . . .'

'Into what?' I ask feebly. 'Into monsters like me?'

Zen's harsh expression immediately softens and he moves closer to me, careful to keep the gun pointed directly at Rio. 'No.' He uses his free hand to touch my face. 'That's not what I meant. I've never thought that about you.'

'Then what did you mean?'

'I didn't—' Zen struggles to find the right thing to say. 'I . . . just mean, you can't ever go back there with them. I won't let you. Because who knows what they'll do to you.'

Rio is mysteriously quiet. I assume he's either hiding something or he's given up trying to argue with Zen and his gun.

Or he's silently acquiescing.

I step up to him, close enough to feel his strained breath on my face.

'Sera,' Zen warns. I hold up a single hand to silence him.

I peer deep into the redheaded man's tired, hooded eyes. They're a faded greenish-grey colour with tiny specks of brown. He holds my gaze. Tenaciously.

As hard as I try, I can't find anything malicious there.

In fact, I only see the opposite. I see the way Heather looks at Cody. The way Kiyana looked at me.

Can you fake something like that?

I wish I knew.

'Is it true?' I challenge Rio. 'Those things he said about you?'

'Sera.' I hear Zen groan behind me. 'I wouldn't lie to you. I'm not *him*.'

'Is it *true*?' I press, ignoring Zen.

Rio's swollen eyelids drift to a close. 'It's true,' he whispers.

I break eye contact and turn to Zen, who appears genuinely surprised by Rio's admission.

'I'll go with you,' I tell Zen. 'But only if you don't hurt him.'

Zen's temper flares again. 'Sera, you don't understand. This won't stop. They'll keep looking for you. This may be the only chance to—'

I raise my hand in protest again and Zen stops talking. Then I reach towards him and turn my palm up. With a sigh, he relinquishes the gun to me. It's heavier than I thought it would be.

'OK, let's go,' I say. Gripping the weapon carefully in my hand, I start walking towards the crumbling doorway. I don't look back at the redheaded man, who stands alone in the middle of the empty barn. I don't know if I have the strength to.

24

ESCAPE

The dry, faded leaves crunch beneath my feet as they pound the dirt floor of the forest. I don't know where we're going but I've deduced that Zen does not own a car. Which must be why we're on foot. His pace is significantly slower than what I now know I'm capable of, but his hard, laboured breaths tell me that this is his top speed. They also tell me that I shouldn't try to speak to him because most likely he will not be able to respond until we've slowed down.

The gun is still heavy and awkward in my hand. I try to slide it into one of the many pockets of my pants, but it's too big.

Finally, after we've been running for fifteen minutes, Zen slows to a stop.

He leans forward and puts his hands on his knees, panting heavily. 'That should do it,' he says between wheezes.

'That should do what?' I ask, my own breath perfectly even.

He takes a moment and a few more strained gasps of air before he answers, rubbing at his damp forehead. I like the way the moisture makes his hair curl. And the way his eyes reflect the moonlight.

'I had to get you far enough away so they wouldn't be able to scan you,' he explains.

I look down at the thin black line on my wrist. I remember seeing the scar-faced man on the sidewalk and feeling my tattoo sizzle. Is that what was happening? Was he *scanning* me? Like a package of food at the supermarket?

'How does it work?' I ask.

'Similar to a bar code. The line looks solid but up close it's actually a unique design that their scanners can recognize and track.'

'And it's tattooed into my skin?'

Zen shakes his head. 'Actually, no. We learned that one the hard way. We tried to remove it once but it simply grew back. Exactly the same. Apparently that design is programmed into your DNA. Like the shape of your nose or the colour of your eyes. So even if someone tries to cut it out, when the skin heals, the same mark will always appear.'

I touch the blackened skin, sweeping my fingertip back and forth. I want to ask more but I'm not sure I can handle the answers right now. So I decide to stick to something simple. Easy. 'Where are we going?'

Zen straightens up and looks at me. The endearing crooked smile I remember from the supermarket and the dressing room is nowhere to be found. Now all I see is a grim expression and hollow eyes. 'We're going somewhere safe. At least for now. Until I can figure everything out.'

I watch his eyes move down my face towards my neckline, and he smiles for the first time. It's a weary smile. 'You're wearing it again.'

I feel for the locket. I had tucked it under my shirt earlier but it must have bounced out while I was running. I bite my lip, unsure what to say. Unsure even what to feel.

'I like seeing it on you.' He steps towards me, extending his hand. 'May I?'

I don't know what he's asking permission for but it doesn't really matter. I find myself nodding to his request, whatever it is.

As he reaches for the locket, his fingertips lightly graze my collarbone, sending tiny prickles over my skin. Having him this close to me is doing peculiar things to my lungs. Only a moment ago it was Zen who was having trouble breathing. Now it seems I'm the one who is out of air.

He carefully unlatches the clasp, and the small heart swings open. Unexpectedly his brow creases and his smile sags into a frown.

I peer down. 'What's the matter?'

'It's empty.'

'I know,' I say. 'It was empty when they found me.'

I watch Zen's mouth contort in disappointment. 'Then it must have fallen out at some point.'

I pull on the chain, drawing the locket out of his hands and into mine. 'What fell out?' I ask desperately.

With a wistful sigh he turns and starts walking. 'A pebble.'

Perplexed, I look after him and then hurry to catch up. 'A pebble? Why a pebble?'

'It was to remind you of what's real.'

'Why would I need to be reminded of what's real?'

He slows slightly and looks to the ground. 'Because not everything in your life was.'

I see a clearing up ahead. We've almost arrived back at the highway. Every few seconds another set of car headlights passes by, illuminating the road for a moment before it returns to darkness.

But I can still see everything flawlessly.

Which is unfortunate because I notice smoke rising above

the trees a few miles to our left and I know immediately that it's the site of the accident. The one I caused. The guilt wrenches through me again and I have to swallow another rise of acid in my throat.

'Why are they looking for me?' I ask, thinking back to the man with the scar who chased me all the way out here.

Zen starts walking towards the road and beckons for me to follow. 'Because you escaped. Well . . . *we* did. Together.'

'Because we're soulmates?' I ask, the unfamiliar term feeling awkward on my lips.

As much as I once wanted to believe that everything he told me was a lie, after all that's happened in the past hour it's decidedly more difficult to do so.

Zen laughs. It echoes beautifully in my ears. 'Well, yes. There was *that* reason. But mostly it was because we figured out what they were doing to you.'

'What exactly *were* they doing to me? I still don't completely understand.'

Zen's smile fades almost instantly. 'Neither do I.'

'But you just said—'

His arm juts out in front of me, bringing me to a halt. We've stopped in front of the highway. There's a lull in the traffic and Zen reaches for my hand. We sprint across together. The touch of his skin against mine makes my entire body hum. I don't want him to let go but he does as soon as we reach the other side.

He doesn't seem to notice my disappointment when his fingers slip from mine. He just keeps walking.

'I know you have a lot of questions,' he begins, as he heads towards the far north side of town. 'But I think it's better if I don't answer them.'

My feet slow to a stop and I scowl in his direction. 'What? Why not?'

He stops too and glances back at me. 'Because knowing you, I honestly don't think you'd believe me.'

His response makes my head spin. How am I supposed to remember anything if he won't even tell me what happened?

'You've always had a tendency to trust only what you can see and touch and define,' he goes on. 'Facts and numbers. They're what you rely on.'

I'm somewhat staggered by how accurate his description is.

'Which is why,' he continues, 'I think it's better if I show you.'

Show me?

He starts walking again and I follow closely behind as he leads me back into the small, sleepy town of Wells Creek. We cross the deserted main street and continue up a hill. I note the street sign as we turn on to a narrow road: BRADBURY DRIVE. And the building we eventually stop in front of is marked by the number 1952.

1952 Bradbury Drive, room 302.

Where Zen told me he was staying. Where he asked me to meet him when he cornered me in the dressing room.

But the part that confuses me is the sign out front that reads MARK TWAIN ELEMENTARY SCHOOL.

Why would Zen be staying at a school?

He taps on a small numeric keypad on the front door and then yanks it open. He beckons for me to enter but I hesitate.

'Sera,' he urges gently, 'I would never lead you into danger. I'm doing my best to keep you *away* from it.' He smiles ever so slightly. 'I promise.'

I walk past him into the building and Zen lets the door swing shut behind us. He guides me up two flights of stairs and down a hallway to room 302.

The lock has been broken. Busted open. He holds the door for me, flips on the light switch, and we step inside. The room is hot and a bit stuffy but I hardly notice. I'm far too distracted by the walls. They're utterly fascinating. Bright and colourful and decorated with hundreds of pictures and drawings and maps of the world.

There are shelves stuffed with books and a handful of small round tables with blue plastic chairs tucked in around them. Every letter of the alphabet is displayed in various colours near the ceiling.

'What is this place?' I ask, spinning in a slow circle, trying to absorb everything.

'It's a kindergarten classroom.'

'What's kindergarten?'

He chuckles. 'It's the first year of school. When children start their education. Typically around age five.'

I smile, immediately feeling a peculiar kinship with the room. After all, I seem to be starting from the beginning as well.

'Sorry it's so warm in here,' Zen says, walking to a table in the centre of the room. 'They don't turn on the air-conditioning in the summer when school is out.'

On the floor near his feet I notice a thin foam pad with a pillow and a crumpled blanket on it. 'Are you . . . *living* here?' I ask.

'Temporarily.'

'Why?'

'I had to find a location that was deserted. So I could stay under the radar. And a kindergarten classroom seemed like the perfect place. There's no one here during the summer and they have blankets and pillows for nap time.'

I stifle a laugh at the thought of Zen sleeping on a pillow belonging to a five-year-old. 'I mean, why aren't you living at home?'

I watch him remove a tiny silver cube from his pants pocket and place it gingerly down on the table in front of him. He's so noticeably delicate with it you would think it was made out of fragile glass.

I move towards him, keeping my eyes on the curious steel object. For some reason, it seems to be calling me. Like the gravitational pull of a large planet. Even though it's barely bigger than my fingernail.

'I can't go home,' he says simply as he presses his thumb against one side of the device. It glows green in response.

I completely forget about our conversation as I'm drawn further and further into the magnetism of the mysterious object, marvelling at how my hands tremble the closer I get. 'What is that?' I ask, refusing to take my eyes off it for even a second.

Zen follows my gaze until we're both staring at the tiny radiant cube.

'This,' he says, picking it up and holding it protectively in his hand, 'is where I've stored your memories.'

25
CONNECTED

The gun slips from my hand and lands on the floor with a loud *thud*. Zen gasps and lunges forward. 'You have to be careful with that!' he warns, scooping it up and placing it on the table next to the glowing cube.

'My memories?' My voice quivers.

'Well,' he amends, 'not *all* your memories. Unfortunately I couldn't get all of them. But these are enough to give you the general idea of what happened.'

He points to the device. 'I stored them on this hard drive until I could convince you to come here.'

His explanation only confuses me more. 'But how did you get them?'

He shrugs. 'I stole them.'

'From who?'

'From the people who took them from *you*.' He studies the bewildered look on my face and then quickly adds, 'To be fair, they stole them first. I was just . . . you know, stealing them back for you.'

My legs feel wobbly and I collapse into the nearest chair – one of the small blue plastic ones clearly designed for a young child. It's a long way down and I nearly lose my balance.

I hold my head in my hands. 'What is going on?' The words barely make it out alive. My throat does its best to suffocate them.

Zen hurries over to me and kneels at my feet. 'I'm sorry. I'm being insensitive. I know this is scary and overwhelming for you. But I promise everything will be explained in a minute.'

He stands up and draws a small wooden box out of his other pocket, flipping open the lid. I crane my neck to peek inside and see that the box contains three very odd-looking discs. Each one is about two inches in diameter and made of some kind of transparent rubber.

He removes the first and leans over me, placing the disc just behind my left ear. It sticks on its own, practically fusing to my flesh.

'These are cognitive receptors,' he explains, removing the second rubber disc from the box. He places this one behind my right ear. 'They will link your brain to this hard drive, allowing you to access anything that's on it.' He taps the miniature steel box gingerly with his fingertip. 'It's a technology that was developed on the Diotech compound. I think they call it re-cognization.'

'And how do you know all of this?'

He shrugs and gives me a sheepish smile. 'The truth is, I don't really. I mean, I don't know the science behind it. I knew the technology existed because my mom was on the team that developed it. And after I went back and stole the memory files from the Diotech compound and erased any backups on their server, I did a little test run on myself, to make sure it worked.'

'Does it hurt?' I ask fearfully.

'No. It's just a little . . .' He pauses, screwing his lips in concentration. 'Weird.'

'Weird,' I repeat, my stomach rumbling with nerves.

He picks up the third receptor and closes the lid of the now empty box. Then he steps behind me. I crane my neck, trying to see him, waiting for what he'll do next. But he just stands there, awkwardly fidgeting with the disc. 'Sorry,' he says, extending his hand tentatively towards my head and then quickly withdrawing it. 'I need to, um, move your hair.'

'Oh,' I say, suddenly feeling as awkward as he looks. 'Right. Sure. Go ahead.'

He slowly reaches towards me and I hold my breath. I don't mean to. The air just kind of traps itself willingly inside my lungs. I feel his fingertips graze the back of my bare neck. His touch causes my skin to prickle and heat up. He gently gathers my hair in one hand and sweeps it over my left shoulder, taking a moment to brush a few loose strands that didn't make it.

The whole movement is so fluid – so practised – that it makes me 100 per cent certain he's done this before. This is not the first time his hands have touched my hair. And I find myself silently hoping that it won't be the last.

'OK,' Zen says, clearing his throat. I jump and my eyes flutter open. I didn't even realize they had closed. He's back in front of me again.

'So,' I say, trying to mask my embarrassment. 'It's done?'

Zen takes a deep breath and sits himself down in an adjacent chair. 'Yes. You should now be directly linked to the drive.'

I wait, wondering if something is supposed to be happening. I'm half expecting a bolt of lightning to strike my brain, but in reality, nothing changes. My mind is quiet. And the room has fallen silent once again.

'I don't feel anything,' I tell him.

He nods. 'You won't feel different. Think of this as an extension of your brain. An external storage container of sorts. But in order to access the information that's in it, the memories have to be triggered somehow.'

'OK,' I say dubiously. 'And how do we do that?'

'There are several ways to trigger dormant memories – key words, objects, images – but the easiest thing is for me to ask you questions.'

'OK,' I say again, feeling less and less confident that this will actually work.

He rubs his palms on his pants. 'Let's start with your house. Tell me about your living room.'

I frown. 'How can I possibly do that? I don't remember my house. I don't remember anything about my life before—'

'What colour is the couch?' he interrupts.

'Beige,' I say without thinking.

My whole body freezes. Apart from my pounding heart. Which I can now hear in my ears.

What just happened?

'And where is the front door?' he continues.

This response comes as quickly as the last one. 'On the opposite side of the room. Next to a tall brown lamp and a coat rack.'

I don't know how I'm doing this. I don't know why these answers are coming so easily. Or if they're even the *right* answers.

I stare wide-eyed at Zen. 'What is going on?'

He smiles encouragingly. 'You're remembering.'

'I am?'

He nods. 'Your brain is accessing the memory that's stored on the drive.'

A rush of euphoria shoots through me, waking me up,

energizing my senses. 'Do it again!' I order. 'Ask me more questions!'

Zen laughs. 'OK, OK. What else is in the room?'

I bite my lip in concentration and close my eyes but nothing is coming. 'I . . . I . . .'

Zen steps in. 'Sorry, you probably need something more specific. What is in the corner, to the right of the front door?'

A grin spreads wide across my lips. I know this. 'It's a plant!'

I doubt anyone in the history of the world has ever gotten this excited about a plant, but I don't care. For me, this plant means everything. It's a piece of me. A piece I thought I had lost forever.

And then suddenly the room starts to take shape. What was a blank white canvas is now becoming a tapestry of colours and objects and furniture. One by one, items materialize out of thin air, filling in empty gaps. A table. Another lamp. A chair. A bookshelf. A fireplace.

It's so magnificent. And so real! I can remember it almost as clearly as I can remember my room at Heather and Scott's house.

'Is this really my house?' I ask Zen.

'Yep.'

I can hardly believe what I'm seeing – or remembering, rather. For the first time in what, for me, seems like forever, I start to feel an undeniable sense of ownership over something.

My living room.

My beige couch.

My house.

And everything I see feels comfortable. Safe. Right. It feels like *home*.

The living room continues to populate with familiar adornments and trimmings. As though a pair of magic, invisible hands were skilfully decorating my memory. Brass candleholders appear atop the mantel and are immediately filled with long tapered green candles. A richly coloured mosaic rug unfurls along the hardwood floor.

The walls, once plain white, are suddenly coated in creamy taupe paint as three dark wood picture frames take shape over the couch. Inside each one, a beautiful oil painting starts to emerge, swiftly crafted by an unseen artist with a concealed brush.

Red opaque curtains glide across the window, blocking out the daylight until, finally, the lamp in the corner illuminates, casting a warm soothing glow on everything, and adding a satisfying finishing touch to the full picture.

But even though the living room seems to be complete, I am hungry for more. I have a burning desire to explore the rest of the house. To push the limits of my newly returned memory.

I notice the beginnings of a narrow hallway leading out of the room and I'm immediately pulled towards it. I squeeze my eyes shut tight and focus hard on the path of the hardwood floor, forcing my mind to walk down it until I see . . .

Nothing.

The world simply stops there. And as hard as I try, as deeply as I concentrate, I can't see beyond it. It's as though the hallway just dissolves into nothing. The floor ceases to exist, the walls disappear, and I'm surrounded once again by that exasperating empty white space that's been haunting me since they pulled me from the ocean.

I squirm in my seat and let out a small whimper. 'I can't . . .' I try to explain, frustration mounting. 'I can't see anything else.' I open my eyes and look desperately at Zen. 'I can't remember what's outside of that room! Why can't I remember?'

Zen puts a reassuring hand on my arm, but this time his touch does nothing to calm me. 'Because you only have access to what's on the hard drive. And unfortunately I wasn't able to get any memories of other rooms in the house. Which means you won't be able to see anything past the living room.'

I toss my hands in the air and launch to my feet so forcefully the little blue chair I was sitting on goes flying backwards. 'So that's it?' I cry. 'That's all I get? A quick glimpse of a stupid living room? What good can that possibly do me?!'

I expect Zen to reach out and try to comfort me again, but he doesn't. In fact, all he does is smile. As though he's thoroughly entertained by my aggravation.

'What?' I demand, my teeth clenching.

He shakes his head. 'Nothing. Sorry. It's just . . .' His voice trails off.

'It's just what?'

'It's nice to see you back.'

My forehead crumples. 'Back?'

'Yeah, you know, the old Seraphina. The feisty, spirited one I fell in love with. I saw a flash of her just then and it . . .' His smile quickly fades, replaced by a much more sombre expression. 'Well, for a while there I was afraid she might be gone forever.'

My rage suddenly subsides and I cast my eyes downward, coming up with nothing more interesting to respond with than 'Oh'.

'But don't worry,' Zen assures me, tapping the steel cube. 'That's not the only memory on here. I promise there's more to see.' He stands up and retrieves the upturned chair from the other side of the room where it landed. 'Sit back down. Relax. I'm going to show you my favourite memory of all.'

Reluctantly I lower myself back into the chair. 'And what memory would that be?' I ask, trying to sound as lighthearted as possible in hopes of counteracting my earlier outburst.

The crooked smile is back. The one that makes me feel like it's the only thing in the world worth remembering. He holds my gaze tightly as he says, 'The day I met you.'

26

CONTAINED

'Close your eyes,' Zen instructs me. 'Go back to the living room and tell me what you see.'

I do as I'm told, allowing my mind to be transported back to the only room I have. I focus hard until I see everything reappear in front of me. The beige couch. The coffee table. The lamp. But this time, there's something new in the picture.

'A book,' I tell him eagerly. 'I see a book. And a hand. It's . . .' The realization comes fast. 'It's mine! It's my hand. I'm holding the book. I just finished reading it.'

'Good,' Zen encourages. 'That's right. You were in the living room reading.'

I can see the book clearly in front of me now. *A Wrinkle in Time*, by Madeleine L'Engle. The cover is ragged and peeling away. As though it's been read a hundred times. And underneath it, I can make out my legs, curled up on the couch, swathed in a pair of dark grey cotton pants. They look surprisingly similar to the ones I was wearing when the rescue boat found me. The ones still folded up in a drawer at the Carlsons' house.

'Now try to let the memory guide you. It may be somewhat stilted at first but it will get easier and start to flow more fluidly the longer you do it. And I'll be here to prompt you if you get stuck. What else do you remember about that day?'

I bite my lip and concentrate, attempting to verbalize everything I see and feel. 'I was getting hungry,' I recount. 'I was going to eat lunch. But then I heard something. A scratching sound. It was coming from outside.'

I watch the scene as it plays out in brief, somewhat hazy fragments. I see it through my own eyes. As though it's happening to me right now.

Standing up. Walking to the front door. Reaching out my hand.

But I'm crippled by a sudden bout of fear and I quickly withdraw it.

'I was scared,' I tell Zen. 'Something scared me.'

'Yes,' Zen replies. 'Do you remember what you were afraid of?'

'The outside,' I say with startling certainty. 'I was afraid to go outside.'

'Why?' Zen prompts.

'Because someone told me not to.'

Who? I immediately wonder. I clench my eyes shut and press my fingers against my temples, trying to find the person's face. Trying to hear the warning. But I just can't. The memory is not there.

'I'm not supposed to go outside when no one is home,' I tell Zen. But I barely recognize my own voice. It sounds flat and lifeless. My words come out like a monotone chant. 'Something bad will happen if I do. But I don't know what.'

'It's OK,' Zen says hastily. 'Keep going.'

I inhale deeply and slide back in.

My hand extends again. My finger presses against a glowing blue scanner. The door beeps and I push it open.

'I didn't listen,' I recall. 'I went outside anyway.'

Zen laughs. 'You were never very good at following rules. Much to the disappointment of the people who made them.'

I think about the Carlsons. How I convinced Cody to sneak out of the house before they woke up. How I disappeared into the night without telling them I was leaving. I find myself comforted by the knowledge that apparently some parts of me were never really lost.

'What did you see when you went outside?' Zen asks, his question inspiring a whole new picture to appear before me.

A white wraparound porch, a small, well-manicured lawn with freshly cut grass and flowers. The air is hot and dry.

'My front yard,' I reply.

'And past that?'

I struggle to remember what was past the yard. But I can't see much.

A tall concrete wall rising ten feet into the air blocks my view. There's a narrow walkway that leads from the base of the porch steps and across the lawn but it stops at a thick steel gate that's been set into the wall.

'I don't know,' I reply, flustered. 'There's a giant wall. It circles the whole house. I can't see anything over it.'

'It's all right,' Zen assures me, resting his hand atop mine.

'What is the wall for?' I ask.

But to my surprise, it's me who responds. Or some variation of me. Once again, I hear my voice drop into an unnerving, inflectionless drone as I callously repeat something I don't recall learning. 'It's for my own protection.'

A debilitating chill runs up my arm. Zen strokes my fingers. 'Don't worry about it,' he says. 'Focus on what happened next.'

I nod, forcing myself back into the scene.

My eyes scan the length of the wall, searching for the source of the strange noise I heard from inside the house. I notice something move off to the side.

'I saw something,' I tell Zen.

'What did you see?'

My gaze whips to the right and lands on a pair of hands that are gripping the top of the wall. I hear a grunt as someone struggles to pull himself up. A head appears a moment later. I can't make out the features of his face but I can see that he's young. My age. Maybe slightly older.

'A boy,' I reply, my excitement growing. 'He was climbing the wall.'

He swings one leg carefully over the top, followed by the other. Then he sits perched on the ledge, staring down. Gauging the distance to the ground. After a moment, he pushes himself off, free-falling for a second, before landing in a crouched position on the other side.

My side.

He stands and dusts himself off. I can see his face now. He has thick, dark eyebrows that are pinched together to form a crease above the bridge of his nose. His eyes are a rich brown. His hair is almost black. It sweeps across his forehead, a few strands tickling the tips of his eyelashes. He shakes his head to brush them away as a single drop of sweat falls from his forehead.

'It was you,' I say quietly, opening my eyes and gazing into the same oval-shaped face.

Zen grins. 'It was me.'

'You climbed the wall?'

He shrugs. 'What can I say? I was curious. You put a giant concrete wall in front of a guy, he's gonna try to find out what's on the other side.'

'I guess I wasn't the only one who was bad at following rules,' I point out playfully before shutting my eyes again.

The sight of the trespassing stranger brings about an ambush of emotions. Terror. Exhilaration. The unyielding urge to run.

I pivot back towards the house, my gaze immediately landing on a flashing red button that is secured to the wall just inside the front door.

'What is that?' I ask Zen.

'What is what?'

'The red button on the wall. What's it for?'

But before I even finish asking the question, the answer has already been triggered in my mind.

It's in case of emergency.

A shudder overtakes me and I mutter, 'Never mind,' before Zen has a chance to respond.

But evidently I didn't consider the appearance of this boy an emergency because as I fall back into the scene, I find that:

I'm still on the porch. I didn't run back inside. I didn't hit the flashing red button. I'm still hiding behind the same pillar. Watching him. Trying to figure out where he came from. Who he is. How old he is.

I open my eyes and look at Zen. 'How old *are* you, by the way?'

'I was seventeen when this took place. I'm eighteen now.'

Content to have something concrete to add to my meagre list of facts, I close my eyes again.

From my hiding spot, I watch the boy as he stares at the house in wonderment. He gazes up and down the facade, his face revealing a dazed, almost endearing curiosity. His presence both fascinates and frightens me at the same time.

'What do you see?' I hear Zen ask from beside me. I think he's moved closer.

'You,' I say, allowing myself just the hint of a smile.

'What am I doing?'

The boy takes a few steps forward but then stops. Very abruptly. He clearly sees something. And it only takes a moment for me to realize what it is.

Me.

I tentatively peer around the pillar and our eyes meet.

'You're looking at me,' I reply.

He laughs softly. 'It's hard not to.'

He's definitely closer now. I can feel his gaze on me. His breath. It's warm and sweet.

My heart starts to pound.

And at this exact moment, I honestly don't know if it's because of the girl in my memory, standing on her front porch, frozen in fear of the stranger who has just unexpectedly infiltrated her life. Or if it's because of me now. Sitting next to that very same stranger. Paralysed by feelings I don't understand.

All at once, everything is tangled.

I can't tell the memory from the reality. I can't separate the emotions.

I can see through her eyes. Hear her thoughts. Feel her fear. Because it was once my own. Because it still is. And because, not so long ago, I felt the same hesitation. I had the same doubts.

Doubts that suddenly seem absurd.

That suddenly seem . . .

Gone.

I open my eyes and he is there. Right there. Closer than he's ever been before.

I feel my lips start to tingle and twitch. I press them together but it does no good. They want to move. They want to go somewhere. They pull me forward. Towards him. Towards *his*.

Like there's a path that was carved out years ago. A direct route. The *only* route.

I don't understand what's happening. Or why every part of my body seems to be acting without my direction. Without my permission. But my instinct is telling me this is something I don't have to understand. I don't even have to try. Because I will probably never succeed.

I'm pulled in even more. Our mouths are almost touching. His hand finds its way to my cheek. And then . . .

'I think we should finish,' he whispers.

Cool air rushes over my skin as his fingers slide from my face and he's suddenly far away again.

I have to blink to bring my surroundings back into focus. Sensation slowly returns to the parts of my body that were momentarily lacking it.

I nod my agreement but don't say anything out of fear that my voice will fail me. Miserably.

I sit up straighter in my chair as I try to tune my thoughts back into the events of that day. To pick up where I left off. But there's not much more to remember.

I watch the boy slowly approach the porch, my uncertainty growing with every step he takes. I eye the alarm a second time. Once again, debating between following the rules and giving in to my curiosity.

The curiosity wins.

'Who are you?' he asks.

I swallow a lump in my throat and slowly part my lips. 'My name is Seraphina.'

Then there is nothing.

The memory is over.

27
ISOLATED

My body and mind are exhausted and craving sleep but I don't want to stop. I'm addicted to the taste of my own memories. The flavour is intoxicating. The thought of finally having answers to my questions exhilarates me. It's enough to keep me wide awake.

'I thought you said that when you first met me I was living in a lab,' I point out.

'You were,' he replies. 'Your house was part of an enormous research compound. Away from civilization. Away from everything. I originally thought the reason Diotech chose to build it so far away was because that was the only place they could find enough space to house all their buildings and staff. But I later discovered it was because they just didn't want anyone to know what they were really doing.'

He makes a vague gesture in my direction that I can't quite interpret.

But he must notice my puzzled expression because he

quickly adds, 'Sorry. As you can probably tell I have sort of a love–hate relationship with Diotech.'

'What does that mean?'

He heaves a heavy sigh. 'I hate them for what they did to you. But at the same time, if it wasn't for them there would be no . . . well . . . *you*. And for that –' he flashes me that beloved lopsided smile again – 'I guess I have to thank them.'

I can feel my cheeks flush with heat. Is this what happens when Cody's face turns red? I quickly avert my gaze.

Zen rubs mercilessly at his eyebrow. 'It's just all so twisted and complicated. You see, I practically grew up on the Diotech compound. It was my home too. My mother was one of the head scientists. We moved there when I was only eight.

'They keep everything on that compound,' he continues. 'All of their research, projects, administration, employees, employees' families. The whole company is there. That way they can keep tabs on everything – and *everyone* – at all times.'

The resentment in his voice is thick and icy. It turns him into someone else. Not the innocent, carefree boy who climbed the wall that day. I have a feeling that boy has been missing for a long time.

'People rarely leave,' he explains. 'Why would you, when everything you need is right there? Schools, stores, restaurants, entertainment.' A bitter smile contorts his lips. 'I suppose it's not much different from a cult.'

'A cult?'

'Yeah. You know, everyone is brainwashed so they'll believe something that's not true. They're lied to. To keep them from fleeing.' He lets out an acidic chuckle. 'But I guess they didn't hide the truth well enough. Because we discovered it. And we *did* flee.' He lowers his head and drops his voice. 'At least, we tried.'

'And that's why they sent people after me,' I state, struggling to make this new information fit with the few things I already know. 'Those men in the barn. Because we ran away?'

He nods solemnly. 'They work for Diotech. Part of Alixter's elite security force.'

'Alixter?' I repeat the name. The sound of it is hauntingly familiar. It sends a tremor of fear through me.

Zen watches my reaction carefully. 'Yes. Jans Alixter. The president of Diotech and the most abominable man in existence. He created the company. Along with Rio. They were the founding partners. Alixter was the business brains of the operation, while Dr Rio handled all the science.'

Rio.

The redheaded man.

The mention of him sparks something in my subconscious.

I sneak a glimpse at the silver cube on the table. It's still on. I'm still connected to it. I wonder if there's anything stored in there that can tell me more about him. About the man who paid for my meal at the diner. Who released me from the chains in the barn. Who Zen tried to kill only a few hours ago.

But nothing comes.

'Are you all right?' Zen asks, studying my face. 'Maybe we should take a break.'

'No,' I reply in haste. 'There's still so much I want to know.'

Zen grins. 'OK. Like what?'

'Like . . .' I pause, scrambling to arrange the multitude of questions swimming around in my head into some kind of prioritized list. 'What happened that day we met? After you saw me behind the pillar. Did I sound the alarm on you?'

'No. Thankfully.' His smile grows. 'We sat on the lawn and talked. For a while actually. You were very wary of me at first. You sat like ten feet away.' He chuckles heartily at the memory.

'It was obvious you didn't trust me. But slowly, little by little, you started to open up. You inched closer. It was adorable.'

'What did we talk about?'

He shrugs. 'Lots of things. Although truthfully, I did the majority of the talking. I was nervous. I just couldn't get over how beautiful you were. And you were talking to *me*. That was the most unbelievable part of it.'

I think about what Cody said on the bus. About girls refusing to talk to him.

'Are you bitter at pretty girls?' I ask.

He breaks into laughter. 'What? No. I . . . Well, I'd never met someone as pretty as you, let's just say that. You were so –' his voice suddenly gets very quiet – 'different.'

I watch his expression shift. The change is perceptible. And I know right away that the darkness has returned.

'What's wrong?' I ask.

He shakes his head, as though he's trying to loosen a thought that's gripping his brain. 'There was just something so unusual about you. I saw it right away.'

'Unusual how?'

'Mostly it was your speech. It was kind of stilted. As though no one had ever taught you to use inflections when you spoke. It was evident you were tremendously intelligent but there was so much you didn't know. Everyday words and phrases and pop-culture references.'

So I've always been like that.

The thought comforts and unsettles me at the same time.

'Then there was that weird mark on your wrist. You told me it was a scar from when you were a baby. But I knew that couldn't be true. No scar looks like that. But I didn't press it. I assumed you just didn't want to tell me. It wasn't until later that I realized you were regurgitating what *they* had told you. You didn't know what it was either.'

I touch the thin black line on my wrist, shuddering as I remember what it felt like when it vibrated and gave away my location.

'But the biggest reason I knew there was something unusual about you,' Zen continues, 'was the fact that I'd never seen you before. You see, all the kids who live on the compound go to the same school. There are only about a hundred of us. You come to know people really well. Like in a small town. So seeing you hiding way back there in that restricted section and knowing that you didn't hang out with the rest of us was pretty strange.'

'Restricted section?' I repeat.

He nods. 'It's in the far back corner of the property. No one is allowed in without proper clearance.'

'So how did *you* get in?' There's more than a little teasing in my tone.

He chuckles, letting a little bit of the lightness back in, and waves away my question as though the answer was trivial. 'Oh, I made a duplicate of my father's fingerprint years ago. Growing up on a technological research compound gives you access to a lot of really cool gadgets. Life is pretty boring there. You find ways to entertain yourself.'

'Like climbing concrete walls?' I ask with a smirk.

'Exactly.'

I eye the small silver box that strangely houses the contents of my life. Or at least *some* of them. I find myself hoping that something in that little device will reveal why I feel so peculiar around Zen. Why my lips felt drawn to his like a magnet. What a soulmate really is. 'So what happened after that?' I ask. 'After we talked.'

Once again, I watch his demeanour shift. The light in his eyes dims. 'You asked if I would come back to see you and I said yes.' He averts his gaze and picks up the hard drive again, cradling it in his hands. 'Then I left and you forgot all about me.'

I blink in surprise. 'That's impossible. I would never—'

But before I can finish the sentence, I'm blasted by a barrage of images. A thousand pictures spinning chaotically, mixed with flashes of milky white.

I know it can only be one thing: the pieces of another memory.

I allow my eyes to close as I watch the scene unfold before me. As I witness it first-hand.

Knock. Knock. Knock.

Panic tightens my chest. My blood runs cold.

No one ever knocks on the door. My father always uses his fingerprint to enter.

Another knock. Then . . .

A voice. 'Sera?'

A voice I don't recognize.

But somehow it knows my name.

How does it know my name?

With shaking hands and uneven breath, I press my finger against the reader. When it beeps, I open the door a crack and peer through it. There's a boy standing on my front porch.

A boy I've never seen before.

I muster my strength, puff up my chest, and demand of him, 'Who are you?'

'Seraphina.' He says my name with such intimacy it makes me tremble slightly. 'It's me. Lyzender. I was here yesterday.'

I open the door a little wider and poke my head out, looking him up and down, trying to jog my memory. But it doesn't work. I don't recognize him.

'No, you weren't.' I retreat back inside and slam the door shut. My breathing still has not stabilized.

Go away, *I think to myself.* Please just go away.

But he doesn't.

He knocks again. 'Sera, please.'

His plea immediately pulls me out. Back to the present moment. Back to now.

I recognize those words. I recognize that desperation. I heard it in the parking lot of the supermarket.

'Please, Sera. Try.'

How many times have I forgotten this boy?

How many times has he begged me to remember?

'I don't understand,' I say slowly, forcing myself to stay calm. 'Why didn't I recognize you? Why was I behaving like we'd never met?'

'Because,' he states in a measured tone, 'they erased me from your memory.'

28
FABRICATIONS

His answer punches me in the chest. And suddenly I feel like I'm back in the ocean. The cold, ruthless waves slapping against my face.

'W-w-what?' I barely manage to squeak out.

'Actually, *erase* is probably the wrong word,' Zen admits. '*Removed* is a better one. Because the memory still existed after they took it from you.' He pats the silver cube on the table in front of him. 'It just didn't exist in your mind any more.'

'Why?' I cry out. My control over my emotions is slipping. 'Why would they do that?'

'Control, Sera,' he says with such gravity I have to look away. 'They tried to manipulate *everything*. Everything you remembered and everything you *didn*'t. They controlled what you knew. What you thought. What you experienced. But most of it was a giant lie. Your childhood, your friends—'

'My friends?' I ask in surprise. 'I had *friends*?'

Zen shuts his eyes and rubs his face. When his eyes open again, I see that they're tormented and bloodshot.

'You *thought* you had friends,' he clarifies. 'You thought you had a whole life outside of the compound. With family and birthday parties and shopping sprees at the mall. But none of it was real. It was all fake.'

'Fake?' I repeat dubiously. 'How do you *fake* friends?'

'By implanting artificial memories of them into your brain.'

I shake my head, refusing to believe it. 'No. I would be able to tell the difference.'

'That's the thing,' he says. 'You can't. No one can. They have computer programs that can generate such flawless memories that the brain can't differentiate them from the real ones. They fill your mind with these happy, comforting experiences that blend right in like they belong there. It's all the same to you. Once the memory has been uploaded, whether or not it really happened is irrelevant. Your brain *thinks* it did.'

I feel hot tears pricking my eyes. 'I just don't understand why anyone would do that,' I choke out. 'Why would they need to implant happy memories in my brain?'

'To replace the unpleasant ones,' Zen replies darkly. 'It was part of a grand illusion. To hide the fact that you were actually a prisoner. They decorated your cell to look like a real house, they crammed your head full of bogus memories. All so they could continue to do whatever horrendous things they were doing to you and you would never even know. Because you could never remember.'

My head is starting to throb. I stand up and pace the floor. Counting the tiles. The tables. The chairs. But it's pointless. Nothing alleviates this sickening feeling in the pit of my stomach.

'What *kind* of horrendous things?' I'm finally able to ask.

'That I don't know,' he admits. 'Although I've assumed it

had to be pretty bad if Diotech went to so much trouble to cover it up. We were never able to figure it out because every time they took you from the house, you came back with a memory of something blissful and benign. A trip to the beach. A sleepover at a friend's house. Always these perfect little excursions.'

My feet slow to a halt. Something is happening. His words must have triggered some kind of reaction because I can feel another memory forming.

I look anxiously towards the hard drive, wondering what horrors it has in store for me now. Wondering if I can even cope with whatever it's about to show me when I can barely handle what I've already seen.

I reach up towards the sides of my face, ready to rip the rubber discs from my skin. But it's too late. The images have already infiltrated my brain. They've already started their dizzying chaotic loops.

My hands fall limp at my sides as I surrender.

I close my eyes and let go. Because I don't have a choice.

'Do you have to leave so soon?'

I recognize my own voice. I'm speaking to someone.

I glance up to see him. Rio. Standing by the front door.

My front door.

It's the same living room.

The same house.

He nods solemnly. 'Yes. I'm sorry, Sera. But I have to get back to work.' He raises his finger to the white plate on the wall. The electronic door beeps.

'When will you be home?' I ask.

Home.

The word yanks me out.

Did he live with me?

In the barn he told me that I was his greatest creation. Does that mean he's my . . .

But I can't bring myself to think it.

Instead I remind myself what Zen said. It was all a manipulation. A lie. None of it was real.

'I'll be back in a few hours,' Rio replies. But he doesn't leave right away. He lingers by the door, hesitating, before turning back slowly and asking, 'Did you have fun today?' His voice is light and cheerful but there's something in his eyes that doesn't match.

Regret?

Sorrow?

Remorse?

Guilt.

The girl in the memory was the one who asked the question but now I'm the one who answers it. I didn't recognize it back then when I was standing in that living room. I didn't have the right frame of reference. But now I do. Because I've been haunted by that very same emotion. And it leaves a mark.

A mark that looks like that.

'Yes!' I say, swooning slightly. 'It was a perfect day.'

He smiles. A sad, tired smile that almost looks like something else entirely. 'Good. I'm glad.'

The room fades to white.

I keep my eyes closed. Even though I know it's over. I can't face reality yet. I'm not sure I even know what that is any more.

'A perfect day.'

That was my response.

Exactly as Zen described.

But Rio wasn't really asking me about my day. He was asking if I believed the lie. He was making sure the memory implant was a success.

My eyes snap open and land directly on the door. The muscles in my legs explode with fire. I heed their request and break for the door, crossing the room in a blur.

I can't stay here another minute.

Zen leaps from his chair but doesn't attempt to chase after me. I think he knows he'll never be able to keep up. Instead he tries to apprehend me with his words.

'Sera. Please. Don't.'

It works. The anguish in his voice brings me to a stop just short of the door.

'You can't keep running away every time you're afraid,' he cautions me. 'At some point you have to stay and fight for what you know is right.'

I stare longingly at the door handle, my fingers twitching. My whole body screaming.

'I stole these memories from Diotech so that I could *show* you. So you could see it for yourself. Because I need you to trust me. And I knew you wouldn't believe me any other way.' His voice cracks, but the intensity never breaks. 'Sera, please,' he implores. 'I need you back on my side.'

Despite every impulse that's urging me out that door, I turn and glance back, moisture pooling on the surface of my eyes.

'I know how hard it is for you to hear all of this,' Zen continues, 'because I've watched you learn the truth before. When we discovered it together. But we had more time then. To let it sink in. We don't have that luxury now. They're coming for you. They won't stop until they find you. And they *will* take you back there.'

The first tear leaks out, tracing a crooked line down my cheek. 'Was *none* of my life real?' I whisper.

He exhales, his shoulders falling. 'I was real,' he says.

He takes one step towards me. Then another. Moving slowly as though he was approaching a frightened injured animal in the woods. And I guess that's what I must look like right now. It's certainly how I feel.

He stops only inches away. Then he reaches out and cups my locket in his hand.

'That's why I put the pebble in here,' he says. 'So if you were ever in doubt, you could touch it and feel it and know that what we had was never fake. It was never generated by a computer and implanted in your brain. It was *always* real.'

I begin to shiver. It starts out small. A delicate tremble. But then it grows. Stronger and harder, until I'm shaking violently. My teeth chattering. My body convulsing.

Zen runs to the makeshift bed in the centre of the classroom and returns with the blanket. As soon as he wraps it around me, I crumple. Every muscle from my head to my feet giving out one by one, like a chain reaction.

Zen catches me just before I hit the floor. Then, in one fluid motion, he drapes my limp hand around the back of his neck, bends down and, with his elbow tucked under my knees, scoops me effortlessly into his arms.

My head sags against his chest as he carries me back to the foam pad on the floor and lowers me to it. I collapse on my side, my legs rejoicing and my head sinking eagerly into the pillow. It's only now that I realize how tired I am.

I peer up at the clock on the wall. It's 3:42 in the morning.

'What about my mother?' I utter dazedly. My voice strangled. 'Did I ever meet her?'

Zen walks back to the table and switches off the hard drive. From here I can see the soft green glow dim and finally extinguish. 'You *thought* you did.'

'Did I even have one?'

'Not like the one you remembered. She was a figment just like the rest of them. But as for a real mother –' he shakes his head forlornly – 'I really don't know.'

'And Rio. Is he . . . was he my father?'

This time, I manage to get the word out.

Zen's fists clench into balls and I can see him eyeing the gun on the table. 'That man is not your father,' he growls.

'But he lived with me?'

'Yes,' he concedes. 'But he was also the one who was controlling your mind. He is *not* to be trusted under any circumstances.'

I think about the person I saw in the barn. When I looked into his placid greenish-grey eyes, I saw something there. Something I couldn't pinpoint. But it made me want to protect him from harm.

Was that just residue from a series of fabricated memories?

Or was it something real?

I wonder if I'll ever know.

Despite the warm blanket around me, my whole body has turned numb. But at least I've stopped shivering.

'Zen?' I ask softly.

He sits down on the floor next to my head. 'Hmmm?'

'If so many of my memories weren't real, how do I know I can even trust the ones you showed me?'

He pulls his knees to his chest and clasps his hands around his ankles. 'You can't,' he admits. 'You can't trust *any* memories. They're too easily manipulated. You can only trust what you feel. What you *know* to be true.'

'But,' I protest, desperation seeping in, 'what if I don't—'

'Shh,' he says. 'A part of you will always know. You just have to figure out which part to listen to.'

He scoots in closer and begins to run his fingers through my hair.

His presence has a calming effect on me. And I'm grateful that he's here. That he's the one telling me all of this. Even though I know how much it pains him to do it. He's like a shield that I'm able to place between myself and the truth. Softening the blow to some extent. Absorbing a tiny fraction of the impact. Making it just the slightest bit less horrible.

And now I understand why I called him Zen.

I can feel my eyelids start to sag. It's getting harder and harder to keep my eyes open.

'Don't fight it, Sera,' he tells me. 'Sleep. I'll stay up.'

But I'm afraid of the silence. Afraid of the thoughts it will bring. And of the memories that I, ironically, once longed for more than anything.

'Keep talking,' I slur through drooping lips.

He chuckles. 'What do you want me to talk about?'

'Tell me more about the locket,' I say.

'I had it especially designed for you.' I can hear the wistfulness in his voice. 'You always loved that symbol. The eternal knot. You said it looked like two intertwined hearts. Forever connected. Forever linked.'

'How many times did I forget you?' My voice is hoarse and barely audible.

He sighs. 'Too many to count.'

'I'm sorry,' I offer weakly.

But he laughs again. 'It's not your fault.' I can hear the soft rustle of his fingers running through my hair. 'Besides, the joke was on them. Because I was never really gone.'

I nod weakly into the pillow.

I want to tell him that I understand. That I'm starting to get it. That I think maybe he's always been there. Lingering somewhere inside of me. Clinging desperately.

Revealing himself in subtle ways that I just couldn't understand.

Even though I still don't remember any of the details he's told me, I feel the shadows of our past together. It continues to run through my veins. It echoes in his laugh. It's reflected in his eyes.

Reminding me that I'm safe here. With him.

Like clues left behind for me to find. Clues that somehow made their mark in permanent ink.

Perhaps some things simply *can't* be erased.

He bends down and whispers softly in my ear, 'Are you asleep?'

'No,' I murmur.

'I want to try something.'

He gently places two fingertips against my forehead, directly above the bridge of my nose.

Instantly the skin between my eyes flares with a soothing white heat. Exactly like it did when I saw him outside the hospital. And in the parking lot of the supermarket. Except this time it's even hotter. It runs deeper. More intense than it's ever been before.

And then, in a flash, I know why.

A memory comes pouring in.

I open my eyes just long enough to see the tiny silver cube sitting on the table above us. No longer lit up. No longer transmitting a signal. Off.

Which means this memory isn't coming from a stolen hard drive. It's coming from me. From somewhere within. Where it's been hiding this whole time. Waiting.

The midday sun is bright in the sky. Shining down on us. Illuminating my tiny world.

A world that has gotten infinitely bigger since he entered it.

Zen and I lie together on the small patch of grass that makes up my front lawn. I'm on my back and he's pressed up against my side, his arm draped over my stomach. The sunlight warming our faces.

The air is quiet. We're alone.

It's my favourite place to be.

Alone. With him.

But I know it won't last for long. It never does.

'What if they erase you again?' I ask. My voice trembles with fear.

I know the truth. About how they've been the ones choosing what I remember. And what I forget.

It terrifies me.

And I don't know what to do next.

Zen shifts beside me and props himself up on his elbow. I can see my own eyes reflected in his. Like two mirrors bouncing light off each other for eternity.

'They haven't been able to completely erase me yet.'

'But they've tried,' I point out. 'What if they try again? What if the next time they succeed?'

'We'll just have to come up with a sign,' he suggests, flashing me that playful, lopsided grin I've come to love so much.

'What kind of sign?'

'Something that they can't take away.'

I feel the tears stinging my eyes. The truth kills me a little more every minute. 'But they can take anything away,' I cry. 'Anything they want. Whenever they want.'

But Zen simply smiles, shakes his head, and reaches out to touch my cheek with the back of his hand. 'They can't take everything.' One tear manages to break free from my eye and he catches it on the tip of his finger. 'They can't take away a feeling. They can't take this.'

Then he presses two fingers to my forehead. I close my eyes and absorb the heat from his skin, letting it sink in. Deep in. Past my mind. Past my overactive, calculating brain. Past my subconscious. Into the place where moments like this live.

Forever.

He leans forward and replaces his fingertips with his lips. The switch is so fluid I never feel the break. The heat never cools.

Then his lips move to meet mine. I anticipate them. I crave them. Our mouths meld together. Our two separate breaths become one inhale and one exhale. I lose myself. I lose time.

When he pulls away, he locks on to my eyes again. 'Now,' he tells me, gently stroking my hair, 'whenever I touch your forehead you'll remember this *moment. Or at the very least, you'll remember that there once was a moment. And that it was perfect.'*

A peaceful aura settles around me. It blocks out every noise. Every sensation. Except the feeling of Zen's touch. I burrow deeper under the blanket and reach up to clasp his hand in mine. I pull it down and tuck it between my arms, close to my heart, squeezing it tightly to my chest.

'Do you remember?' he asks, leaning in and pressing his lips to my cheek.

'Yes,' I whisper. 'Always *yes*.'

PART 3

THE SURRENDER

29
AIR

I'm on a beach. I watch three faceless figures play in the water. Swimming further and further away. They call to me.

'Sera! Come on!'

But I don't go to them. Despite the fact that they are my best friends.

I just watch as they get smaller and smaller.

A giant wave crashes down, sucking all three of them into its powerful undertow. One of them manages to surface and scream. But her voice is quickly snubbed out by the sound of water. She struggles against the current but it's merciless. Whipping her this way and that. Never letting up. Never surrendering.

She is no match. And I watch her go down again.

I jump to my feet and run towards the water, bracing myself against the cold as another large wave buries my feet. I dive headfirst under the next one, the horizon disappearing in a flash of blue.

I am submerged now. Paddling hard. Frantically.

I open my eyes.

I can see everything clearly. The seaweed. The coral blowing in an underwater breeze. A small school of sand-coloured fish.

Their perfect harmonious formation breaks and they scatter as I swim through them, searching for my friends.

I can still hear their screams.

Even down here.

My hair swirls around my head, blocking my view. I push it back and search harder. They have to be here somewhere!

But they are nowhere. Vanished. Swallowed by the ocean.

I see light above me. It's an unusual colour. Not yellow like the sun. But fluorescent white.

I swim towards it, feeling my lungs slowly contracting.

I need to breathe.

My arm reaches up to break the surface. I anticipate the feeling of the warm beach air. But it never comes.

My hand smashes against something hard. A smooth, solid surface. A glass ceiling. Holding me captive under the water.

I flatten my palm and press upward but it doesn't budge. I feel around for an edge. An opening.

There is none.

I glance up and see my own terrified reflection.

I press harder, banging with my fist but I hear only the hollow echo of my efforts reverberated back through the salty water.

I need to breathe!

Then suddenly through the thick sheet of glass, I see someone. Walking above the surface. I bang again, hoping to capture his attention.

He leans over and peers down at me. I see his eyes. They are cold. Ruthless. They send an explosion of tingles down my already tingling body.

'Alixter, I think that's enough,' I hear a vaguely familiar, muffled voice call from somewhere behind him.

He stands up. His movement sharp. Chilling. 'No,' he responds callously. 'She's not ready.'

I make one last vain attempt to break through the glass but it's too thick.

I open my mouth to scream and water floods my lungs.

I wake up gasping for breath. Choking.

The familiar surroundings of room 302 blur in and out of focus as sweat drips into my eyes.

This is my second dream.

30

FOUND

The sun is bright in the sky when I awake. It filters through the blinds on the windows, lighting up the entire room. It's probably midmorning by now. I wonder how long I've been sleeping.

I stretch and glance around me. As I take in the small tables and chairs, the colourful walls and my makeshift bed on the floor, the events of last night come racing back to me.

The small silver hard drive.

The memories.

The truth.

That's when I realize that Zen is gone. And so is the gun.

'Don't move!' I hear someone yell. I immediately recognize the voice as Zen's. It's coming from just outside the door. 'Who are you!?'

I leap to my feet and run, kicking the door out. It flies off the hinges and clatters to the ground on the other side.

Zen jumps slightly at the noise but then regains focus. He's holding the gun at arm's length. Pointing it at someone down the hallway.

I follow the direction of his aim and gasp when my eyes land on Cody, cowering against the wall. His eyes are shut tight. His body is shaking.

'Zen!' I scream, running to Cody. 'What are you doing? Put the gun down!'

'Sera,' Zen starts to argue.

But I don't let him finish. I flash him the most menacing look I can muster. 'Put. It. Down. Now.'

Reluctantly Zen lowers his arms. The gun comes to rest against his thigh. 'Sera,' he tries again. 'You can't trust *anyone*.'

I sigh. 'And you can't distrust *everyone*. This is Cody. He's my thirteen-year-old foster-brother. I assure you, he's harmless.'

I reach out and touch Cody lightly on the back. He jumps. 'It's OK,' I tell him.

But that doesn't seem to reassure him at all. Instead I watch his eyes grow very wide.

'Who the hell *are* you?' he demands. 'Why are you kicking down doors and hanging out with people who carry guns and . . .' His breathing quickens to the point where he can no longer speak.

I try to touch him again but he jerks away. 'Cody, relax.'

'Ask him how he found you,' Zen yells from down the hall. He's started to pace.

Cody looks uneasily from me to Zen, then back at me. 'I went through your search history. On my laptop. I saw that you Googled this address.'

'You left it on the computer?' Zen screams. *'For anyone to find?'*

The stress of having to pacify both of these boys is fraying my nerves. I hold up my hand to attempt to quiet Zen. 'Please.' Then I turn back to Cody.

'My parents totally freaked out when they woke up and you were gone,' Cody explains. 'They had to call Social Services and tell them you were missing. My parents blamed me. They assumed I had helped you run away again. Even though I swore I knew nothing. But of course they didn't believe me. I guess I have a track record now.'

I lower my head. 'I'm sorry about that, Cody. I really am.'

He shrugs. 'Whatever. I went through your room looking for clues, thinking that if I could find out where you were and bring you back, I could clear my name.'

'She's not going back there.' Zen's voice is firm and protective.

I shoot him another pleading glance and he bows his head and falls quiet again.

Cody eyes the gun, still grasped firmly in Zen's hand. Then he looks back to me. 'What is going on here? Who is *that*?'

'That's Zen,' I explain. 'He's . . . a friend. From my past.'

Cody snorts. 'Some friend. What is he doing with a semiautomatic weapon?'

I bite my lip as I struggle to find an answer. An answer that will make sense but that won't put Cody in any danger. I finally decide on, 'It's complicated. Zen is just being extra-careful.'

Cody's eyebrows rise. 'Does this have anything to do with the people who came to the house looking for you this morning?'

In an instant, Zen is by my side, glaring down at poor Cody. 'What people?' he demands.

I push against Zen's chest, urging him to take a step back and give Cody some room to breathe. He obliges. But his ominous glower never falters. 'What people?' he asks again.

I step between them and try again to put my hand on Cody's shoulder. This time, thankfully, he doesn't flinch.

'Who was looking for me?' I ask, careful to keep my voice much calmer and gentler than Zen's.

'I don't know,' Cody admits. 'I was already heading out the door when they arrived. I just heard them say they were scientists and that they wanted to talk to you.'

Zen and I exchange a look. We both know what this means.

He's right. I can't go back there.

'Did they follow you?' Zen asks.

Cody shakes his head. 'I don't think so.' He looks at me again, pleading with his eyes. 'Violet, what's going on? Are you in trouble? Did you do something illegal?'

I sigh. 'I can't explain. I'm sorry. I don't even have the entire story myself. I just know that I'm in danger and I can't stay here. I have to leave town. If I tell you anything more than that, it will only put you in danger as well. And I can't do that. I've already caused you and your family enough trouble. Please tell your parents that I'm sorry.' I can feel tears spring to my eyes. I blink them away. 'And thank you.'

I face Zen, taking control of the situation for once. 'Come on. Let's go.'

'Wait!' Cody calls. 'Maybe I can help you somehow.'

I turn back and smile. He looks so scared. Yet so eager. 'Thank you, Cody. But you can't help. The best thing you can do for us is go home and tell your parents and whoever else comes to the house that you don't know where I am and that you haven't seen me.'

'But—' Cody tries to argue.

'Please,' I stop him. 'Please just go home.'

'If you're in trouble I want to help.'

I shake my head sadly. 'Cody, there's nothing you can—'

'Actually –' Zen steps up beside me – 'there might be something he can help us with.'

Cody's eyes light up. I think it's partly out of fear of Zen and partly out of anticipation of what he might say.

I shoot Zen a disapproving stare. 'What?'

Zen looks hopefully from me to Cody. 'We could really use a car.'

31
DRIVEN

I watch as Cody carefully steps over several unconscious bodies lying on the floor, bending down to examine each of their faces. The scene in front of me is a frightful one. The family room of this unfamiliar house that Cody has brought us to is covered in plastic bags, food crumbs, aluminum cans, various items of clothing, and, most unnerving of all . . . people.

They look dead.

And I'm instantly reminded of the water.

Waking up in a salty wasteland. Surrounded by an ocean full of dead airline passengers.

And I realize I still don't know how I ended up among them.

I still don't know a lot of things.

But for the first time since I woke up on that floating piece of debris, I am optimistic that my questions will finally be answered.

I suck in a sharp breath. 'Are they dead?' I ask, afraid

of what the response might be.

But all I hear is laughter. Cody's laughter. 'Dead?' he repeats. 'No. Just passed out.'

'Deactivated?' I clarify, remembering the strange device that Rio showed me.

Cody laughs again. This time even Zen joins in. But his laughter is much more scornful in nature.

'Sure,' Cody allows. 'Deactivated. Drinking all night will do that to you.'

I glance around the room again. 'Drinking?'

'Yeah. You know, alcohol.' Cody crouches down and peeks behind a red square pillow that's covering the face of one of the inert bodies. I steal a glance as well. The young man looks to be the same age as Zen. He has longish brown hair that appears to be acting as some kind of trap because it has several bright orange pieces of food stuck to it. As soon as the pillow is removed, he groans at the sudden blast of daylight and clumsily reaches up to pull his hair over his eyes.

His hand lands on one of the orange objects and, without opening his eyes, he picks it from his hair and pops it in his mouth, chewing languidly.

Cody rolls his eyes. 'A friend told me his older brother was coming to a party here last night.' He walks over to a person lying on a nearby couch and leans over to peer at his face, grimacing slightly at what he sees. 'And from the looks of it, it was a big one.'

He stands up and turns to me, taking in my puzzled expression. 'Lemme guess. You don't remember alcohol either?'

I look to Zen for help but he just flashes a quick smile that I can't interpret. 'No,' I admit. 'I don't. What is it?'

'It's a substance that makes you act like a total dickhead,' Cody explains.

I open my mouth to ask what that is, but Zen jumps in. 'It's slang for someone who is mean or rude.'

'Or in high school,' Cody says with a shrug. He stoops to pick up one of the empty aluminum cans that's been crushed in the middle. 'See?' he says, brandishing it towards me. 'This is beer. A very common form of alcohol. Some people drink it to relax. While others –' he motions towards the handful of deactivated teenagers – 'like these jerkwads, drink it to become even bigger jerkwads.'

'I'm getting the feeling you don't like these people,' Zen remarks.

Cody steps over another body and tilts his head to get a look at her face. 'How'd you guess?'

I glance down and instantly recognize the girl Cody is standing over. It's Lacey, from the dressing room at the mall. And she's wearing the very skirt I saw her holding when she disappeared into the stall with her friends.

But for some reason, she's not wearing a shirt with it. Just the skirt, a white belt – presumably the one her friend recommended – and a bra.

I shake my head in bemusement, wondering if I'll ever understand normal teenagers.

'Are you looking for someone in particular?' I ask Cody.

'Yeah,' he mumbles, his tone becoming instantly more hostile. He lifts the brim of a baseball cap off a person who's asleep on the dining-room table and calls out, 'Aha! Here he is.'

'Who?' I ask, making my way over and studying the guy's features. He doesn't look familiar.

'Trevor Stoltz. The biggest jerkwad of them all. And also the richest.'

Cody leans in close to Trevor's face and then grimaces, as though he's just smelt something extremely unpleasant. 'Not so tough now, are you, *Trevor*?' He pronounces the name with unmistakable disgust.

'I'm sorry,' Zen says, taking a step forward. 'But how exactly is this going to help us get a car?'

Cody's tongue hangs out of his mouth as he concentrates hard on digging his hand deep into the pocket of Trevor's jeans. Trevor doesn't even flinch. Apparently alcohol is a very strong deactivator.

A moment later he withdraws a set of keys and dangles them high in the air. 'Trevor Stoltz's very expensive and very *fast* Porsche. A gift from Daddy. His favourite pastime is to chase middle-schoolers down the street in it.'

I look from Zen to Cody. 'Are you sure about this?'

Cody just shrugs. 'The guy has been tormenting me for *years*. He owes me one.'

Zen and I follow Cody out of the sleeping house. The driveway is filled with cars but it's easy to spot the one that goes with these keys. I don't even know what a Porsche is, but the bright red, sporty-looking vehicle parked crookedly on the lawn immediately jumps out at me. It's the only one I would describe as 'expensive and fast'. The thing just *looks* fast.

Zen jabs at a button on the keys and the headlights of the car flash. He hurries to the driver's-side door and yanks it open, plopping down in the seat. He sticks the key in the ignition and then his entire body sags in disappointment.

'What's the matter?'

'This is a manual transmission. I don't know how to drive this.' Zen closes his eyes, then bangs his hand against the steering wheel.

I touch his arm. 'It's OK. We'll figure something out. Maybe we can find another car somewhere.'

He shakes his head. 'No, there's no time.' He swiftly reaches across the console and opens a compartment on the passenger side. 'You'll have to drive.'

'Me?' I ask, watching in horror as he pulls out a shiny, rectangular booklet.

He hands it to me and gets out of the car, gesturing to the now-empty driver's seat. 'Come on. Get behind the wheel. Hurry.'

I'm completely perplexed by his directive but I reluctantly grip the booklet in my hand and lower myself into the driver's seat while Zen runs around to the passenger side.

'But,' I protest as soon as he sits down, 'I don't know how to drive.'

He nods towards the book in my hand. 'Not yet anyway.'

I stare at him in bewilderment. 'What are you talking about?'

Cody sticks his head in my open door. 'What's the matter? Why aren't you guys leaving?'

Zen holds up a hand to quiet him. 'It's fine. She's just getting a little crash course in driving.'

I toss the booklet into Zen's lap as though it was red-hot and burning my skin. 'No. I've never driven before.'

'Sera,' he warns, handing it back, 'it's the quickest way to get out of here. It'll take too long for me to figure out how to drive a stick shift. You can learn in a matter of seconds.'

'Sera?' Cody repeats. 'Is that your real name?'

I shrug. 'I suppose so.'

He nods approvingly. 'I like it.'

Zen groans. 'That's very nice but we really don't have time for this. Sera, just read it!'

'But,' I protest again, flipping through the booklet from beginning to end. The pages fan by in a blur. There are over three hundred of them. 'It's going to take me *hours* to read this.

Let alone understand it all. I can't simply—'

I freeze, my voice coming to a dead halt. The booklet drops into my lap as an explosion of images crashes into my mind, shaking my entire body.

I don't know how it's possible but I suddenly know exactly what to do. My limbs act entirely on their own. My right foot thrusts down hard on the brake while my left foot depresses the clutch.

Wait a minute, what's a clutch?

The voice in my head answers before I even finish asking the question.

It's the pedal that engages the transmission.

My arms move next. Without my brain even having to tell them what to do. My left hand grasps the steering wheel while my right hand turns the key in the ignition and swiftly manoeuvres the gearshift into first gear.

Terrified by my involuntary actions, I throw both my hands in the air and pull my feet from the pedals. The car jerks violently, tossing my head back into the seat, and the engine sputters and stalls.

Cody jumps out of the way. 'Whoa!'

'What was that?' I ask, my voice and hands trembling.

Zen smirks. 'You read the owner's manual.'

I peer down at the glossy book in my lap and shake my head. 'No. I didn't.'

'She didn't.' Cody backs me up. 'I saw it. She only flipped through it.'

Zen chuckles softly to himself. 'Trust me, you read it.'

'He's right.' I point at Cody. 'I only flipped through it.'

'How many pages are in it?' Zen asks, raising his eyebrows as though he's challenging me.

I feel my throat constrict. '322.'

Cody snorts. 'Well, that's easy.' He reaches in through the still-open door and grabs the booklet from my lap. 'The pages are obviously numbered . . .' But his voice trails off as he flips to the end and his mouth falls open.

I grab the book back from him. 'What?' I glance at the last page and immediately understand Cody's reaction.

To my astonishment, the number 322 isn't written on the bottom corner. Instead, the number 10-18 is written.

The book is labelled in sections. And subsections.

Not in pages.

'How did you know there are 322 pages in there?' Cody asks.

'I counted them,' I reply softly.

'No one can count that fast,' Cody argues.

Zen remains quiet, waiting for the realization to hit me. And even though it's starting to sink in, I still can't bring myself to believe it.

'That's impossible,' I argue feebly. 'There's no way I can read something just by glancing at it for a split second.'

'Like it's impossible for you to speak multiple foreign languages and add large sums in your head and—'

'OK!' I say, wanting nothing more than for him to stop talking. 'I get it.' I reengage the clutch and brake, and turn the key in the ignition again, desperate for the sound of the engine to drown out Zen's voice . . . and my own thoughts. 'Let's get out of here.'

Cody, still wide-eyed and open-mouthed, stumbles dazedly away from the car as I reach out and grab hold of the door handle.

'Wait! I almost forgot.' He digs into his pocket and pulls out a cellphone. 'Here. You might need this.' He tosses it into the car. It lands softly on my lap, atop the owner's manual. 'I took it from my good friend Trevor back there. I programmed my number in, just in case.'

I slide the phone into one of my pants pockets. 'Thanks, Cody,' I say earnestly. 'For everything.'

Then I slam the door, jam the transmission into first gear again, and peel off the grass, leaving a cloud of smoke and a spray of dirt visible in the rear-view mirror.

32
IMPEDIMENTS

'Where are we going?' I ask.

We've been driving for twenty minutes and Zen hasn't said a word other than to direct me where to turn, when to speed up and pass other cars, and how to read the signs on the side of the highway. Because although the Porsche's owner's manual taught me how to operate the car, it didn't teach me anything about the rules of the road.

'Somewhere we can stay under the radar,' he replies.

'How do we stay under the radar?'

Zen points to a sign that reads 55. 'That's the speed limit.'

I check the odometer on the dash – 83 – and gently apply the brakes.

'For one,' he replies, 'we don't get any speeding tickets. Because you don't have a licence and they'll be monitoring police reports and radio traffic.'

'Diotech?' I confirm.

He nods. 'But most important, we have to keep you away from the press. And nosy people in general. No photographs can be taken of you. Anything that gets posted on the Web or in any news outlets can be used to track down your location. They'll be monitoring for that too. So we just have to find a remote place to lay low. I figure if we head inland we can camp out in the desert for a while.'

'Until what?' I ask.

'Until I can figure out how to get us out of here.'

I shake my head, downshifting into fifth gear. 'But if they can find me anywhere, where are we supposed to go? How can we ever escape them?'

Zen rests his hand on mine on the gearshift. 'We can,' he assures me. 'I just need some time.'

'Time to do what?'

'Sera,' he begins, his voice turning very solemn and serious, 'something happened when we tried to escape.'

'You mean the fact that I lost all my memories?'

He sighs. 'Yes, *that* – although I'm still not quite sure *how* you lost them.'

I glance at him out of the corner of my eye. 'What do you mean? Didn't Diotech steal them?'

He shakes his head. 'Not this time. At least I don't think so. You were perfectly fine that morning, before we escaped. Your memories were fully intact. Or as intact as they could be given the circumstances. I know for a fact Diotech hadn't messed with your brain for weeks. Which means something must have happened between the time we left and the time I found you in the hospital.'

'I don't understand,' I complain. 'If it wasn't Diotech, then what could have happened that would erase my memories? And how did I end up floating in the ocean with a bunch of plane wreckage if I was never actually *on* the plane?'

'That's the thing,' Zen says, anxiously rubbing his chin. 'I don't know. I've been racking my brain trying to figure it out but I can't. All I know is, something went wrong. You weren't supposed to be at that crash site. You were supposed to be with *me*. But somehow you ended up here and I ended up . . . there.'

I frown. 'You're not making much sense.'

'I know. I'm sorry.' He sighs. 'I just need to come up with a way to explain it to you.'

He presses his lips together so hard they're white when he opens his mouth to speak again. 'After we figured out what Diotech was doing – what you were involved in – we knew we had to get as far away from there as possible. It was the only way you could have a normal life and we could be together. Because it was clear that they weren't going to let that happen.'

I nod. 'So we tried to flee the compound. You already told me.'

'Yeah. But our escape plan was much more elaborate than that.'

'OK,' I encourage him.

He is visibly struggling, kneading his hands. 'Maybe I should start with the poetry.'

I shoot him a glance. 'Poetry?'

'Yes. Sonnet 116. Remember?'

'"Let me not to the marriage of true minds admit impediments . . ."' I recite softly.

Zen smiles and I feel him relax somewhat.

'Cody says it's about eternal love,' I prompt him.

'It is,' Zen whispers. 'It's about constant, unchanging love. That no one can stand in the way of.' He stops and peers out the window. 'They implanted so much in your brain. Languages, math skills, everything they thought someone would need in order to be considered exceptionally intelligent. But they left out a lot of important things.'

'Like poetry?' I guess.

He sighs. 'Yeah. Like poetry. And the ability to comprehend it. I used to bring you poems to read when I would come to see you. We would spend hours deciphering them. At first, it was very hard for you to understand. You took everything so literally. Like a computer. It took you a while to learn how to attach your own emotion to someone else's words. That's one of the things I taught you.'

'And Sonnet 116?'

'Sonnet 116 was your favourite.'

I feel my fingers tighten around the steering wheel. The silence in the car is almost thick enough to touch.

'But it eventually became more than that,' he explains. 'It became the inspiration for a very complicated plan.'

Beep!

The car makes a strange sound and I jump in my seat. Zen leans over and looks at the dashboard. 'We're low on gas. You should probably get off at the next exit.'

I merge into the right lane and veer on to the next off-ramp. Zen directs me to a gas station. I park in front of the contraption that Zen calls a pump and kill the engine.

'I'll go inside and pay for the gas and buy some snacks,' he says. 'I'm assuming you're hungry.'

My stomach rumbles right as he says that and I laugh. 'I guess so.'

'Wait here,' he commands. 'Don't get out of the car.'

I watch him disappear into the building and then I lean back in my seat and try to take deep breaths. Everything I've learned over the past two days is swimming frantically around my head, trying to find solid ground.

There's a knock on the window, startling me, and I turn, expecting to find Zen standing there. But instead I see a stranger. A young woman.

She's smiling animatedly and bouncing up and down. 'You're that girl!' I can hear her shrieks even through the glass. 'The one who survived the plane crash!'

Then there's a bright flash and I watch in horror as she lowers her cellphone and begins tapping on it. 'I *have* to tweet this!' She turns and walks away, a slight skip in her step.

Tweet?

Zen warned me to stay in the car. But he also warned me *not* to be photographed by anyone. And that's exactly what just happened.

So should I get out of the car and tell him?

No. I should wait until he comes back.

Nothing can happen in the few minutes it takes him to pay for some food and gas. Even if Diotech is able to track the girl's photograph, we've been driving for thirty minutes. It would take them just as long to get here. If not longer.

Right?

The answer comes almost instantly.

A trembling sensation tickles the inside of my wrist. I look down at my tattoo. It's vibrating again. Which can mean only one thing.

I glance in the rear-view mirror and see two men dressed in black approaching the car. I recognize them as the two men who were lying unconscious on the floor of the barn last night.

And they look more determined than ever.

'Sera!' I hear Zen's panicked voice soar across the parking lot. I turn and see he's stepped out of the gas station, about five hundred feet away. I watch several items drop from his arms and clatter to the ground as his eyes widen in terror. He has only one directive for me now.

'Run!'

33
DESERTED

I heed his advice. But I don't run *away*. I run straight to him, bounding out of the car and crossing the long parking lot in a matter of seconds. The men stalk after me, but their limited speed gives me a considerable lead.

'You need to get out of here,' Zen tells me urgently. 'Get as far away as you can.'

I shake my head, eyeing their ominous approaching figures. 'I can't leave you here alone.'

'Sera.' Zen's voice is dark and grave. 'They don't want me. They want you. And I'll only slow you down. You can outrun them. I can't.' He looks towards the car. 'I'm going to make a move for the gun in the centre console to try to divert them. Get at least two miles away so they can't track you.'

'But—'

'I will find you. I promise.' Zen places his hand on my hip for a brief moment. Then he gives me a shove. 'Now GO!'

I bow my head and sprint forward, surrendering my thoughts, my doubts, my fear to the power of my legs. My fast, perfect, questionably human legs.

They don't fail me.

The scenery whizzes by in a blur as I manoeuvre behind the gas station and head for the vast plains in the distance. The wooded mountain landscape is slowly morphing into desert. The early-afternoon sun is hot, beating down on my face and bare shoulders, but it doesn't slow me.

I take a moment to glance behind me. One of the men is chasing after me. But he's not fast enough. For every second that passes by, I put another fifty feet between us. The other man is . . .

I don't see him.

Then I hear the loudest *bang!* I've ever heard in my life. It startles me and I let out a quiet whimper.

With a sick feeling in my stomach and a foreboding sense of darkness, I slow to a stop and turn back towards the gas station, squinting against the bright sun. I can just make out the second man, staggering around the side of the building. He moves with difficulty, and upon closer inspection I can see that he's dragging something.

He dips in and out of view as he weaves around a series of large black dumpsters. When he clears the last one, I can finally see what he's towing behind him.

And despite the blazing heat, my whole body turns to ice.

No.

It can't be.

I take a step forward, hoping the minor shift will somehow drastically alter my point of view. Transform what I'm seeing into something less horrific.

But it doesn't.

Just like with the memories on that tiny silver cube, I can't change anything. I can only see what is there. I am powerless to do anything about it.

I watch as the man hoists the unconscious body and tucks his hands under its armpits, before continuing to heave it across the asphalt parking lot.

From this great distance – nearly a mile away – the body is tiny. Not much bigger than an insect. But there's no denying who it belongs to.

'Zen!' I cry out, and then quickly cover my mouth.

Is he dead? Or only deactivated? Did they use the same device on him that they used on me? Or was that loud noise I heard Zen's gun going off?

Oh, please don't let him be dead.

I'll never be able to survive knowing they killed him. Because of me. The guilt will surely kill me too.

I have to go back for him. I have to do something. I can't just stand here and watch.

I shift my weight, preparing to dart back towards the gas station. But I feel a sizzle on my wrist, freezing me in place. My tattoo. It's pulsating again.

I hear heavy footsteps approaching. Accompanied by strained, ragged breathing. My pursuer has identified my location and now he's closing in on me.

I take one last longing look in the direction of Zen's lifeless body and tear myself away. Heading for the sprawling crimson desert before me. Tears stinging my eyes as I go.

The ground is uneven – a jumble of rocks, mounds and small holes. My ankles swivel smoothly in every direction to keep my body stabilized as I navigate the rough terrain. Once again, I'm astonished at how easy it is. How little effort it takes on my part. After running for twenty minutes at top speed, my breathing is steady and even. My muscles still feel strong and agile. I feel like I could run for days and never tire.

I don't move in a straight line. I make sure to zigzag, changing my direction randomly and frequently so that I can't be followed.

Once I'm sure he's no longer behind me, I come to a stop.

I'm in the middle of nowhere. A stretch of open silent space. Without a soul around for miles. The wind blows, whipping my hair and spraying small pebbles against my bare arms and legs. The air is dry out here. And laced with dust. It burns my throat.

I fall to my knees and rest my forehead against the scalding-hot sand.

The tears gush out in a torrential downpour, plunging directly from my eyes into the dirt, creating small muddy pools beneath me. As hard as I try to pull myself together and think straight, I can't stop crying.

I can't stop picturing Zen's body being dragged across the parking lot.

I could have done something. I could have stayed behind and fought. I already know I'm stronger than they are. So why did I run? Why did I listen to Zen?

Why did I choose to save myself when I could have saved us both?

Is it really because of my DNA? Because some scientist programmed me to flee? I can't bear the thought of it. I can't stand to think that Zen might be dead because I was too weak to defy my impulses.

What's the point of remembering someone if you're only going to lose him again? What's the point of clinging to something if it's only going to be ripped away from you?

My eyes burn. My head pounds. Everything is spinning.

I fall on to my side and curl into a ball, hugging my knees to my chest, begging for someone – *something* – to come and take this moment from me. Steal it from my memory. Store it somewhere I'll never find it.

I don't care.

I just want to forget.

I stay like that for a long time – maybe even hours, I don't know – but no one comes.

The memory of Zen's lifeless body stays locked in my brain. Condemned to play on a never-ending loop. To torture me forever.

Eventually a voice comes from deep in the back of my mind, telling me to get up. To stop crying and start formulating a plan.

But it feels hopeless.

I know nothing about these people or what they're capable of. I have no information to act upon. If Zen is still alive, what will they do to him? Where will they take him? I don't even know where to start looking.

You're wrong, the voice argues.

And it's enough to make me sit up and wipe the tears and dirt from my face.

'I am?' I ask aloud.

You know exactly where they would take him, it replies.

And I immediately realize that the voice inside me is right.

I *do* know. They would take him back to where he came from. Back to the place where we met. Where we read poetry together. The place we tried to escape from.

The Diotech compound.

At that instant I know that I have to go there. If he's alive, then I have to help him. I don't know where this unyielding sense of necessity is coming from but it's there. It's not something I can touch or define or even remember. And yet I trust it blindly. It's an undeniable part of me. A force I can't fight. No matter how strong I am. A power I cannot run from. No matter how fast I am.

It's as though I don't have a choice.

I pull myself to my feet and dig the cellphone out of my pocket.

When I searched for Diotech on the Internet, I came up with nothing. But maybe the Diotech compound isn't listed on the Internet for a reason. If they're as secretive as Zen described, maybe they're purposefully not publishing their whereabouts.

Or maybe I simply don't know how to search for it. Maybe there's another way. A *better* way.

If there is, there's only one person I can think of who would know about it.

I fumble through the phone's various on-screen menus until I find what I'm looking for. An entry in the address book that reads *Cody*.

I press Call and hold the phone up to my ear.

'Hello?' comes the familiar voice after the second ring. The sound of it comforts me.

'Cody,' I say, sniffling, 'it's me. I need your help.'

There's a stunned silence and then, 'Already?'

I let out a weak and tired chuckle. 'Something went wrong. Someone has –' I search for the right word; it pops into my head a split second later, feeling all too appropriate given who's on the other end of this call – '*kidnapped* Zen.'

'What?' Cody shrieks.

'Can you come meet me?' I plead desperately.

Cody sighs. 'Fine. Tell me where you are.' He then proceeds to walk me step by step through the process of using the GPS on the cellphone to identify my location.

'OK,' he says, after it's been determined that I'm about three miles from a city called Bakersfield. 'There's a train that goes there. I'll try to get on the next one. Meet me at the coffee shop next to the station in two hours.'

'OK,' I agree. 'And Cody?'

'Yeah?'

'Bring your laptop too. I need help finding a top-secret compound.'

I hear him laughing quietly and I can picture him rolling his eyes as he mumbles to himself, 'I should have just stayed at science camp.'

34
INCOMPLETE

I don't have any sort of disguise to shield myself from inquisitive stares and wandering eyes, so I find a table in the back, pull my hair down around my face and try to keep my head low to avoid eye contact with anyone.

The last thing I want is to be recognized – and photographed – again. I'm starting to see a very disconcerting pattern here. The last two times I was photographed, those creepy men in black somehow managed to appear almost instantaneously.

When I left the diner and the news vans and reporters were there taking my picture, I saw the man with the scar as soon as I tried to run. And then again a few hours ago at the gas station: the second that girl took my photograph with her phone, they appeared. Seemingly out of nowhere.

I pull the cellphone Cody stole for me out of my pocket and place it on the table in case he tries to call. Then I reach down the front of my shirt and take out the locket.

I hold the heart-shaped locket in my hand, gently stroking the grooves of the clasp and the raised surface of the symbol on the front – the eternal knot – then my fingertips graze the engraving on the back.

S + Z = 1609.

I know for certain that the S and Z stand for Seraphina and Zen. And 1609 must be a reference to the poem. *Our* poem.

Sonnet 116. First published in 1609.

Zen said it was my favourite. And now I know why.

Because it was about us.

But even though the pieces are slowly starting to fall into place, there are still lingering questions that I can't answer. Like, why would Zen engrave the year the poem was written on the back of the locket? Why not 116 after the name of the poem? Or a key word from the poem? A more direct reference.

What does the *year* the poem was published have to do with anything?

Despite the information I've managed to collect, my instincts are telling me that I'm still not seeing the entire picture. That there's still one very large piece missing. Perhaps even more than one.

And now I worry I might never find it.

I might never have more than a half-finished story and an empty locket.

I finger the clasp, preparing to open it and take a peek at its hollow core, when I hear footsteps approaching my table. I glance up to see Cody standing over me. I stuff the locket back under my shirt and launch to my feet, throwing my arms around his neck.

'Oh thank you!' I cry. 'Thank you so much for coming!'

My actions clearly take him by surprise because his body gets very rigid and he pats me awkwardly on the back until I release him.

'How did you get away from your parents?' I ask.

He shrugs as though the solution was easy. 'I told them I

was going to Marcus's house for the night.' He jerks his thumb towards the entrance. 'Where's Trevor's car? I didn't see it out front.'

I cringe, that ugly guilt feeling creeping into my chest. 'I'm so sorry, Cody. I had to leave it.'

'Where?'

'A gas station.'

Cody purses his lips in concentration.

'Are you going to get in trouble?' I ask anxiously.

He shakes his head. 'I highly doubt it. Trevor has no idea I was the one who swiped the keys. Plus, the police will find it soon enough. It'll probably be back in Wells Creek before he even realizes it's gone.' He nods in the direction of the counter. 'Do you want something to drink?'

I return to my seat, feeling relieved. 'Sure.'

'What do you want?'

I shake my head. 'Can you order something for me?'

'Sure.' He heads for the cash register, only to turn around a few seconds later. 'Oh, I almost forgot,' he says, reaching into his backpack. 'I brought you this.' He pulls out Scott's familiar navy-blue-and-white baseball cap and hands it to me.

I breathe out a deep sigh of relief and take the hat, jamming it down over my head and pulling the brim low. I already feel safer. As though it's not just a hat, but rather a set of full-body armour to shield me from the harsh world and all the camera-bearing people in it.

'Thank you!' I say again.

'I thought you might need it. Your picture has been all over the news today.'

That warm and safe feeling disintegrates instantly and I feel my heart start to hammer. 'What?'

'Yeah,' Cody says, pointing to a TV mounted near the ceiling in the far corner of the coffee shop. 'Social Services has issued a press release. Everyone's out looking for you now.'

I shake my head in disbelief as I watch the television. Just as Cody said, my face is there. Filling up half the screen. It's the same picture they showed right after the crash. When I was stuck in the hospital. As though nothing has changed.

When in reality *everything* has changed.

Cody leaves to get our drinks and I continue to watch the TV. The sound has been muted but there are words scrolling across the bottom of the screen:

> Jane Doe, also known as Violet, the sole survivor of the crash of Freedom Airlines flight 121, went missing from her foster-family's home this morning. Sources believe that she might have run away but that has yet to be confirmed. Social Services reported in their official statement to the press that the sixteen-year-old girl is in danger on her own as she has still not regained her memory. California police are currently on a statewide hunt for the girl, and anyone with any information is encouraged to call the number on this screen.

My mind reels as I watch the text go by.

Social Services is the organization that placed me with the Carlsons. Are they working with Diotech? Are they part of this?

No. That's impossible. Otherwise, they would have simply turned me over to Diotech the moment they pulled me out of the ocean. Instead of placing me with a foster-family.

The two entities must be separate.

Add in the California police and that makes *three* groups of people that are looking for me.

Could things possibly get any more complicated?

I instinctively pull the brim of my hat down even further over my face.

Zen returns a few minutes later with two large steaming mugs of liquid. He slides one across the table to me. I pick up the cup and sniff it. It has a sweet, spicy odour. 'What is it?' I ask.

'Chai tea latte,' Cody responds. 'It's my mom's favourite. And a bunch of girls at school drink it so I guess it must be a chick thing.'

'A chick thing?' I repeat sceptically.

'Sorry. A *female* thing.' He pronounces *female* with a funny accent that makes me laugh.

It feels good.

And for just a moment I almost forget why we're here. But then Cody removes his laptop from his backpack and places it on the table between us and I'm dragged back into the reality of our visit.

Zen.

He's gone. And it's up to me to find him.

I take a reluctant sip of the drink. It's delicious. But I can't enjoy it. The delectable flavour feels empty in my mouth.

Everything feels empty without Zen.

Cody takes a sip of his own drink and immediately gets to work on his computer. 'OK, tell me about this secret compound of yours.'

'It's a research facility owned by a company called Diotech.'

'Diotech?' Cody asks curiously.

'Have you heard of them?'

He shakes his head. 'Not even a little bit.'

My shoulders fall. 'Oh.'

'But that doesn't mean anything,' he interjects quickly, seeming to sense my disappointment and attempting to reassure me. 'I mean, this is America. There are like a billion corporations out there. No one's heard of every single one. What do you know about them?'

I open my mouth to speak but quickly close it again, opting to take another sip of my drink instead. I'm undecided about how much to tell Cody. If I tell him everything I know about Diotech – everything Zen has told me – then I might have a better chance of finding it. Of finding Zen. But if I tell him too much, I might endanger him.

The last thing I want to do is unintentionally harm Cody. If these Diotech people are as evil as Zen says they are, then there's no way I can bring him into this. I'm torn between my desperation to find Zen and my impulse to protect Cody. He may have only been a temporary little brother to me but he still feels like family.

Plus, I don't even know if I fully understand what Diotech is. Or what they do. I just have these strange bits and pieces of information.

All I know is that they did something to me.

Something that made me who I am. Or *what* I am.

Something horrible enough to make me want to escape.

But until I figure out what that is, I think it's probably best if I stick to the simpler details. The ones I'm more certain about.

'They're some kind of technology conglomerate,' I tell him cautiously, repeating the words Zen used to describe the company to me for the first time. 'Apparently located in a remote location. Away from civilization.'

I think back to the memory I saw. The hot arid breeze that dried out my throat. 'Maybe in the desert. That's all I know.'

Cody nods and starts typing. My stomach is churning as I watch his fingers fly over the keyboard. I take a large gulp of my chai tea latte and wait.

A few minutes later, Cody sits back and scowls at the screen. 'Well, that's weird.'

I sit up straighter. 'What?'

'I found something, but it doesn't seem to make any sense.'

I crane my neck to look at the screen. 'What did you find?'

Cody shrugs. 'Some post on a random conspiracy-theory website by a guy named Maxxer. But it's just a bunch of gibberish rambling.'

I sigh. That's exactly what I found when I tried to search last night. I'm about to take another sip of my drink when something about the web page that Cody is looking at catches my eye.

'What?' he asks, reading my expression. 'What's the matter?'

But I don't answer. I set my drink down and lean in closer, scrutinizing the screen. At first glance, it *looks* just like the post I found yesterday. But there's one very distinct difference.

Under the post, in the line that reads *Tags*, a new string of words appears:

Diotech, technology conglomerate, remote, desert

My jaw drops.

These are the exact search terms I just gave Cody a minute ago. Once again, word for word.

But when I searched last night, the tags that were listed under the post were completely different. They were my *own* search terms.

How is that even possible?

Are there two different postings that say the same thing? Or did the author change the tags sometime between now and then?

Yesterday I was convinced it was Zen who wrote that post. But a lot has changed since yesterday. And now I'm really not sure.

I'm not sure about anything.

'What's so important about this company anyway?' Cody interrupts my thoughts. 'What makes you think that's where Zen is?'

I know what he's asking. He's asking for the truth. He can sense that I'm hiding it from him. But I can't give it to him. 'Cody,' I say ruefully.

He raises his hand to stop me. 'Hey, it's OK.'

'I'm sorry—' I try again.

But again he interrupts. 'Look, I know there's something going on with you. I knew it the moment you walked into my bedroom and solved that conjecture practically with your eyes closed. I knew then that you weren't a normal girl. But that's OK. I don't like normal girls anyway. Which is probably a good thing since they don't seem to like me much either. You don't have to tell me anything if you don't want to. I'm fine just continuing to believe the fantasy I've created in my head.'

I smile tenderly at him. 'And what fantasy would that be?'

He straightens up in his chair. 'That you're a megahot alien from a far-off planet *full* of supermodels who's come to earth on a scouting mission because men have gone completely extinct on your planet and you're looking for another species to breed with in order to keep your superhot alien race from going extinct.'

I giggle. 'That's very imaginative.'

He shrugs. 'I read a lot of sci-fi.'

He clears his throat loudly and focuses back on the computer. 'So anyway, this Maxxer guy seems to be full of it.' He squints at the screen, reading aloud from the text that I've already committed to memory. '"The rise of Diotech will be the fall of humankind. This massive corporation will fascinate some and infuriate many."' He snorts. 'The guy makes it sound like the company doesn't even exist yet.'

'What do you think that means?' I ask.

Cody shakes his head. 'I have no idea.' He clicks the track pad below the keyboard a few times with his index finger and then slides the laptop towards me. 'But here. Why don't you ask him yourself?'

I stare speechlessly at the screen as a small white box pops up on the website. 'What are you talking about?' I say. 'Ask him *how*?'

Cody takes a long sip of his drink, finishing off the last drop and then tossing the empty cup into a nearby trash can. He points nonchalantly at the screen. 'He's online. You can chat with him.'

'Chat?' I repeat, confounded. 'What does that mean?'

But Cody doesn't have to answer. Because just then a single line of blue text magically appears in the box. As though typed by a pair of invisible hands.

Maxxer: Hello, Sera. I've been expecting you.

35
CHAT

My heart is pounding. My hands are shaking violently. I look at Cody with wide, panic-stricken eyes. 'What do I do?'

Cody's mouth is hanging open. He looks just as shocked as I feel. 'I guess you write back?' he says, his voice squeaking. 'You can sign in as a visitor.'

I nod uncertainly and pull the laptop closer to me, placing my fingers on the keys. I take a deep breath and start tapping out letters. Cody points to the Enter key and I hit it, watching my words appear in red below Maxxer's blue text.

Visitor: Who are you?

Cody and I both sit completely still and speechless as we watch the screen. A few moments later, the laptop beeps and a reply appears.

Maxxer: An old friend.

An old friend? I wasn't aware I had any old friends. Zen made it sound like all of my friends on the compound were just figments of my imagination. Fake memories implanted in my brain. The computer beeps again, startling me, as another line of text emerges.

Maxxer: I've been sent to help you.

I immediately lunge for the keyboard.

Visitor: Help me with what?

More seconds tick past, and then:

Maxxer: Help you find what you're looking for.

The excitement builds inside me. For the first time since I saw them dragging away Zen's lifeless body, I feel a twinge of optimism. I try to steady my trembling hands so that I can type out a response. But it takes several tries and backspaces before I'm successful.

Visitor: I'm looking for Diotech. Do you know where they're located?

I hold my breath while I wait for a response. It's taking longer than I anticipated for such a seemingly simple question. I look to Cody for help but he only shrugs. Finally there's a soft *beep* and a reply appears. Although it's not exactly the answer I was hoping for.

Maxxer: Further than you would think. But growing closer every day.

I frown at the screen. Cody verbalizes my confusion. 'What is *that* supposed to mean?'

I shake my head. 'I have no idea.'

I rest my fingers on the keys, preparing to request more detail, when the computer beeps again.

Maxxer: We should not be having this conversation here. It's not safe. We must meet.

A heavy, terrifying pause.

Maxxer: In person.

Before I can contemplate his response, the computer is

ripped out from under me. 'Don't even think about it!' Cody shrieks, hugging the laptop possessively to his chest. 'Look, you had your fun little chat session but this is where I draw the line. Everyone knows you're not supposed to meet up with people you find online! That's like Internet rule number one. Especially guys who post things on conspiracy theory websites. I mean, that's like the official breeding ground for nutcases. I mean, just look at the guy's picture. He's clearly a loony.'

I glance at the photo on the screen, once again taking in his long silvery hair and the creepy glass eye that sends a shudder through me.

'For all we know, he could be a serial killer,' Cody goes on. 'He probably puts up these vague, mysterious posts to attract curious young minds. Then he lures them in with fancy talk and the promise of answers but instead of answers . . . he slaughters them.'

'He knows my name,' I point out. 'My *real* name.'

Cody scoffs at this. 'Big deal. These Internet predators have their ways.'

'I don't know how to explain it, Cody,' I say. 'I just have a feeling he can help.'

Beep.

Cody and I peer at the screen simultaneously.

Maxxer: I *can* help.

I gasp and glance around the coffee shop, fully expecting to see the man from the photograph sitting at the next table, listening in on our conversation. How else would he know what I was saying?

But no one looks even vaguely familiar. Nor does anyone seem to be paying attention to us.

Beep.

Maxxer: But first . . . I think someone else is trying to get in touch with you.

Cody and I exchange another look as an eerie silence falls between us.

I start counting the seconds. I can't help myself.

Before I reach five, the silence is broken by the shrill ring of my stolen cellphone.

36
WANTS

'Are you going to answer it?' Cody asks, nudging me with his elbow.

I shake my head numbly as I stare down at the ringing cellphone on the table. The screen is illuminated with the words *Caller Unknown*.

'Aren't you curious?' he prods.

With trembling hands, I reach out and pick it up. I press the green button and bring it to my ear.

'Hello?' I squeak.

'Sera.'

These two syllables send an ice-cold prickle all over my skin. The voice is male. Rough. Cruel. He doesn't have to say anything else. Hearing him pronounce my name is enough to make the connection. It's the voice I keep hearing in my dreams.

The dark stranger.

The man I saw through the glass ceiling of the ocean as I panicked and struggled for air.

Alixter.

Zen said he was the president of Diotech.

The most abominable man in existence.

And now he's here. On the other side of this call.

'Who is this?' I ask, wanting to be sure. And at the same time, praying that I'm wrong.

A *tsk* comes through the phone. 'I'm so disappointed that you don't remember my voice. It's your dear friend Alixter, of course. Your *raison d'être.*'

Raison d'être: reason to be, or, reason for being.

I guess I can add French to the list of languages I speak.

'It's nice to hear your voice again,' he says.

A knot forms in my stomach. My chest convulses and that acidy bile fills my mouth again. I swallow it down.

'Although,' he continues, 'I do wish it were under different circumstances. You can imagine I'm not very happy about having to come all the way here to get you.' He sighs. 'But alas, it is what it is.'

I have only one question to ask him and so I don't waste any time. 'Do you have Zen?'

He chuckles. It's a cold, callous sound that makes my ears ring. 'Wow, you really do have a one-track mind, don't you?'

It doesn't matter that he didn't answer the question. I already know the answer is yes. 'Where is he?' I demand. 'Is he alive?'

'He's perfectly safe.' There's a long, dead pause. 'For now.'

'Please don't hurt him.' I wish I had the strength to yell, make all sorts of angry threats and demands. But really the only thing I'm capable of is pathetic begging.

'Well, that depends,' Alixter says.

'On what?'

'On you.'

The knot in my stomach tightens and then doubles in size. When I don't reply he keeps talking. 'It's you I want, Sera. Not him. You're the trillion-dollar investment. And he's . . . Well, he's just the fool who fell in love with you.'

My forehead burns with the memory of Zen's touch. The mark he left. It's as permanent on my skin as this tattoo.

'I can't say I blame him,' Alixter goes on. 'You are . . . quite breathtaking.'

I close my eyes and fight to regain my composure. But my entire body is shivering.

When he speaks again, his voice is lighter. More casual. But it still chills me to the bone. 'Which is why I'm willing to negotiate a trade.'

'A trade?' I ask, and I feel Cody stiffen beside me. 'What kind of trade?'

'Well, you for him, of course,' he replies swiftly.

'I agree,' I reply immediately.

He laughs. 'You may be the smartest human being on the planet, but you're not a very good negotiator, are you?'

I ignore his insult. 'Just tell me where you are.'

'See,' he says, sounding very proud of himself, 'I told my agents that it would be so much easier to let *you* come to *us*, instead of them chasing you all around the state, making idiots of themselves and leaving behind nothing but a trail of messes to clean up. And I was right. You *are* willing to come to us. You just needed the right . . . motivator.'

'*Tell me where you are!*' I scream into the phone, causing a few people to turn and stare. I lower my head.

'Patience,' he soothes in a voice that's far from soothing. 'Good things come to those who wait. Isn't that how the saying goes? Although I'm not sure how much I believe that any more. After all, I waited five long years for you to come into my life and then you simply deserted me.'

I don't reply. I'm not going to play into his taunting any more. I have a feeling he's enjoying it far too much.

'We're in the process of relocating to a more remote position. My agents have already attracted too much attention, chasing after you in public places. Not to mention all the attention you've managed to draw to yourself.'

I glance around the café. Everyone who turned to stare at me has gone back to their own conversations.

'You're quite the publicity whore, aren't you?' Alixter says with another disturbing chuckle. 'Although it was that very popularity that helped us locate you in the first place so I suppose it's a catch-22.' He pauses, seeming to contemplate his next words.

'Anyway, we can't afford to attract any more attention to ourselves. We will be in touch once we arrive at our new location. Until then, I guess you'll have to wait.'

I'm about to slam the phone down when I hear, 'Oh, and Sera?'

'Yes,' I seethe through gritted teeth.

'I'm very much looking forward to seeing you again. It's been far too long.'

There's silence on the other end of the line and I hear a tiny *click*. I throw the phone down on the table. It bounces and slides off the side. Cody catches it before it falls to the floor.

'What was that about?' Cody asks.

But I don't answer. I just grab the laptop back and start typing. I don't hesitate. I don't stop to think. There's no longer anything to think *about*.

Visitor: Where do you want to meet?

I drum my fingers impatiently on the table as I wait for a response. Fortunately it doesn't take long.

Maxxer: I'll be outside in ten minutes.

37
TRUSTING

I rise from my chair and dash towards the front door of the coffee shop, shoving it open with my shoulder and exiting on to the street. The warm sunlight is a welcome distraction. I gaze up into it, and for the briefest of moments everything goes pale pink. My eyes water. The world disappears. And I can pretend that none of this is really happening.

But that brief moment is over far too quickly.

I blink and look away. Cody is hurrying out the door, his laptop tucked under one arm. 'Sera, or whatever your name is, you *can't* do this,' he insists. 'I've seen this horror movie and trust me, it doesn't end well. Let's just get out of here while we still can. We'll figure something else out. We'll keep searching the Internet until we can find more information about this Diotech place.'

'He *has* all the information I need,' I say with complete confidence. 'I know it.'

'But what if he works for *them*?' Cody argues. 'The very

people who are after you. Who took Zen! You could be walking right into their trap.'

'Then at least I'll have no trouble finding him.'

Cody fumes, making a variety of grunting sounds in response.

I won't deny that I'm afraid, but I allow my fear to be overpowered by my yearning to find Zen. I already made a huge mistake by running away instead of staying to fight and protect him. I let him be captured. I let them take him. This whole thing is entirely my fault.

And there's no way I'm going to run away again.

I don't care what Rio said about my instincts or what's in my DNA. I won't flee this time. I'm going to do whatever it takes to find him. Including this.

It's just like Zen said to me back in the kindergarten classroom when I made a dash for the exit. I can't keep running away every time I'm afraid. At some point I have to stay and fight for something I know is right.

And I know this is right.

A grey car pulls up to the kerb and stops. A window rolls down and a woman I don't recognize sticks her head out.

'Sera,' she commands in a stern voice. 'Get in.'

I look to Cody but he's still brooding and doesn't offer me any help.

The woman has thick wiry grey hair that's cut bluntly across her forehead. Her skin is pale and loose. As though it's been stretched too far and then released. Her narrow dark eyes are hidden behind a pair of glasses with thick black frames.

'But you're not . . . Where's Maxxer?'

She glances suspiciously up and down the block. 'I am Dr Rylan Maxxer. The photograph on the website is a cover. I'll explain everything later. But right now you need to get in the car.'

I peer over at Cody again. 'So? Are you coming or not?'

He rolls his eyes and finally releases his tightly crossed arms, letting them drop down to his sides. 'Well, it's not like I can let you go alone.'

We approach the car together. Cody gets into the back seat and I walk around the front to the passenger side. I yank on the handle and slide in, pulling the door closed behind me.

The woman steps on the gas before the door has fully shut, screeching away from the kerb and causing me to be thrown backwards against the seat. I peek behind me to see Cody pulling his seat belt across his body and fastening it. I reach up and do the same.

'Where are we going?' I ask the person claiming to be Maxxer.

'Probably to a murder house,' Cody responds under his breath.

Dr Maxxer peers anxiously in her rear-view mirror but doesn't answer my question. Instead she jerks her thumb over her shoulder and asks a question of her own. 'Who's the annoying kid?'

'Hey!' Cody interjects, sounding offended. 'I'll have you know, I'm thirteen. I'm not a kid.'

'OK,' Maxxer amends. 'Who's the annoying thirteen-year-old?'

'He's my foster-brother,' I tell him.

'Right,' she responds, slowing at a yellow light and obsessively checking her rear-view mirror again. 'The good news is I don't think they're following us.'

'Who?' I ask.

'Diotech,' she replies, and I can almost hear her voice tremble at the mention of their name.

I shake my head. 'They're not. They're waiting for me to come to them.'

'Well, you can never be too careful,' she muses.

'Are you going to tell us where we're going?' I ask again.

The car comes to a stop at an intersection. 'Like I said,' she begins, reaching into a compartment in the driver's-side door, 'you can never be too careful. Especially in a world where not even your *memories* are safe.'

'What does that mean?' I ask suspiciously, straining to see what she's holding in her hand.

'It means, when you don't want to be found, you better not leave behind any trails.'

She moves so swiftly I barely have time to process what's happening. She turns around in her seat, lunging towards Cody. The concealed hand lashes out, touching the side of Cody's head.

I watch in horror as Cody's body slumps. The seat belt continues to hold him upright but his eyes close and his head droops forward. As if he simply fell asleep.

Or someone *put* him to sleep.

By the time I make the connection, it's too late.

Dr Maxxer has already turned the Modifier on me. And I'm conscious only long enough to see the familiar device in her hand moving towards my neck. It makes contact directly under my jaw. I hear a faint sizzling sound and before I even have time to scream everything around me fades to black.

38
WINTER

The air outside is warm and dry. The sun has almost disappeared over the wall. I lie on the small patch of grass in front of my house, with my head in Zen's lap. He strokes my hair. Beginning at the roots and gently weaving his fingers down to the tips before starting over again.

'One more time,' I say.

He stops to tickle behind my ears, his voice taking on a playful annoyance. 'Again? But you must have it memorized by now.'

'Of course I have it memorized,' I tell him. 'I've had it memorized since the first time you read it. But it sounds so much better when you say it.'

He laughs, removing his hand from my head. He picks up the tattered hardback book lying on the grass next to him and opens it to the earmarked page.

I reach up and affectionately touch the spine, loving the way the soft, aged cloth feels against my skin.

'Where did you get this?' I ask.

He peers down at me. 'From the Diotech historical archives,' he says tenderly. 'Is this the first time you've seen a real book?'

I shake my head. 'Rio collects them.'

I can feel the perceptible shift in Zen's energy at the mention of his name. His face hardens and his smile vanishes. I change the subject quickly, before his reaction has a chance to stick.

'So are you going to read it or not?' I tease. 'Because I don't have all day, you know.'

He chuckles, taps my nose with his finger and focuses back on the book. Then he clears his throat and starts to read in a silly pompous accent. '"Let me not to the marriage of true minds admit impediments."'

I reach up and swat his arm. 'No! Not like that.'

He smiles down at me, our eyes connecting for a brief but intense moment. Then he returns to his coy, playful self. 'What? You don't like my British accent? I'm just trying to give you a real authentic experience. Shakespeare was British, you know, so that's probably how it sounded in his own head.'

I swat at him again, unable to control my giggles. 'No,' I insist. 'Read it your way.'

His expression turns serious as his gaze returns to the book. 'OK,' he concedes.

There's a brief pause, and the anticipation of hearing the words on his lips is almost too much to handle. I feel flutters in my stomach. A longing on my lips. My breath becomes shallow.

When he finally speaks, his voice is soft and focused and powerful.

It sets the world around us on fire. Everything is ablaze. Nothing is safe. I listen to the entire poem in a state of expectation. That any minute, I might go up in flames too.

'Let me not to the marriage of true minds
Admit impediments. Love is not love
Which alters when it alteration finds,
Or bends with the remover to remove:
O, no! it is an ever-fixèd mark,
That looks on tempests and is never shaken;
It is the star to every wandering bark,
Whose worth's unknown, although his height be taken.

Love's not Time's fool, though rosy lips and cheeks
Within his bending sickle's compass come;
Love alters not with his brief hours and weeks,
But bears it out even to the edge of doom.
If this be error and upon me proved,
I never writ, nor no man ever loved.'

When he finishes I close my eyes and bask in the warmth of his voice and Shakespeare's lyrics, wishing that it would never end. That it would always stay this warm.

But I know that is impossible.

Because soon he will leave. Like he does every day. And I will be cold again.

'Shakespeare couldn't have written that poem today,' I resolve after a moment of mutual silence.

Zen has put down the book and resumed stroking my hair. 'Why not?'

'Because love like that can't exist today.' The sad reality of that truth scoops out a large chunk of me and leaves me feeling hollow.

'That's not true.' Zen bends down and kisses my forehead. 'What about us?' he whispers in my ear. 'You are my ever-fixèd mark. Just like in the poem.'

I feel the tears glistening in my eyes as I hold my wrist in front of my face and trace the thin black line with my fingertip. 'We will always be kept apart. As long as we're here, we can never be together. They'll never let us.'

I gaze up into Zen's eyes and I can see the sorrow that shadows them. Like a cloud. He knows I'm right. Even if he refuses to admit it.

I push myself up to my knees and face him. 'Shakespeare was lucky,' I go on. 'He was born in a time before computers and brain scans and DNA sequencers. Love could survive because technology wasn't around to destroy it. Science wasn't powerful enough to ruin people's lives.'

Zen doesn't agree with me, but he doesn't argue with me either. He stays very silent. Pensive. His eyes fixed on something far in the distance.

'That's the only place we can be together,' I say, reaching out and resting my palm against his cheek.

He blinks, as if breaking from a trance and refocuses on me. 'Where?'

I smile. '1609.'

I expect him to laugh. I wait for it. Because I know the notion is ludicrous. A fantasy. The kind of adventure you only read about in books.

But he doesn't laugh.

His eyes glaze over again and he continues staring out at that far-off point in the distance.

'Zen?' I turn his head back to me.

'Hmmm?' he replies distractedly.

I lean forward and press my lips against his. He kisses me back, reaching up to hold my face between his hands and then wrapping them around the back of my head and pulling me closer.

His kiss is delicious.

Just as it always is.

But something is different this time. I can sense it.

His mind is elsewhere. His thoughts are far away. And I don't know why.

When the kiss is over, Zen rises to his feet and then offers his hand to help me up.

'What are you doing?' I ask.

'I-I-I . . .' he stammers. 'I need to go.'

'But it's not time yet,' I insist. 'We still have another thirty minutes before Rio comes home.'

Zen struggles visibly, torn between the idea of staying and whatever else is competing for his attention. 'I know. But there's something I have to do.'

I bite my lip. 'OK,' I say softly.

He studies my expression and smiles, wrapping his arms around me and drawing me into him. 'Don't worry,' he tells me. 'I'll be back tomorrow.'

Then he pulls me close and whispers in my ear, 'Close your eyes.'

I do. But not willingly. Because I know what it means. It means he's leaving me and the bitter cold is near.

But I also know it's better than the alternative: watching him go.

His lips brush delicately against mine and then I hear the all-too-familiar heart-wrenching sound of his footsteps retreating, the scraping of his shoes against the concrete as he hoists himself to the top of the wall and the soft thump of his feet as he lands on the other side.

I wait, shivering slightly as I count slowly to fifty like I always do.

It's just enough time for the sound of his footsteps to completely disappear. A calculation I once had to make and have despised ever since.

48 . . . 49 . . . 50.

When I open my eyes, my ever-fixèd mark has vanished.

39
TEMPORAL

I wake up to the feeling of the cold hard ground beneath me.

The room is small and dark. There are no windows and no doors. A single lamp illuminates the tiny space. It takes me a moment to realize that I'm lying on a cement floor. I turn my head to the left and see Cody lying beside me, still unconscious.

What happened?

I try to remember how I got here. Or even where *here* is.

I remember getting into the car with a woman who claimed to be Maxxer. She said she didn't think we were being followed but that you can never be too careful. We stopped at a red light, and before I could react she turned and deactivated both of us.

Then I was . . .

Where was I?

I seem to remember being with Zen. Yes, we were back on the Diotech compound. We were reading poetry on my front lawn. Sonnet 116. My favourite poem. Everything was wonderful. Then he started acting very strange and he left.

But wait. Did that really happen?

It couldn't have happened. Zen was captured. I saw it.

Unless . . . I sweep my eyes around the room again. Unless I'm *on* the Diotech compound now.

But that doesn't make sense. Why would Maxxer bring us there? In the car, it seemed like she was *afraid* of Diotech.

The floor trembles and I glance upward to see two feet stalking towards me. From this strange angle, I can only barely make out her features although I'm fairly certain it's the woman from the car.

'You're awake,' she says.

I push myself to a seated position and rub my eyes. 'Where are we?' I ask groggily.

'My storage unit.'

I glance around the small, dank space. There's nothing in it except the lamp, a mattress that appears to be filled with air, a shabby metal table and one metal chair behind it. On the table is a collection of mostly unfamiliar devices. The only one among them that I recognize is a laptop.

'You live in here?'

'Temporarily, yes,' she says. 'I tend to move around a lot. Storage units are easiest. You can rent month to month and there are no nosy neighbours.'

'Why did you deactivate us?' I ask.

'I had to make sure you had no memories of where this place was. Nothing for Diotech to steal later. It's safer that way.'

'When will he wake up?' I nod to Cody.

'In a few minutes,' Dr Maxxer replies. 'His brain chemistry is slightly different than yours. It will take a bit longer for the effect of the Modifier to wear off.'

I rub the back of my head, which is somewhat sore from

lying on the cold concrete floor. And that's when I feel the small rubber disc at the base of my neck. My hand darts to my left ear and then my right. The cognitive receptors. I never took them off.

'What else did you do to me?' I ask frantically, standing now and looking around.

'Just returned what was rightfully yours.' She reaches into her pocket and pulls out a small silver cube. I immediately recognize it as the hard drive Zen used to store my stolen memories. It's glowing green again.

I gasp and take a step towards her. 'How did you get that?'

She looks at it and then back at me. 'I found it when I searched you.'

'Me?' I ask in surprise.

She nods. 'It was in your pocket.'

I shake my head. 'But that's impossible. The last time I saw it, Zen was putting it in his *own* pocket. Right before I fell asleep. Then those men showed up at the gas station and they took him and I never saw it again.'

Maxxer raises her eyebrows tauntingly at me. 'Maybe you should take another look at that gas station.'

I hastily play back the scene in my mind. Moment by moment.

Zen told me to stay in the car while he paid for the gas. Then the girl with the cellphone took my photograph. A second later the men appeared. I ran to Zen but he pushed me away. He placed his hand on my hip and told me to get as far from there as possible.

On my hip.

I reexamine the action more closely and, suddenly, now I can feel him slip something into my pocket before he shoves me away. I didn't even notice it at the time because I was so distracted by everything that was happening around us.

But Zen was clearheaded enough to make sure I had the drive before I left.

He wanted me to have access to the rest of the memories.

He wanted me to have the final pieces of the story.

And most of all, he wanted to make sure Diotech didn't.

'You,' I say with sudden realization, blinking at Maxxer. 'It was *you* who triggered that memory? The one about the poem?'

'Actually,' she replies, 'I didn't have to. You triggered it yourself. I just turned on the drive.'

I blink. 'How did I do that?'

She shrugs. 'You must have been thinking about Zen when you were unconscious. Clearly that was enough.'

I can't help but smile at this.

'It should make my explanation a bit easier though,' Maxxer says.

'What explanation?'

'The one you're about to ask of me.'

I stare at her in astonishment. 'How do you know what I'm about to ask you.'

She smiles, her slender eyes crinkling at the corners. 'I know a lot more about this conversation than you might think.'

This whole exchange is making no sense whatsoever. My head is starting to pound. I shut my eyes tight.

'Go with your instinct,' she advises. 'Ask whatever question pops into your mind first. I promise, it will be the right one.'

'Where is Diotech?' I ask without thinking.

'It's not a question of *where*,' she says. 'It's a question of *when*.'

'Huh?' I'm so confused now, the walls feel like they're closing in.

'Keep asking,' she encourages. 'You'll get there.'

I take a deep breath and ask the next thing that pops into my mind. 'How do you know so much about Diotech?'

She lowers herself into the chair and folds her hands

in her lap. 'Because I used to work for them.'

'*Used* to?'

'Yes. I was one of their lead scientists.'

'Why didn't you want me to know how to get here? Are they after you too?'

She nods enthusiastically, as if to tell me I'm on the right track. 'Yes. Keep going.'

Her little game is exciting me and frustrating me at the same time. 'Why are they after you?'

'Because when you work at Diotech, especially on such a high-profile project as I did, you don't get to simply quit. They don't let you.' She leans forward, holding my gaze. 'You see,' she continues, 'I escaped too.'

She takes a deep breath and presses her hands together. 'When I started working for Diotech they were a small company. Innovative. A collection of forward-thinkers who wanted to take science to the next level and use it for the betterment of humanity. I liked that. But then things started to change. Motivations started to change. And I no longer agreed with where the company was heading. So I left.'

'Why, on the message board,' I begin tentatively, 'did you talk about Diotech as though it doesn't exist yet?'

She nods, as though this is the *very* question she expected to hear next. 'Because it doesn't.'

I blink rapidly. 'What?'

She leans back in her chair again and sighs. 'Diotech won't be created for another hundred years.'

My muscles start to go numb. The feeling drains from my arms first.

'When you said you "escaped",' I say cautiously, 'you meant . . .'

But my voice trails off. I can't finish the thought.

She seems to find amusement in my reaction, which elicits

a soft chuckle. 'Sera, I got here the exact same way you did.'

I think about the memory I just saw. The one that was triggered while I was lying on this floor. I told Zen that I thought Shakespeare was lucky. Because he lived in a time without technology. When life was simple and eternal love was possible. I told him that was the only place we could truly be together.

My mind automatically drifts back to the conversation I had with Zen in the car today. When he tried to explain to me how we fled the compound. A few crucial sentences suddenly stand out in my mind. Sentences that are now starting to form a very different story.

'Maybe I should start with the poetry.'

'Sonnet 116 was your favourite.'

'But it eventually became more than that. It became the inspiration for a very complicated plan.'

'Something happened when we tried to escape . . . something went wrong.'

'You ended up here and I ended up . . . there.'

The feeling in my legs is the next to go. My body is crashing, falling down, down, down, until once again the cold, cement floor is beneath me. I reach desperately for the locket hanging around my neck and clutch it tightly between my fingers as the truth hits me like a bolt of lightning.

There isn't a place. It's a *year*.

40
EXISTENCE

1609.

The number that's been haunting me from the very beginning.

The year I said it was when they pulled me from the ocean.

Because evidently it's where I *thought* I would be going.

That was the elaborate plan Zen tried to tell me about in the car. Before we got ripped apart. We were planning to escape . . . to the year 1609. A time of renaissance and love poems. A time without technology. Without Diotech.

Which is why Zen engraved it right on to my locket. Right on to my heart.

S + Z = 1609.

Seraphina plus Zen . . . in a time when we could actually *be* together.

I want so badly not to believe Maxxer. To discount everything she's saying, but I can't. As much as it frightens me, my logical brain welcomes the ridiculousness of her claim. Because, ironically, it makes perfect sense.

It miraculously explains so much of what I haven't been able to explain.

Why there's no mention of Diotech anywhere on the Internet.

Why Cody had never heard of it.

Why they have technology that seems so futuristic.

Which means all those stolen memories – everything I've been watching in my mind – the compound, my house, the day I met Zen – those things didn't happen in the past. They happened in the future.

Dr Maxxer rushes over and helps me up. She puts me in her chair and tells me to try to relax and take deep breaths. I'm so overcome by emotion and confusion that it takes me a few moments to be able to ask the most important question yet.

'How is that even possible?'

Maxxer perches on the edge of the table. 'You mean, how did you manage to journey one hundred years into the past?'

I nod dazedly. 'Well . . . *yeah*.'

'The science of it is actually quite complicated. But I'll try to simplify it as much as I can. You see, I'm a quantum physicist. One of the best in my field. That's why Diotech originally hired me. And several years later they asked me to spearhead a new, highly secretive project. Its code name was Project White Flower. I was saddled with the daunting and seemingly impossible task of determining if and *how* human beings could relocate themselves across time and space. We called it *transession*, or, in the verb form, to *transesse*. It's a word based on the Latin roots *trans*, meaning "across", and *esse*, meaning—'

'To be, or exist,' I say softly.

She smiles. 'Very good. Transession literally means to cross-exist. Or to change where, or *when*, you exist. The full, official term evolved to become *chrono-spatial transession*. To exist across space and time.'

She takes a deep breath and stands up. 'We immediately abandoned the usual suspects that scientists had been trying for decades – wormholes, travelling faster than the speed of light, etc. And we focused more on genetics.'

'Genetics?' I repeat. 'You mean a gene that allows you to transplant yourself to another time?'

'*Transesse* yourself,' she corrects with a playful grin. 'But yes. The transession gene. We were able to develop it in only a few short years. But we could never get it to work in any of our test subjects. We tried to implant the gene in mice and send them a few seconds into the future, or simply across the room, but they never left. And all of them ended up dying a few weeks later. The gene was literally eating them from the inside.

'Let it suffice to say we weren't making much progress and Diotech was thinking about shutting the project down. Looking back, I should have just let them.'

'But obviously you didn't,' I confirm. 'Because we're both here.'

She nods solemnly. 'Exactly.' She presses her hands together and starts to pace in front of the table. 'One night when I was alone in my lab, I made a major breakthrough. I figured out why the gene wasn't working. What we had been doing wrong. I was so confident that I had fixed the problem that I implanted the gene directly in myself. Without even testing it on anything else. And I actually was able to send myself two minutes into the future.'

'*Transesse* yourself,' I correct with the same playful grin.

She chuckles. 'Of course. By that time, however, I was already starting to have serious doubts about the integrity of the company. And the people who were making all the decisions.'

'People?' I echo. 'I thought Alixter is president of the company.'

'He is,' she confirms. 'On paper. But I had suspicions that it was more complicated than that. That there were other people pulling the strings. People much more powerful and dangerous than Alixter.'

'What made you think that?' I ask.

'Diotech started out very small. A five-person company running out of Dr Rio's basement. And then suddenly, out of nowhere, there was this *massive* influx of capital. Alixter was very cagey about where the money came from or what it would be used for. But the next thing I knew, we were being moved to an enormous compound in the middle of nowhere. Hundreds more scientists and staff were hired. Security was ramped up to the point of ridiculousness. We couldn't go anywhere without scanning our fingerprints. We weren't allowed to leave without clearance, or talk to anyone outside of the compound who wasn't on a preapproved list. And even then our conversations were all recorded. The whole thing was just . . . eerie.'

Maxxer gets a far-off look in her eyes before shaking her head clear and continuing. 'Anyway, it wasn't until we moved to the compound that some of these very expensive (not to mention *secretive*) endeavours were initiated. Like my own Project White Flower and the project that created you. I know for a fact Alixter couldn't have funded those on his own. Which means someone – or some *group* – must have been sponsoring them.'

'Do you know anything about the project that created me?' I ask hastily. 'Like what they were doing to me? Or even *why*?'

Maxxer shakes her head. 'Unfortunately not. Your project was kept highly confidential. Only Rio and Alixter were given full clearance. No one else on the compound even knew that the first synthetically engineered human being was living among us. In fact, I didn't even know you existed until very recently. But I'll be honest, I'm not optimistic. Alixter is fueled by one thing: money. And whoever he's working for – well, who knows what's fuelling them. Whatever the reasons were for creating you, I'm fairly certain it goes beyond just you.'

'What do you mean?' I ask numbly.

'I mean, why create the perfect human only to keep her locked up in a cell all day? I know they didn't spend trillions of dollars just to admire a pretty face. If they're trying this hard to find you and bring you back, then the project is not over. I have a feeling you're just a small piece of a much larger plan.'

I feel my chest tighten to the point of pain. I want to run. Run far. My eyes dart around the poorly lit space for an exit but the only door I see has a steel lock on it. I force myself to stay put and breathe. The inhales and exhales seem to calm me. Not completely. But enough.

Maxxer starts to pace. 'So like I said, when my breakthrough in the lab came, I was already having misgivings about what Diotech had become. And I was starting to wonder what my research was really going to be used for. It was funny – since the time I started working on White Flower, I never stopped to think about what a technology like transession would do. What kind of repercussions it could have. Especially if it was used for the wrong purposes. I guess in my heart, I never really thought it would work.

'But it did work,' she continues. 'And so then I was burdened with the idea that if I turned my research over to Alixter, I really had no idea whose hands it would end up in. And if something horrible happened, the responsibility would fall on me. I had horrific nightmares about waking up to find that Hitler had won World War II, or that the planet had fallen into a nuclear winter because someone had intentionally changed the course of history. I couldn't let that happen. So I destroyed the evidence of my success, submitted the final report containing a mock-up of the older, flawed version of the gene, claimed that transession would never successfully work and recommended that the project be shut down. Then I left. And I've been hiding out ever since.'

'But,' I begin pensively, 'clearly somebody else figured out how to manufacture the gene correctly. Because I'm here. And Zen. And Rio.'

'Precisely,' she says, pointing at me. 'Of course, you're not the only ones.'

I know right away who she's referring to.

The men who took Zen.

The thought of them makes my fists tighten and my teeth clench.

Maxxer must be able to read my reaction because she nods understandingly and says, 'Diotech security agents. Ruthless ex-military men that Alixter hires to do his bidding. They're probably the only people at that company who are more depraved than he is. And if they're here, it means Diotech has the correct code for the transession gene.' She lowers her head and whispers, 'And God help us all.'

'So this is *my* fault,' I whisper.

She lets out a soft laugh. 'This is not your fault, Sera. This is so much bigger than you.'

'But they're here because of me!' I rage. 'Because I tried to escape. If it wasn't for me, none of them would even know about transession. They followed *me* here.'

But a thought suddenly stops me and I glance down at my tattoo. 'Wait a minute,' I muse. 'Zen said they could only track me within a two-mile radius.'

Maxxer nods. 'Zen is mostly right,' she admits. 'Now – in *this* time – yes, they are limited to a two-mile radius. But one hundred years from now, Diotech has satellite systems in place that allow them to track you anywhere on the planet. However, those satellites won't be sent into orbit for nearly a century. Which means when you're here – in this time, or any other time before the satellites are created – their tracking technology is extremely limited.'

My eyebrows knit together. 'But they have some way of tracking what *year* I'm in?'

Maxxer smiles knowingly. 'Not at all. That was the beauty of your escape plan. You would never have been able to escape the compound and live in that time period. They would have been able to find you anywhere. But time is so vast and limitless, it's nearly impossible to locate anyone within it. Once you disappear into the past, that's it, you're gone. You can't be tracked by any technology.'

'But then how were they able to find me here?' I ask.

'The same way Zen was able to find you,' she replies.

I shake my head, starting to feel frustrated again. 'I don't understand.'

'You see, even when someone disappears into the past, unless they're extremely careful, they almost *always* leave a trail.'

'What kind of trail?'

She pulls her laptop closer to her and starts typing on the keyboard; then a second later, she spins it around to face me. On the screen, I see a very familiar photograph staring back.

A photograph of *me*.

It's the one I remember seeing on the news when I was lying in my hospital bed. And again at the coffee shop today. The one that was used to encourage people to call in with any information about my identity.

'I'm confused,' I say. 'How did my photograph leave a trail?'

'Any public record, news story, Internet posting, even Facebook upload is stored on a server somewhere indefinitely. All you need is the right search criteria and you can find anyone. Anywhere. Any*time*.'

'Are you saying this photograph showed up in an Internet search one hundred years from now and that's how they knew I was here?'

'It's possible.' She tugs her ear thoughtfully. 'It's quite easy to figure out though. When did you first see Zen here?'

The memory returns instantly. His face blurred by my drug-induced haze. I can still feel the warmth of his hand as he touched me.

'He came to see me at the hospital,' I say longingly.

'And let me guess,' Maxxer says. 'That was *right* after they showed your picture on the news and revealed what hospital you were admitted to.'

'Yes!' I cry eagerly. 'That's right!'

'You see,' she says. 'The best chance he had of finding you was to appear *exactly* where the newscast said you were at the *exact* moment it said you were there. One minute later, and you could have been somewhere else.'

'But Zen went to 1609. He told me. How could he have seen the newscast from way back then? It didn't happen yet.'

'He was only there for a moment,' Maxxer clarifies. 'Once he realized you didn't make it, he went directly back to Diotech to find you. When he saw that you weren't there either, he spent the next *two months* searching for you. He had no idea where you were. You could have ended up anywhere. And because your name was never reported on the news, due to the fact that no one here *knew* your real name, finding you became a full-time job. He scanned the digital news archives for hours a day, searching for someone who matched your description. And once he found the story about the plane crash and the sixteen-year-old survivor with eyes the colour of violets, he went straight there to get you.'

In utter disbelief, I replay the scene from the hospital in my mind, searching for evidence that what Maxxer is saying is true.

Kiyana tells me to shut off the television and get some rest, but I refuse. So she administers drugs to help me sleep, then she leaves.

The room becomes fuzzy.

I see someone in the doorway. A silhouette. It moves towards me. Fast. Urgently.

'Can you hear me? Please open your eyes.'

He touches my hand and I struggle to stay awake.

'Please wake up,' he pleads, from far away. His voice echoes in my ears.

I can barely make out his face. Hovering inches from mine. It blurs in and out of focus.

'This wasn't supposed to happen,' he says. 'You're not supposed to be here.'

He moves quickly, removing my IV, the tubes from my face and chest.

I hear footsteps down the hall, coming from the nurses' station.

'Don't worry,' he says. 'I'm going to get you out of here.'

The touch of his hand slowly dissolves and I fight to open my eyes one last time before the darkness comes.

He is gone.

'Wait,' I say, standing up. Now it's my turn to pace. 'Zen found me in the hospital. But the Diotech security agents didn't show up until I stepped out of that diner and walked into a sea of press. Then they showed up again at the gas station after that girl took a picture of me with her cellphone. Why wouldn't they just come to the hospital too? If that was the first time my picture appeared in the news. How did they miss that?'

Maxxer smiles. It's obvious she takes great pleasure in relaying what she's about to say. 'Because Zen was watching out for you.'

I feel an instant warmth spread through my entire body and that magic spot in the centre of my forehead burns again. But the heat is short-lived. It cools the moment I think about how fast I abandoned him. How fast I ran away to save myself. After everything he did for me.

'He tried to cover your trail,' Maxxer goes on. 'He knew it was only a matter of time before Alixter figured out that you had transessed and came looking for you too. So once he discovered you were here, in this year, he hired a professional to hack into the digital news archives and erase the evidence of your whereabouts.'

'Then why didn't he also remove the photograph taken outside the diner or the one taken by the girl on her cellphone?' I ask.

Maxxer shakes her head. 'Because *those* events happened after he was already here. In fact, they happened as a *result* of him being here. You only ran away from the Carlsons' home and ended up at the diner because Zen told you there were people following you. And then you were only at that gas station because you escaped *with* Zen. Those events and photographs didn't exist until *after* he came here to find you. Which means it would have been impossible for him to erase them because the technology doesn't exist here.'

My head is starting to hurt again and I rub my temples with my index fingers.

'Don't worry,' she says. 'It will start to make sense eventually.'

I laugh. 'Somehow I doubt it.'

'Trust me,' she says. 'I . . .' Maxxer's voice trails off as something seems to catch her eye. And then a strange shadow passes over her face.

'What?' I ask, glancing around. 'What's wrong?'

But I don't have to wait for her to answer. My gaze falls upon the empty space on the floor where Cody's unconscious body once lay.

Maxxer looks from one end of the room to the other, coming up with nothing. She turns to me and with panic-stricken eyes asks, 'Where's the kid?'

41
BETRAYED

'For the last time,' I hear a voice yell, 'I'm *not* a kid!'

We both spin to see Cody crawling out from under the table, holding the Modifier in his hand and pointing it at Maxxer.

'Cody,' I say gently, stepping towards him. 'Please put that down.'

But he waves it frantically, forcing me to back away. 'Don't come near me!' He looks scared and overwhelmed. His eyes are wider than I've ever seen them. His breathing is strained.

'Be careful with that,' Maxxer warns, nodding towards Cody's hand. 'Modifiers can be very tricky to operate and extremely dangerous if you don't know how to use them.'

But Cody ignores Maxxer, pushing her against the wall with a few threatening flicks of his hand.

'What is this place?' he asks, his voice breaking. 'It looks like the inside of a storage unit.'

'It is,' Maxxer replies patiently.

Cody's face contorts in fear. He shoots an accusatory glare at me. 'I told you! I told you not to get in that car! I knew this was bad news. But did you listen to me? Noooo! Who listens to the thirteen-year-old *kid*? No one! And now we're about to be murdered and left to rot in a storage unit!'

I shake my head and try to approach him again. 'Cody, you've got it completely wrong. Dr Maxxer is on our side.'

But Cody shoos me back right away. '*Our* side!' he screams. 'Our side? You and I are *not* on the same side. I don't even know who or *what* you are!' He gazes at me with such hurt in his eyes it makes my chest ache.

'How much of our conversation did you hear?' I ask him, trying to stay calm.

'Enough,' he replies sharply. Then with his other hand he reaches out and cranks up a small dial on the side of the Modifier.

'No!' Maxxer calls out to him, rushing forward. 'That setting is too strong!'

'Shut up!' he yells back.

'Cody, please,' I beg. 'You've got to trust me.'

'I'm done trusting you,' he resolves. 'It's gotten me into nothing but trouble.'

I look to Maxxer, who gives me a subtle nod. I know what I have to do. As much as I hate to do it.

'Cody,' I say. 'I'm sorry.'

'Save it,' he snaps. 'What's done is done.'

'I mean,' I say softly, 'I'm sorry for this.'

His forehead crinkles as he regards me with confusion. 'What are you talk—'

I lunge towards him with such speed that he doesn't have time to react, nor finish his sentence. I go for his arm first, thrusting it upward, praying I don't hear any bones crack.

Cody cries out in pain and the Modifier goes flying up into the air. Maxxer leaps forward to catch it.

I kick Cody's legs from underneath him and hold his body as it falls to the ground, protecting his head from crashing against the concrete.

Maxxer fidgets with the dial on the side of the device while Cody squirms against my grip, whipping this way and that. I pin his shoulders down with my arms while I use my knees to keep his legs in place. It's not difficult to restrain him. His puny strength is no match for mine.

It's his eyes that I have trouble with.

He glares up at me with such hatred, such loathing, I have to look away. He thinks I betrayed him.

'Hurry!' I tell Maxxer, who sprints over with the Modifier.

Cody struggles harder. 'You . . . you . . . bitch!' he shouts.

'Do it!' I cry to Maxxer.

Maxxer kneels down. Cody thrashes his head back and forth, refusing to give Maxxer direct access to him. I lean forward and press my forearm across his face, attempting to hold it still while Maxxer places the metal tip of the device under Cody's left ear.

I hear a small buzzing sound and then Cody's body goes limp again.

I sigh and push myself back to my feet. When I glance down at his unconscious form, the tears instantly start streaming down my face.

Maxxer puts a hand on my shoulder but it does little to comfort me.

'Now the only thing he'll remember about me is this,' I snivel. 'This is what I'll always be to him. The monster who attacked and restrained him while someone deactivated his brain.'

The thought makes me sob harder.

Maxxer squeezes my shoulder. 'It won't be that way,' she says.

'Yes, it will,' I say quietly. 'You didn't see the way he looked at me. He thinks I betrayed him. And he always will.'

'I promise you, he won't.' Maxxer says this with such conviction my tears dry almost instantly. I sniffle and look up at him. 'What do you mean?'

Maxxer steps away from me and returns to her table. From a small wooden box, strikingly similar to the one that Zen carried in his pocket, she pulls out three small rubber discs – receptors – and kneels back down next to Cody.

'He's heard too much,' Maxxer explains, shifting Cody's head so that she can properly place one disc behind each ear and the other on the back of his neck, near his hairline. 'The information he knows will only put him in danger.'

'You're going to erase his memories,' I say with a numbing realization.

Maxxer sighs and stands up again. 'We don't have a choice. If he tells anyone about what he's seen or heard today, he'll be putting his life in jeopardy. As well as his parents'. Not to mention the ridicule and social consequences for a thirteen-year-old boy running around claiming he met people from the future.'

I wipe my eyes and nod. 'How much will you take?'

She walks back to her computer. 'Everything that happened today.'

'But his parents,' I say. 'They think he's at his friend Marcus's house – that's what he told them.'

Maxxer nods. 'OK. I'll replace today with a memory of that. I can access a similar past experience and create a template from them.'

'Computer games,' I say softly. 'He likes playing computer games. Put that in too.'

'OK,' Maxxer says, and immediately goes to work.

I breathe a sigh of relief but I'm still an emotional mess. Although I'm grateful that Cody won't remember any of this, that he'll wake up tomorrow morning still thinking of me as some kind of 'amnesiac supermodel', as he called me, I will know the truth. I will still remember the last time he looked at me, and the horror I saw in his eyes.

And I will never be able to forget it.

But I suppose I deserve that.

I should never have gotten him mixed up in this. I should have left him at that coffee shop and gone with Maxxer alone. Or better yet, I never should have called him for help in the first place. This is my fault and now I'll have to live with the memory of the consequences.

Even if he doesn't.

A shrill beeping sound interrupts my thoughts. Maxxer looks up from her computer in alarm and I glance around the dark room for the source. I follow the sound to Maxxer's table, where I find the cellphone Cody gave me.

I reach for the phone and peer curiously at it.

'What is it?' Maxxer asks.

'A new text message,' I say, tapping at the screen.

'What does it say?'

After a few attempts, I finally figure out how to open the message and read it. But I don't understand what it means.

'It's just two long numbers,' I say with a frown.

'Numbers?' Maxxer repeats, walking over to me.

'Yeah,' I say, confused. '35.35101 and -117.999523.'

Maxxer freezes. 'Who is it from?'

I look at the screen again. 'It says "unknown number".'

'And what number did Alixter call you from last time?' she asks.

I feel the colour drain from my face. 'An unknown number.' I glance back down at the phone. 'But what do these digits mean?'

'Those are GPS coordinates,' Maxxer informs me. 'Alixter is telling you where to meet him.'

42
GOODBYES

Maxxer's car is parked in a dimly lit garage next to the storage facility. I help her carry Cody's unconscious body to the car and strap him into the back seat before hurrying around to the passenger side. Maxxer slides in behind the wheel.

She turns the key in the ignition and the engine revs to life. She takes my borrowed cellphone out of her pocket and shows it to me. The image on the screen doesn't look like much. Shades of red layered with light browns. And a blinking blue dot marking a spot right in the centre. 'According to this, the location is close to a place called Red Rock Canyon,' she explains. 'But these exact coordinates are in the middle of nowhere. About ten miles from any road or state highway. My guess is Alixter is leading you somewhere remote to avoid causing a public scene.' She hands me the phone. 'I can get you close but you'll have to travel the rest of the way by foot.'

'That's fine,' I agree.

'And just to be safe . . .' she begins, flashing me an apologetic look.

I nod. 'I know.'

She pulls the Modifier out and spins the dial counterclockwise. 'I'll put it on a low setting. You'll only be out for fifteen minutes. Just until we're away from here.'

I close my eyes and lean back against the headrest, inviting her to do what she has to do.

I feel the prick of the cold metal and the faint vibration of the electricity flowing into my nervous system and then . . .

When I wake up, we're on a dark, empty highway. I didn't even realize how late it had gotten. The day is already gone. Maxxer drives in silence, her eyes focused on the road.

'How far away is this place?' I ask.

She jumps slightly at the sound of my voice but quickly composes herself. 'About forty-five minutes.'

As we drive, I think about Zen.

About what I'm willing to do for him.

After tonight I'll be back there. At the Diotech compound where I came from. Where this all began.

Except this time, Zen won't be there.

There's no way they'll ever allow him to come back. There's no way they'll ever allow me to see him again.

But it's worth it. As long as I know he's alive, I'll be able to live with my decision.

The meaning of the poem has never been clearer to me than it is right now.

'Love is not love which alters when it alteration finds.'

Circumstances cannot change how you feel. When you truly love someone – on a level that goes deeper than your mind, deeper than your memories, all the way to the very thing that makes you human – you do whatever it takes.

You save him.

I just hope I get to see him one more time.

'Are you scared?' Maxxer asks me.

I contemplate his question. I guess I really hadn't thought about it until now. I've been so preoccupied with finding Zen. Saving Zen. Protecting Zen. I didn't even stop to think about my own future. About what it will be like when I return to the Diotech compound.

The truth is, I have no idea what my life will be like after tonight. I don't know what they'll do to me, since I have no recollection of anything they've ever done.

I only know that I won't be with Zen.

And that's the most terrifying thought of all.

'Yes,' I finally reply. 'I'm very scared. But I have to do this.' I breathe in. 'I love him.'

Maxxer nods. 'I know.'

I turn and study her face, the dashboard lights reflecting off the lenses of her glasses. I don't know where I'd be without her and yet she's still so mysterious to me. An enigma. There's so much about her I don't know. And then it suddenly dawns on me just *how* much she seems to know about *me*. Practically everything, actually. She knew it was me chatting with her in the coffee shop. She knew where to pick me up. About the phone call with Alixter. My entire story with Zen. How I got here and everything that's happened since. She knew exactly *what* I wanted to know.

It's as though she's been one step ahead of me this entire time.

And I didn't even think to question it until now. I was so wrapped up in *what* she knew, I didn't even stop to think about *how* she knew.

'What's wrong?' she asks, evidently sensing me staring at her.

'How do you know so much about me?' I ask. 'You left Diotech before me and yet you've been talking about everything as though you were *there*. You had *all* the answers. And at some point, you even seemed to have the questions too. Plus, when we were chatting online, you knew it was me. You knew where I was and you even knew when my phone was about to ring. You couldn't possibly know all of that unless . . .'

'Unless what?'

'Unless . . .' I begin again, but I can't seem to come up with a logical response.

'Unless I can see the future?' she says, flashing me a shrewd smile.

I turn and gape at her.

'Don't look so surprised,' she says. 'You know how transession works now. And I already explained this to you during our online chat.'

'You did?'

'You asked who I was, and I said I was—'

'An old friend,' I finish, quoting her exactly from the transcript that's now etched into my memory.

'You just assumed I was a friend from the *past*.'

'You mean, we met in the future?' I venture, completely unsure of the words coming out of my mouth.

'Yes,' she says. 'Although technically it's *your* future, not mine. For me, the meeting has already happened. That's how I knew so much about you. Or even that you existed. Because *you* told me everything. About the phone call, about Zen, about when you would contact me, and what you would ask. You even told me what search terms you would use on the Internet. That's how I knew how to set up the message-board posting so you would find it. And find me. The only thing you conveniently managed to leave out was the kid.' She jerks a thumb over her shoulder and I glance back again at the still unconscious Cody.

'I'm still confused. When is all this going to happen?'

'For you, the meeting will take place . . .' She pauses, biting her lip. 'Well, you'll find out soon enough. Let's just say you and I are destined to play a very important role in each other's lives.'

I struggle to follow her explanation. 'So you're saying that sometime in the future – *my* future – I'm going to travel back to somewhere in the past – *your* past – and I'm going to tell you how this day happened?'

'Yes. But not only that, you're going to *send* me here – to this point in time – to help you.'

I shake my head. 'This is crazy.'

She laughs. 'Welcome to my world.'

Twenty minutes later, Maxxer pulls the car to the side of the road and kills the engine. I peer through the windshield but there's really not much to see. Through the darkness, I can make out nothing but miles of jaggedly cut red-rock mountains.

Maxxer takes the phone from my lap and shows me the screen. 'As you can see, we're currently at 35.34128, -117.971756. Which means you have to travel approximately three miles north-west to get to the coordinates Alixter sent.'

I nod, feeling my stomach start to churn. 'OK.'

'You should take this phone with you. It'll help lead you to the right place.'

I grab it and stuff it in my pocket. 'Thanks.' Then, with a deep sigh, I step out of the car. I open the back door and duck inside. Cody is still out. His body is sprawled across the seat, the side of his face pressed into the black leather upholstery.

'Are you sure he's going to be OK?'

'He'll be fine,' Maxxer assures me. 'After I drop you off, I'll drive him home and put him to bed. When he wakes up in the morning, he won't remember any of this. Or me.'

I know I will probably never see Cody again. Or Heather.

Or Scott. The thought saddens me but I understand it's the way it has to be.

I bend down and whisper into his ear. 'Goodbye, Cody.' And even though I know he can't hear me and won't remember any of this anyway, I add, 'When I get back to my home planet, I'll be sure to send you the hottest thirteen-year-old girl I can find.'

Then I plant a soft kiss on his exposed cheek. It's the first time I've kissed anyone since I lost my memories. And although I know it's not the same kind of kiss I witnessed between Zen and me when we were on the compound, it still fills my body with warmth.

I give his blond hair a ruffle and shut the back door. I walk around the front of the car, and Maxxer rolls down the window.

'Well,' I say with a weak smile, 'I guess I'll see you later?'

She chuckles. 'Yes, you will.' Then she reaches out the window and grabs my hand. 'Be careful.'

I nod. 'I will.'

I start to turn but stop when I hear Maxxer say, 'Actually there's one more thing I'm supposed to tell you.'

'What's that?'

'Just a little piece of advice that you asked me to relay to you.'

'That I asked you?' I confirm.

'Yes.'

'OK,' I say warily. 'What advice did I have for myself?'

She closes her eyes for a brief moment, as if trying to remember the exact words. When she opens them again her expression is serene. Placid.

'Trust your heart,' she says, her gaze drifting downward for a moment, in the direction of my chest, before returning to meet mine again. 'It's the only thing that will never lie to you.'

43
FALLEN

As I start to run, gaining speed by the second, I feel the cool prick of moisture on my cheeks. I hadn't even realized I'd started crying again.

But the warm wind whisks against my face, roughly brushing the droplets away, and the arid desert climate immediately dries my skin. Leaving behind no trace of the tears. Or the emotions that summoned them.

I run as fast and as hard as I can. Although the map is still displayed on the cellphone in my pocket, I don't need to look at it. I already memorized it. Plus it's almost as though my mind knows exactly where to go anyway. As though I have some kind of internal GPS system working as well. My body steers itself.

I reach the base of a towering rock formation and slow to a stop. The facade is spectacular. Painted in thick stripes of burnt red, grey and sandy white. Large turrets seem to be carved right into the face. Like hundreds of miniature castles stacked side by side. The result is both magnificent and creepy at the same time.

I glance up at the peak. Looming ominously. Rising several hundred feet in the air. Made even more daunting by the dark night and the faint moonlight reflecting off the top.

From how far I've run and what direction I'm facing I know that the coordinates are leading me right there. To that summit.

That's where the two numbers meet: 35.35101 and -117.999523.

Where they intersect.

Collide.

Where *everything* collides.

My past and my future.

The one I love and the one I despise.

His freedom and my imprisonment.

It's the memory of Zen's face that pushes me forward. The feeling of his arms wrapped around me, his lips pressed against mine, the sweet sound of his voice as he promises that they will never be able to take him away from me.

As I find a groove in the rock and position my foot to take my first step upward, I know that he was right.

No matter what happens next, no matter what they do to me, he will always be there. Even if I can't remember him.

The ascent is difficult. At times I'm forced to scale the side of the butte using only small indents in the cliff to place my hands and feet. My strength proves advantageous several times. I slip more than once, nearly plummeting to the ground hundreds of feet below. But I still reach the top in less than twenty minutes.

I pull myself up with my hands and throw my legs over.

I'm not sure what I expect to see when I stand up and brush the red dust from my clothes, but the sight still surprises me.

It's empty.

There's absolutely nothing here apart from a miraculous

view of the stars and a brilliant red-rock mountain range.

I walk in a small circle, taking in every square inch of the summit, but can find no sign of life.

Was it a trick?

Are they not even coming?

But then why lead me all the way up here for nothing? If it's really me they want, why wouldn't they be here to apprehend me?

I walk to the other side of the peak and glimpse over the edge. There's nothing but sharp, jagged, rust-coloured rock as far as I can see. The drop down into what I suppose must be Red Rock Canyon looks infinite. As though there's no bottom. It just keeps going until you fall out the other side of the earth.

But it's not the depth of the canyon that catches my attention.

It's the large crevice that seems to be cut out of the side of the wall directly below me. It looks like the mouth of a cave.

I take the phone out of my pocket and check my location. Just as I suspected, I'm standing right on top of the blinking blue dot. And then it hits me. GPS coordinates are only two numbers. Two dimensions. Longitude and latitude, X and Y. There's no Z.

And because there's nothing right here, it can mean only one thing.

The actual destination must be *below* me.

Inside that cavern.

I glance over the side again. The entrance to the cave is about ten feet down. And the opening has a lip that protrudes a few inches from the rest of the canyon wall. If I hang off this edge and allow myself to drop, I will theoretically end up right on that rim. That's *if* I can manage to land on the tips of my toes and keep my balance long enough to duck forward into the cave.

I return the cellphone to my pocket and unclasp the locket from around my neck. I wrap the chain around my arm a few times, until only the smooth black-and-silver heart-shaped emblem is dangling under my wrist.

As soon as I'm safely on that ledge, I'm going to drop it into the canyon.

Diotech will surely confiscate it if they find it on me and I can't stand the thought of it in their possession. It's too valuable.

If I can't be with Zen, then the locket has no real purpose.

And I'd rather it be at the bottom of this void than in the hands of the people who tore us apart.

I take a deep breath as I drop to my knees and slowly crawl backwards. My left foot finds the edge first, slipping over the side and dangling precariously. I feel for any kind of rock or uneven surface to use as a foothold but find nothing.

A few pebbles tumble over the side and I wait to hear the sound of them hitting the ground but it never comes.

The canyon is too deep. Even for my ears.

I push my right foot over next, strengthening my grip on the rugged ground. I continue to slither backwards on my stomach until I'm hanging completely over the edge of the canyon wall.

I don't want to look down but I have to in order to align myself with the opening of the cave so that I can make sure to drop right on to the protruding ledge.

The sight of the infinite abyss below me sends tremors of terror through my body, tensing my muscles and numbing my brain.

I breathe in and out, fighting to maintain my composure.

I only have one chance to make this. I need to stay calm.

With a deep swallow and a large gulp of air, I point my toes, picture Zen's beautiful brown eyes, and let go.

It feels as though I'm falling forever. In my mind I manage to convince myself that I've missed the edge of the cave completely and will be descending until the end of time. Or until I reach the bottom of this canyon. Whichever comes first.

I also manage to convince myself that, without me, they'll have no use for Zen. That my death will set him free. And that maybe this wasn't the worst option in the world.

But then my toes slam against something hard. My eyes focus just in time to see a dark tunnel in front of me and I realize that I've landed right where I wanted.

However, I also realize that the acceleration of the fall has knocked me off balance, and I feel myself tipping backwards. My heels dip into nothingness and I thrust my weight forward, fighting to stay on my toes . . . and on the ledge.

But I must have tried to offset my fall too strongly because while the top half of my body is flung forward, the bottom half is flung back. My legs drop into the void and I feel the rest of me being dragged down with them.

My chest hits the ground hard, knocking my breath away. I scramble to grab on to something, clawing my nails into the unhelpful scarlet-coloured dirt.

Pop, pop, pop, pop, pop.

One by one, each of my long, shapely fingernails snaps in succession. And now I only have my fingertips to use for traction. But they're too smooth to grip on to anything.

Gravity is no match even for me. It's too strong and too relentless. The rough rock beneath me scrapes away the skin on my stomach, chest and forearms. I slip further and further, losing willpower and hope with each passing second.

Until I have nowhere else to go but down.

44
HOLLOW

I close my eyes and surrender to the pull of the abyss. Once I stop struggling, I fall much faster. It's a liberating feeling. My hands, instead of grappling to hang on to something, slide smoothly and effortlessly through the amber dust.

It's so easy to simply let gravity take control of my fate, it almost doesn't seem real.

And who knows, maybe it isn't.

Maybe this whole thing is just another implanted memory and when I open my eyes I'll be back on the compound with Zen, telling him stories about our attempted escape into the past.

But I know I'm only kidding myself.

Nothing in my life has felt more real than this moment.

Death is not a memory you can fake.

My hand unexpectedly hooks around the sturdy frame of something smooth and leathery and I'm jolted back into the moment. My fingers instinctively wrap around whatever they just touched and my fall is halted right as I'm about to disappear over the edge.

My body wrenches to a stop. One hand grips the mysterious object of salvation while the rest of my body dangles precariously above the endless chasm below. I twist and pull until I'm able to wrap my other hand around the same surface.

I strain my neck to look up until I can finally see what it is that saved me. The smooth, leathery object that I'm hanging on to for life.

It's the heel of a large black boot.

Attached to an even larger man.

I immediately recognize his harsh blunt features, scarred face and short cropped hair.

He reaches down with one of his massive chapped hands, wraps it around my arm and pulls me up.

He moves fast. And as soon as I'm back on my feet he yanks my arms behind my back and clasps them together with the same thick metal chains they used to detain me in the old, run-down barn. The ones Rio released me from.

He must not notice the necklace wrapped around my arm or the locket dangling from the underside of my wrist because he doesn't try to remove it. And I manage to cup the heart-shaped amulet in my hand, hiding it from view.

I don't tell him that the chains are pointless. I'm not going to fight. Or run. Despite every fibre in my body screaming for me to.

Perhaps some human emotions are simply stronger than DNA.

Besides, I agreed to be taken. I'm surrendering. And that's exactly what I came here to do. Resisting would only drag the process out longer.

Once he's finished securing my arms behind my back, he shoves me forward and we walk into the cave. It goes deeper than I thought and we walk for at least five minutes. Eventually we both have to duck until we reach what I assume is the centre.

The tunnel opens up into a large roundish room. It's lit by four blazing torches. The ceiling is dripping with long, icicle-shaped rock formations that hang perilously above me, seemingly poised to break off and impale someone at the subtlest movement.

Another agent stands in the middle of the chamber. A thinner, darker version of my current escort. I identify him as the man who apprehended me in the barn.

Directly at his feet, sitting on the ground, I see Zen. His hands are also tied behind his back. Nasty cuts and bruises mar his beautiful face and his left cheek is caked in dried blood.

Emotion overtakes me and I try to run to him but I'm forced to a halt when a short middle-aged man with light blond hair, icy blue eyes and smooth tanned skin emerges from the shadows and places a Modifier inches away from Zen's temple.

'Hello, Sera,' he says, in a deep, unnerving voice that I recognize from the phone call and my nightmares.

'Alixter,' I breathe.

'So you *do* remember me,' he says, looking pleased. 'Do you know what this is?' He gives the Modifier a small flick.

I nod.

'Good,' he says icily. 'Then you won't come any closer. Because I have it programmed to a setting I like to call scramble. One zap from this and he won't be of much use to you any more.'

I get the point and back away. 'What did you do to him?' I ask, my voice shaking as I take in his assortment of injuries.

Zen lifts his head and our eyes meet for the first time. I see so much pain in his face but still he manages to flash me that exquisite uneven smile that I love so much.

Alixter shrugs and takes a few steps towards me. 'Nothing time won't heal. And a little antiseptic.' He motions to the ground behind me. 'Why don't you take a seat?'

I drop to my knees and lean back against the rock wall. It feels cool on my sweat-stained shirt.

Alixter nods to the agent who led me in here. 'Search her,' he commands.

As the scar-faced man ominously stalks his way over to me, I squeeze the locket in my hand, wishing I had thrown it over the edge when I had the chance.

Now, it appears, Zen's gift – just like me – will end up in the hands of Diotech.

He grips me by the elbow and starts to yank me back up. I say a sad, silent goodbye to the locket and everything it stood for – eternal love, freedom, escape – and slowly let it slide from my fingers. It makes a soft *clank* against the stony surface and I pray it will go unnoticed.

The guard reaches into all of my pockets, removing my borrowed cellphone. Zen watches carefully from across the room, his eyes registering panic. He thinks I might still have the drive.

But at least I was smart enough to leave that behind with Maxxer.

When the guard comes up empty-handed, I see Zen relax somewhat.

'She's clean,' he announces to Alixter. 'Just the cellphone.' Then he pushes me down to the ground.

'Gentle,' Alixter reproaches silkily. 'Don't damage the merchandise.' Then he grins cunningly at me. 'And I wouldn't try to break free if I was you. I know exactly how strong you are. And those chains are customized to your specifications. Just out of your reach.'

I glare back at him. The sight of him makes me tremble with fear, but I try not to let it show. 'I have no intention of escaping,' I tell him. 'I came here to fulfill my end of the agreement.'

'Ah yes,' Alixter replies sinuously. 'Our *agreement*. Of course. But you must understand, it's hard to trust you, given your –' he wheels his hand around in a slow circle – 'well . . . *history* of insubordination.'

He glances from me to Zen and then back again. 'Tell me,' he says, 'where *were* you two planning to go? Because I *know* it wasn't here.'

'Don't tell him,' Zen urges me, his voice strained and raspy.

I remain quiet. But not on Zen's orders. There's no way I'm telling this man *anything*.

Alixter studies the two of us again. 'Such solidarity,' he muses. 'Right to the end.' He exhales a long, drawn-out sigh. 'No matter. Once we get you back to the lab, we'll be able to find all the information we need.' He taps his forehead.

I can feel the three receptors still attached to my head. No doubt, once I get back, they'll use them – or something similar – to dig out all the memories they want. In fact, I wouldn't be surprised if they reset my mind completely. Back to square one.

After I've come so far.

The thought makes me shudder.

'And then,' Alixter goes on, 'maybe we can figure out how to fix this little weakness you seem to have.' He gestures to Zen, who's so frail and battered he's barely able to sit up. 'It was something we definitely didn't anticipate.'

Alixter pinches his chin between his thumb and forefinger. 'You see, when we set out to create you – a perfect genetic specimen with speed, strength, brainpower, beauty, immunity to disease – we honestly didn't expect you to have many human characteristics. In fact, we purposefully programmed you to be docile and obedient. With all the brain and gene modifications we made, our research indicated that you'd behave much like a robot. A willing servant. Incapable of insubordination or feeling much emotion. And certainly incapable of falling in *love*.'

He says the word as though it physically sickens him.

'But clearly something in our calculations was amiss, because here we are.' He spreads his arms out wide and chuckles sinisterly. 'It became most obvious that you weren't what we expected you to be when you fled the compound. And then ran from my agents. Instead of coming willingly. That's when I knew that apprehending you was going to be a bit more complicated than I had originally hoped.'

He starts to pace, keeping a close eye on me the whole time. 'I should have realized the truth sooner though. You had a certain zealous spirit about you right from the start. A rebellious streak. I suppose that's why Rio always called you Seraphina – meaning "fiery one" – instead of the name we gave you.'

As revolting as Alixter's words are, I still find a peculiar satisfaction in hearing them. At least I *had* a rebellious streak. At least I fought.

'Of course it wasn't really a name,' he muses. 'It was just an abbreviation for the sequence of DNA that finally took. You see, we had several failed attempts before you came along. But sequence E, recombination *A* was the successful one. S:E/R:A. But like I said, no one really expected you to *need* a name, given your anticipated nature. But once it was discovered that you were, in fact, quite human, we figured Sera was as good a name as any.'

He stops pacing long enough to run his fingers through his silky white-blond hair.

'Looking back,' he continues, 'we really should have used our resources to create an *adult*. Then maybe I wouldn't be in this predicament. Teenagers can be so irresponsible. So reckless and misguided. All because they *think* they're in *love*.'

His voice suddenly takes on a high-pitched singsongy

quality and once again I hear the disgust he infuses in the word.

He stops pacing and approaches me, bending down and coming close enough to my face that I can smell his breath. It nearly makes me gag.

'We chose sixteen because it's such a perfect age,' he says, his voice smooth like glass. He reaches out and hooks a strand of my hair around his finger. 'When a human being – especially a woman – is most healthy, visibly striking and physically fit.' He leans in and inhales the scent of my hair, breathing deeply before letting it fall limp against my shoulder.

'But clearly it was a mistake.' Repulsion seeps back into his voice as he rises to his feet. 'A mistake we'll be certain to remedy as soon as possible. This time we'll have to make *sure* you don't have the ability to think for yourself.'

I hear a soft noise from the opening of the tunnel and my eyes dart in that direction. Is there someone else here?

'Sera, just run!' Zen screams, taking advantage of the lull in the conversation. It's obvious he's using every ounce of depleted energy he has left. 'Forget about me.'

'I'm sorry,' I say, looking to him and trying to convey exactly how I feel about him with a single glance. 'I can't.'

Alixter seems to find humour in this exchange. He smiles contentedly. 'You see, this is what I'm talking about,' he explains. 'Despite every modification we made to your DNA to ensure you would be suspicious of strangers, you still continued to fall for him time and time again, trusting him so blindly, going against every instinct that warned you not to.' He clucks his tongue against the roof of his mouth. 'Free will is simply not your strong suit, Sera. Math and science and languages, *that's* where you're exceptional, but making wise, sensible choices based on reason and logic? Not so much. It's quite the dichotomy.'

He looks at Zen and plasters an artificial frown on his face. 'Unfortunately he's right though. You really *should* save yourself. I mean, don't get me wrong. I'm very fond of Lyzender. His mother is an integral part of my team. But *you* –' he points to me with both hands, a look of pride flashing across his face – 'you are worth trillions of dollars. There's simply no comparison.'

I hear another sound from the cave opening. And this time, it would seem, Alixter hears it too, because he glances up and a sly smile spreads across his lips.

'Rio,' he states, sounding pleased. 'How delightful of you to join us. Welcome to our little party.'

My head jerks up and I see Rio stepping into the cavern, clutching a shiny black gun in his hand. It's pointed directly at Alixter's head.

The dark-skinned agent standing near Zen reacts, readying himself to charge.

'I wouldn't,' Rio warns, with a wave of his hand.

Alixter calls off the agent with a nod, and he withdraws.

'Sera,' Alixter says formally, 'you remember my business partner, Dr Havin Rio.'

'Hand her over,' Rio demands. His voice is grave and unyielding. A stark contrast to the way he spoke to me.

Alixter chuckles at this. 'Oh, Rio. Always the idealist. Now why on earth would I do that?'

Rio takes a step forward, brandishing the gun. 'Because I'll kill you if you don't.'

Alixter teeters his head from side to side, seemingly considering the validity of this threat. 'You do appear to have the advantage here,' he admits nonchalantly, gesturing to the wide gap between him and Rio. 'After all, we both know the Modifier –' he hoists up the black device in his hand – 'only works upon direct contact, whereas *that* –' he nods to the gun – 'can be used across distances.'

Rio stays silent, but it's fairly clear this was his exact strategy.

'Which means I could *try* to deactivate you, but I'd be dead before I could even reach you.' Alixter clucks his tongue again. 'Hmmm. Quite the dilemma we have on our hands here.'

'There's no dilemma,' Rio states evenly. 'Put down the Modifier, hand her over to me, and no one gets hurt.'

Alixter raises his eyebrows and shrugs before finally conceding and placing the device on the ground by his feet.

'Good. Now tell your goon over there to release her,' Rio encourages.

Alixter inhales pensively. 'I *could* do that, yes,' he allows. 'However, I should note there is one advantage I have over *you*.'

Rio's eyes narrow. 'And what would that be?'

'Your foolish need to protect her,' Alixter says matter-of-factly. Then, in a blur, he reaches behind him into his waistband and produces a gun of his own. He extends his arm, aiming the gun straight at me, causing Zen to moan in agony and Rio's stony facade to crumble.

'Alixter, don't,' he pleads, the former menace in his voice suddenly gone.

I cower further back against the rock wall, trying to tuck my face to my chest.

'Funny how life works,' Alixter observes callously. 'We confiscated this gun when we apprehended Lyzender.' He chuckles. 'I find it so ironic that *he* would be the one to help me in the end.'

A look of pure hatred flashes over Zen's face.

Alixter looks at the weapon in his hands, examining it with great curiosity. 'Huh,' he muses. 'I always thought these things were so outdated. So *archaic*. Not to mention absurdly heavy.' He screws his mouth to the side. 'It's no wonder they stopped making them fifty years ago.'

'Alixter,' Rio warns, 'you don't want to do this. Think of the people you have to answer to. She's worth too much to you.'

Alixter smiles. 'This is true, but she's clearly worth more to you.' He lowers the gun a few inches and takes aim at my left leg. 'I can repair any surface damage I cause and she'll be as good as new. But would you really be able to stand seeing her in that much pain? Having an entire limb blown off can't be comfortable.'

'Wise choice.' Alixter motions to the dark-skinned agent, who sprints across the cavern, scoops up the abandoned gun and grabs Rio by the arm, jamming a knee into his stomach. Rio groans and doubles over.

'Please don't hurt him,' I whimper, tears springing to my eyes.

But no one seems to be listening to me. The guard leads Rio over to Alixter, kicking at the backs of his legs until they give out and he falls to his knees.

Alixter sighs and tucks Zen's gun back into the waistband of his pants. 'I'm sorry, Rio. But after this, I don't think we can be business partners any more. I question your loyalty.'

Rio doesn't respond. He bites his lip, seemingly in an effort to hold back another cry of pain.

'We started Diotech together,' Alixter explains wistfully, addressing me. 'We had such high hopes and so many aspirations. I had the business background but he was the genius and brains behind the whole operation. The most brilliant scientist of his day, there's no doubt about that. But I'm afraid, dear Rio –' he peers down at him with a look of longing – 'that you went a little soft during our biggest and most important experiment to date.' Alixter nods his head ambiguously in my direction. 'You broke the cardinal rule of science: never *ever* become attached to your test subject.'

I study Rio's body language. His shoulders are slouched

forward, his head hangs low. If it wasn't for the bright red beard, I would say he looked like a scared little boy.

'He put his emotions before his science,' Alixter continues, looking at me again. 'When it was discovered that you weren't exactly what we anticipated, that you were more humanlike than any of us expected, I suggested you be repaired right away. There was just too much at stake to allow you to have a mind of your own. To form thoughts and opinions and escape plans. A few tweaks here and there and we could have easily avoided all of this. But Rio convinced me that the procedure was unnecessary. That you could be controlled with daily memory modifications. He became so fond of you, so *protective*, that at one point he even tried to convince me to release you, if you can believe it.' He huffs. 'It was almost as if he really did *believe* he was your father.'

I shoot a glance at Zen. He meets my eye and offers me an apologetic shake of his head.

'Well,' Alixter says with a small grunt of repugnance, 'we can't have trillions of dollars' worth of research and scientific advancement – not to mention trillions more in potential profits – resting in the hands of a softy, can we?'

Rio lifts his head again. His eyes – where I once saw kindness and genuine remorse – now appear tired and conquered. 'Seraphina,' he says weakly, 'I hope you'll find it in your heart to forgive me.'

Then, for a brief moment, an unmistakable intensity blooms across his weary face and he stares at me with such pointed determination I find myself leaning forward slightly, being pulled into his sudden renewed willpower.

His gaze flickers down to my neckline briefly before returning to meet my eyes. And then he says it again. This time with an almost disconcerting conviction. 'I hope you'll *find it in your heart* to forgive me.'

I'm so overwhelmed by his message and its strange delivery that I barely notice Alixter handing his Modifier over to the agent who's holding Rio. And by the time I do notice, it's too late.

'NOOOOO!' I attempt to stumble forward but the other agent moves fast, thrusting me back with his leg. Everything seems to be moving in some kind of slow motion. The dark-skinned agent's hand extends, the tip of the Modifier makes contact with Rio's cheek and his entire body starts to convulse. It writhes violently as the electricity is shot into his brain and travels down the length of his body.

He falls hard to the ground, his bones making a horrific cracking sound upon impact.

Then the twitching stops and everything is silent.

45
OPEN

I stare, aghast, at Rio's lifeless figure. His eyes are closed but his face is frozen in a state of sheer terror.

I know he's not dead. He can't be. I've seen the Modifier in action several times now. It doesn't kill you. It only shuts down your brain for a few minutes, maybe a couple of hours at most.

But then again, never in the handful of times I've witnessed that device being used on another human being, did I see it elicit a reaction like that. His body shook so hard and so cruelly I thought he was going to explode.

'Is he . . .' I try to speak but I'm sobbing so hard now I can barely get the words out. 'Is he dead?'

Alixter seems completely unfazed by any of this. 'Trust me, he's better off,' is all he says.

'Now, back to our little arrangement,' he continues. 'I'm a man of my word, so as soon as you and I are safely back on the Diotech compound, I'll send notice and my agent will release Zen.' His lips tug into a scowl. 'Of course, you do understand that we can't allow him to continue to transesse. He'd only come back to Diotech and try to kidnap you again. So I'm afraid, before we release him, we're going to have to disable his gene. He will be forced to remain here, in this time period, but I assure you he'll be unharmed.'

He approaches me and leans forward. 'Do those sound like amenable terms to you?'

I sense that I don't really have a say. But as long as Zen is alive, I have fulfilled my purpose for coming here. So I sniffle up the last of my tears and say, 'Yes.'

Alixter claps his hands. 'Excellent! Then we're all in agreement. It's so much cleaner that way, isn't it?'

'You'll never be able to take her back,' I hear a broken voice murmur. Alixter and I both turn to Zen, leaning against the wall behind him, barely able to hold up his head, his strength depleted.

'What's that?' Alixter asks, clearly faking his interest in whatever Zen has to say.

Zen visibly struggles to speak louder. 'I said you'll never be able to take her back.'

Alixter continues his charade of entertaining this conversation. 'And why is that?'

'Because her transession gene is broken.' Zen painfully hoists his head up and supports it against the wall. 'It's not working. I think it was damaged when she came here.'

For the first time, genuine emotion seems to register on Alixter's face: fear.

'And how do you know this?' he asks, irritation trickling into his tone.

Zen's eyes close as he winces. 'Because I tried to take her with me the moment I found her, and several times after that, but it didn't work.'

My mind jumps back to the memory from the hospital. When Zen came into my room.

I'm going to get you out of here.

That's what he said. And a moment later he seemed to vanish into thin air.

Then I remember what he said in the car as we were driving away from Wells Creek.

We just have to find a remote place to lay low . . . Until I can figure out how to get us out of here.

Was that what he needed time to do? To figure out what was wrong with my gene and try to repair it?

The thought fills me with simultaneous hope and dread. Hope that if what Zen says is true, there might be another way out of this predicament. And dread that if I'm unable to transesse back to Diotech, Alixter might renege on his end of the agreement.

'I'm not sure I believe you,' Alixter says, glowering at Zen. 'I think you might just be buying time.'

'Try it yourself,' Zen challenges in a hoarse whisper. 'Try to transesse with her.'

Alixter refreshes his smile, but I still see the traces of frustration around his eyes. He doesn't like to be told what to do. 'It's a fairly new technology, of course,' he admits. 'But from the way I understand it, if you have the transession gene, all you have to do is focus fully on your desired destination and you'll be transported there.'

He gives the scar-faced agent next to me a subtle nod, and he wraps his thick, brawny fingers tightly around my biceps and pulls me back up to standing.

'It's also my understanding,' Alixter goes on, interlacing his fingers, 'that anyone in direct contact with the transessor, who *also* carries the gene, will be transported with them.'

Alixter nods again. I shut my eyes tight and hold my breath. I can feel the agent's hand vibrate slightly against my skin, and then I slowly feel his grip loosen. I open my eyes to watch his hand blur in and out of focus, becoming more and more translucent until it's gone completely. When I peer up, I see that the rest of his body has vanished too.

I drop back to the ground and let out a sigh of relief and a whimper of astonishment at the same time.

Alixter stares open-mouthed at the spectacle. I expect him to get angry, to start throwing things, but he's exactly the opposite. He calmly rubs his chin and says, 'Very interesting.' His gaze flickers to Zen. 'It seems Lyzender might be right.'

Then he glances at Rio's body on the ground. 'It's too bad the man who knows the most about your genes is –' he lets out a vile laugh, amused by his own depraved sense of humour – 'well, it appears we may have dealt with him prematurely.'

He stops laughing and tilts his head pensively to the side. 'Although it's not as if he would have divulged any of his secrets to me. It would seem that he's been *keeping* far more secrets than he's been sharing lately.'

He presses his hands together and rests them under his jaw. 'An intriguing predicament indeed.'

For the first time since he collapsed I allow myself to look at Rio once more. The sight nearly makes me start shaking with sobs again but I fight back the emotion and force myself to examine his face.

What kind of secrets has he been keeping?

And what was that intense look he gave me supposed to mean?

I hope you'll find it in your heart to forgive me.

But the truth is, I've already forgiven him. I don't blame him for anything. And even though I don't fully remember, I'm certain I never did. It's obvious who the true monster is in this situation.

Find it in your heart.

These five words play over and over in my mind. I can't

seem to shake the feeling that he was trying to tell me more. That he was trying to divulge one of his secrets.

I lean back against the stone wall and my bound hands touch something cold. With curiosity I run my fingertips around it, trying to identify what it might be. It's small and smooth with a raised surface, attached to a long chain.

I gasp softly.

Of course! I dropped it here only a few minutes ago. In the commotion I completely forgot about it. It's my locket. My . . .

Heart.

Find it in your heart . . .

My mouth falls open. Could he really have been talking about my necklace?

But the locket was empty. Dr Schatzel said they found it that way. And even Zen confirmed it used to have a pebble inside of it.

I glance up to see that Alixter is pacing again, seemingly contemplating how to fix this unforeseen glitch in his plan.

Zen is watching me carefully. He can tell I've stumbled on to something but he's waiting for a sign from me to tell him what it is.

The problem is, I don't know what it is. I don't know if it's *anything*.

But I suppose it's the only clue I have at this point.

With a pounding heart and shaking hands, I manage to unclasp the small heart behind my back and pry it open.

And as soon as I do, I feel the familiar rush. The blast of information. The sudden influx of images into my brain. The small vibrations at the base of my neck and behind my ears.

What is going on?

The images spin and spin, eventually aligning to form a complete scene. A full picture.

A *memory*.

That's been stored inside my locket. And is now being triggered by my brain. Because I still have the receptors on.

I take another long look at Zen and then close my eyes, letting the movie in my mind play.

I am back inside my house. I sit on the couch in my living room. Alone. So alone.

Rain streams down the windows. Pounds the pavement outside.

I feel anxious. My knee bounces. I can't make it stop.

I've never done anything like this before. I've never kept anything from Zen.

But I'm doing this for him. For us. Because I love him.

If it works, if I'm right about Rio, then we will finally be together. Forever. Like the poem.

If I'm wrong . . . Well, I don't even want to think about that.

I stare at the front door, jumping with every tiny creak the house makes.

When the beep finally sounds, I leap from the couch and rush towards the door, swinging it open wide.

Rio stands on the porch, soaking wet. I can't read his expression. It's as though the rain has washed it away.

Does he look happy?

Sad?

Regretful?

I step back, allowing him to come in. I hold my breath as he shrugs off his raincoat and hangs it on the rack. 'Well?' I ask, unable to take the suspense any longer.

He sighs, lowering his gaze as he reaches into his pocket and produces a tiny vial filled with clear liquid.

'Is that . . . ?' I start to ask but I can't even bring myself to say the words.

He nods. 'Yes.'

I jump up and down. 'Thank you! Thank you! Thank you!' I can't stop smiling. I throw my hands around his neck and squeeze, inhaling his familiar sweet scent. It instantly settles me down, returning me to a calmer, more collected place.

'You saved my life,' I whisper in his ear.

I feel his body sag. He wraps his arms tightly around me and holds me. 'It was the least I could do.'

Then he reaches up and gently disengages my grip, holding me at arm's length and forcing me to look at him. 'Seraphina,' he says, his expression turning grave, 'I have to warn you. The transession gene is highly unstable. There's so much I don't know about it yet. And there have been absolutely no tests yet to investigate its long-term effects.'

I nod, matching his serious demeanour.

'If something goes wrong and you have no way to disable it, the gene could destroy you. Slowly eat you alive from the inside out. You wouldn't even know until it was too late. I have to insist that you let me construct some type of deactivation mechanism that will allow you to turn the gene on and off. Just to be safe.'

'But what about Zen?' I ask.

Rio shakes his head. 'Unless you can get him to meet me, I can't—'

'He won't,' I reply hastily. 'He won't do it. He didn't even want me coming to you. If he knew, he would be furious. He doesn't trust you.'

Rio sighs. 'I can't say I blame him.' He places the vial ever so carefully in my hand. 'But if he won't come to me, then you're going to have to take a chance.'

'I understand,' I say.

There's a long pause and I watch Rio's eyes start to glisten with tears. 'Sera,' he begins, his voice raspy, 'I'm sorry about everything. Everything I did to you.'

'Dad—' I try.

'Don't call me that,' he interrupts. 'I don't deserve that title. And you and I both know it's not a rightful one anyway.' He presses his fingertips against the corners of his eyes. 'You've been such a gift to me, but I hate that this had to be your life.'

I can feel my own tears start to well. I blink them away.

'I just wish there was a way I could make it up to you,' he says.

'You already have,' I say, holding out the vial. 'This is all I've ever wanted.'

He presses his lips together. 'I know. I mean, I wish I could take back what I did.'

I fall silent, running my thumb along the smooth glass of the tiny bottle in my hand. My salvation.

'Actually,' I say, my own voice sounding suddenly rough and uncertain, 'you can.'

He gazes down at me with enquiring eyes.

'Take it all,' I tell him, gaining conviction as I speak. 'Every memory I have of this place. Everything. It's the only way I can truly start over. The only way I'll ever be able to forget.'

'But, Sera . . .' he objects.

'I don't want to remember any of it.'

He places a warm hand on my shoulder. 'I don't think you understand. If I take everything, that will include Zen.'

I smile knowingly. 'Zen can never be forgotten. He lives in my blood. In my soul. We'll *be together and that's the only thing that matters. Eventually, with his help, he'll come back to me. I know it. I'll always remember him.' I gently squeeze the vial between my fingers. 'Because I always have.'*

The first thing I see when I open my eyes is Zen.

Despite his various scratches and wounds and possibly broken bones, he's the most beautiful sight I've ever seen.

But there's so much he doesn't know. That I now know.

Rio was the one who got us access to the transession gene.

He was the one who put the memory inside my locket.

Then he erased everything. At my own instruction.

Diotech didn't *steal* my memories. They weren't accidentally lost. I gave them up willingly.

Because I assumed it wouldn't matter. That I'd arrive safely in the year 1609 and I'd be with Zen. That's why I wrote myself the note. Trust him. To give myself a head start.

But instead, something went wrong and I ended up here. Alone. Without a single scrap of memory in my mind.

Fortunately, however, I know how to fix it. I finally know how to make it right.

I look directly into Zen's eyes, trying desperately to convey a silent message across the dimly lit cave.

Don't worry, I tell him. *It's going to be all right.*

Then I jump to my feet, catching Alixter and the dark-skinned agent by surprise. They both pivot quickly in my direction. The agent holds the Modifier poised and ready.

'I know how to fix the gene,' I tell Alixter.

Zen looks in alarm from me to them, then back to me.

'Do you now?' Alixter asks, seemingly intrigued.

'Yes,' I say. 'Rio told me before I left. He said something like this might happen and he told me how to repair it if it did.'

Alixter folds his arms over his chest. 'I'm listening.'

I look fleetingly at Zen and then back at Alixter. 'It's very easy. A quick and simple fix. Once I tell you, you'll be able to transesse me out of here in a matter of minutes.'

Alixter nods. 'Go on.'

'But I have one condition.'

He breaks into a sinister smile. 'Of course you do.'

'I want to talk to Zen.'

I watch Alixter's mouth fall into a frown and so I quickly add, 'To say goodbye.'

He appears to be considering my offer.

'Then I'll tell you how to repair the gene and I'll go with you,' I promise.

Alixter's eyes dart between us. I keep my face as sombre as possible. He drums his fingertips across his forearm, weighing the decision.

'All right,' he finally agrees. 'You have one minute.' He jabs a finger in the direction of the agent and motions for him to follow me.

With the open locket clasped tightly in my hand, concealed from view, I walk twelve short paces across the care and kneel down next to Zen.

The agent is right on my heels, hovering over me. He taps the Modifier against his open palm in long, menacing beats, warning me not to try anything.

'Don't do it, Sera,' Zen begs me. 'Don't go with them. Get yourself out of here. Get as far away as you can.'

'Shh,' I soothe, leaning closer to him, our faces inches apart. I inhale the air he exhales. 'Close your eyes.'

He shakes his head, knowing what that means. Knowing because he was the one who always used to say it. Before he left.

It means goodbye.

'Trust me,' I whisper.

He silently pleads with me, his expression anxious and fearful. I give him an encouraging nod, and reluctantly his eyes drift closed.

I immediately press my lips to his, kissing him hard. He falls into it and I feel our bodies joining. Melting together. The kiss is just as delicious as it was in my stolen memory. Just as consuming. Just as perfect. And for a moment, everything around us disappears. Nothing else exists in the world but this.

This one amazing, lifesaving kiss.

I have been yearning for this sensation – this beautiful moment – for longer than I can even remember. But the truth is, I have another motivation for this kiss. With our hands tied behind our backs, this is the only way we can touch.

And Alixter said it himself . . . You *have* to be in direct contact.

I squeeze my eyes shut and repeat the same phrase over and over again in my mind, focusing all of my thoughts, all of my energy on this one, simple salvation.

Get us out of here. Get us out of here. Get us out of here.

As I feel the ground start to disintegrate beneath us and the soft *hum* of our bodies converging with the air, I can hear Alixter's voice growing further and further away.

'*Damn it!*' he screams.

But it's too late. We're already gone.

46
FAITH

When I open my eyes we're standing at the mouth of the cave, looking over the edge into the abyss. I try to tear the chains from my hands but they don't break easily. Alixter was right. They seem to be just out of my reach.

But after a few seconds, combined with the force of my adrenalin, I'm able to contort the metal enough to squeeze my hands through.

Apparently I'm stronger than he thought.

In more ways than he could imagine.

I turn to Zen. His hands are tied together with a thin piece of rope. I rip through it effortlessly. He rubs his wrists and looks at me, a huge grin spreading across his face. 'How did you do it?'

'It was Rio,' I tell him breathlessly. 'He told me he was going to create a way to deactivate my gene. As a safety precaution. And I figured there was only one place he could have put it. I only had one thing on me when I arrived here.' I open my clenched palm and reveal the necklace.

'But how does it work?' Zen asks.

'Well, at first I wasn't sure,' I admit, 'but then I remembered you telling me that you put a pebble inside the locket. But it was empty when I got here, which means it must have fallen out. And the only way it could have fallen out—'

'Is if the locket was open.' Zen finishes the thought.

I nod eagerly. 'He put the deactivator in my locket. It has to be open for the gene to work.'

Zen glances around, taking in our surroundings. 'But how did you get us *here?*'

I shrug. 'I don't know. I just focused all of my energy on getting out of the cave. So I guess –' I giggle – 'we got out of the cave.'

He laughs too, his smile brighter than I've ever seen it before.

He slides the locket from my palm, reaches up and clasps the chain around my neck. Then he leans in and kisses me again, gently touching his lips to mine. I'm instantly pulled into him. Craving him like oxygen. I can no longer feel the ground beneath my feet. But then again, I no longer need it to be there.

I hear a noise. Feet pounding against rock. We break apart and I glance behind us, into the dark tunnel that leads back to the chamber. I listen intently. The footsteps are coming fast.

'He'll be here in less than fifteen seconds,' I calculate.

Simultaneously we both lean forward and peer over the edge again. Into the great black void. Into eternity.

'There's only one place we can go,' he says, looking hopefully into my eyes.

I nod and gently touch the open locket that rests against my chest. 'Only one place where we can be together.'

The footsteps get louder. Alixter's agent is getting closer. A voice behind us yells, 'Don't move!'

Zen reaches down and slips his hand into mine. 'Do you trust me?'

I smile. 'With all my heart.'

'Don't let go,' he tells me.

I interlace my fingers with his, squeezing tightly. 'Never,' I vow.

We take one step towards the edge and then, together, we leap.

ACKNOWLEDGMENTS

Memory is a tricky thing. At least when it comes to my own. But regardless of how much I manage to unremember (and it's a shocking amount!), the following people can never be forgotten.

Janine O'Malley, my editor. You have put up with me for four books now. That might be a bigger accomplishment than physically writing the books. I know how I can get.

Bill Contardi, my agent. This book would not be in existence without those three little words you wrote to me: 'very cool idea'.

Simon Boughton, Joy Peskin, Kate Lied, Angus Killick, Elizabeth Fithian, Kathryn Little, Karen Frangipane, Ksenia Winnicki, Lucy Del Priore, Holly Hunnicutt, Jon Yaged, Lauren Burniac, Vannessa Cronin, Courtney Griffin, Jean Feiwel, Caitlyn Sweeny and all the fantastic people at Macmillan Children's Publishing Group. Thank you for continuing to support me, pamper me and make my books look good. I'm grateful to be working with such a dynamic group of book enthusiasts.

And thanks to Elizabeth Wood, who couldn't have designed a more perfect cover for this book!

Ruth Alltimes, Polly Nolan and all the simply marvellous people at Macmillan Children's Books UK who believed in this story from the beginning – before I even finished it. Now that's faith!

Allison Verost. An extra, super-duper thanks goes to you because you are a total rock star and because you somehow miraculously manage to never look stressed out.

Meg Cabot, you are an idol and a total sweetheart. Thanks for supporting my book!

Thank you to the fantastic people who worked on the book trailer for *52 Reasons to Hate My Father*. The beautiful cast: Alanna Giuliani, Hunter Blake, Micky Shiloah, Tom Wade, Javier Lezama, Wesley Rice and Lishmar, the horse! The hard-working, talented crew: Jason Fitzpatrick, Jason Bell, Terra Brody, Anna Bratton, Jackie Fanara and Charlie Fink. The musicians and bands who contributed music: 'Time Will Tell', 'Shhh! It's a Secret', Matthew Clark, Sarah Meeks-Clark, Tommy Fields and Nikki Boyer. The generous people who allowed our little production to crash at your places of business/residence: Brian Braff, Steve and Zina Glodney, Jennifer and Ryan Bosworth, Lisa and Lisa at the Lionheart Ranch and Ike Pyun at the Parlor. And the awesome people who helped make the trailer shine: Ryan Bosworth, Jerry Brunskill, Shane Harris, Thatcher Peterson, Matt Moran and Ella Gaumer.

Liz Kerins, thank you for being there and for saying, 'Send me more!' Marianne Merola, thanks to you I now seemingly speak several languages. Nicki Hart, the master swag designer! Deb Shapiro, publicity and marketing genius. Also, thanks to Kim Highland, Kathryn Bhirud, Christina Diaz, Lisa Nevola Lewis, Leslie Evell, Brittany Carlson, BJ Markel, José Silerio, Rich Kaplan and Mark Stankevich.

Huge gratitude goes to Ruth Haas and Stan Wagon for walking me through complex mathematics that was way over my head, Tara Playfair for teaching me how to be Jamaican, Dr Julianne Garrison for the med-school crash course and Lynn and Rob at the Tealeaves Café, for allowing me to sit in your beautiful restaurant for hours without ever complaining (or threatening to kick me out) and for introducing me to the magical qualities of Mayan cocoa tea.

All the teachers, librarians, principals and students who

have invited me into their schools. Thank you for welcoming me with such open arms and making me feel as though I have halfway interesting things to say. Thanks to all the librarians and booksellers who stock my books on the shelf and hand-sell them to readers. And to the foreign publishers who bring my stories to life all over the world.

Writers are crazy people. And, ironically, it's other crazy people who keep us sane. Thank you to my support team of fellow writers who have managed to keep me on the ledge (as opposed to falling over the side of it): Alyson Noël, Robin Reul, Joanne Rendell, Brad Gottfred, Mary Pearson, Gretchen McNeil, Leigh Bardugo, Lauren Kate, Amanda Ashby, Carol Tanzman, Carolina Munhóz and Raphael Draccon. And an überspecial thanks to Jenn Bosworth, who read this book way before it was readable and who puts up with me far more than she should.

Terra Brody. You continue to impress me with your strength, creativity and ability to watch an entire season of *Vampire Diaries* in one night.

Michael and Laura Brody, I'm quickly running out of ways to tell you what cool parents you are.

Charlie Fink. Thank you for making me laugh, letting me cry, fixing broken plots and humouring me when I swear I'll never write another book again.

And most important, and never ever forgotten, the biggest, fluffiest, warmest, shiniest, sparkliest thanks go to my readers.

That means you. Yes, you. Don't look so surprised. You really think I'd be able to do any of this without you? Think again.